THE
LOST SOUL
of
LORD
BADEWYN

THE ORDER OF THE *M*.U.S.E

THE
LOST SOUL
of
LORD
BADEWYN

THE ORDER OF THE M.U.S.E

MIA MARLOWE

Entangled Publishing, LLC
2614 South Timberline Road
Suite 109
Fort Collins, CO 80525
Visit our website at www.entangledpublishing.com.

Select Historical is an imprint of Entangled Publishing, LLC.

Edited by Erin Molta
Cover design by Louisa Maggio
Cover art by The Killion Group, Inc.

ISBN 978-1-68281-050-7

Manufactured in the United States of America

First Edition November 2015

For my sisters: the keepers of my secrets and my partners in crime.

Welcome to the Order of the M.U.S.E.

His Grace, the Duke of Camden, has recruited (some say coerced) gifted individuals from all strata of society to join his Metaphysical Union of Sensory Extraordinaires. Their purpose is to protect the Crown from arcane weapons of a psychic bent. The duke fears that one such malicious object may have slipped by them and is responsible for King George III's periodic descents into lunacy. There may be no help for His Majesty, but Camden intends to see that a similar fate doesn't overcome "Prinny," the Prince of Wales.

Meet the M.U.S.E.s

Meg Anthony — a former ladies' maid and a psychic "Finder." Her ability to locate misplaced items and people is uncanny, but not without danger to her, a fact she tries to hide. She's in awe of the Duke of Camden and fears disappointing him if she can't learn to act the part of a proper lady instead of a domestic. She hides the truth of her parentage because she's on the run from her uncle who used her abilities for profit and to ruin others.

Edward St. James, Duke of Camden — Founder of the Order of the M.U.S.E., Camden is the protector and mentor of those who display unusual sensory and metaphysical gifts. In addition to safeguarding the Crown from psychic attack, he's searching for a way to make contact with his deceased wife. He's exhausted all natural means of investigating the mysterious deaths of Mercedes and his infant son. Now he has turned to the supernatural.

Vesta LaMotte — Top-tier courtesan who is also a fire mage. She's called in to educate Cassandra in the ways of her gift… and the ways of men. She and the widowed Camden have had an on-again, off-again "arrangement" for years.

Cassandra Darkin, Lady Stanstead — Second daughter of Sir Henry Darkin who was an unwitting fire mage. Cassie risked losing her place in Society when she accidentally set Almack's on fire. But since the horrific event brought Garret Sterling into her life, she blesses the accident now. She's in full possession of both her psychic ability and Garret.

Garret Sterling, Lord Stanstead — Recently elevated to his new station after the death of his uncle. Garret is able to implant a thought in another's mind with such seductive force, his suggestions are irresistible. Garret is a libertine who carouses to avoid sleep because his nightmares have the bad habit of becoming someone else's waking reality. Usually. Cassandra Darkin seemed oblivious to his gift, which made the fact that the duke asked him to help her control her accidental fire-starting a difficult assignment.

Pierce Langdon, Viscount Westfall — a telepath whose skills are the mirror image of Garret Sterling's. If Sterling is the universal dispenser of unwanted thoughts, Westfall is the universal receiver of everything rattling around in the heads of others. Unfortunately, he hasn't learned to filter anything out. Because of his propensity to "hear voices," Westfall was only recently released from Bedlam on the condition that the Duke of Camden be responsible for him should his "voices" urge him to violence.

I watch the heavens by night because they both instruct and bewilder me. When a star streaks across the sky, hurled to earth in a flaming death, it makes one wonder what sin a ball of fire could possibly commit to earn such a devastating fall.

~ from the journal of Samuel Templeton, Lord Badewyn

Chapter One

Meg Anthony stood tiptoe on the top of the chimney, the highest point above the gambrel roof of the Duke of Camden's town house. She leaned on the iron weathercock. More than four stories down, people and carriages moved up and down the broad Mayfair street. They seemed like child's toys. No one glanced up at her.

Well, they wouldn't, would they?

She spread her arms and took a flying leap.

The ground rushed to meet her, but before she could crash headlong into His Grace's miniscule front garden, Meg willed herself to slow and come to a complete stop above the hydrangea, heavy with blooms. For a blink, she hovered, wishing she could detect scents in her spirit form. Then she floated upward, light as a soap bubble and as free of care.

It was always like this when she exercised her gift. The abandon, the exhilaration, the sense that anything she could think, she could do—flying free of her body was the closest thing to heaven she could imagine. Unfortunately, she had to be mindful that while her spirit soared during these times, her empty body died a little as it waited for her essence to return. She needed to be quick.

Especially since this was an unsanctioned use of her *Finding* ability. If the duke discovered she'd done it, he'd pitch a fit. Of course, it might be considered disrespectful to think of such an important person as His Grace doing something as common as pitching a fit, so she set that idea aside. Besides, more than she feared his anger, she feared he might wash his hands of her entirely and ban her from the Order.

It would be the worst that could happen.

She'd never felt she belonged anywhere until His Grace brought her into his household to join his band of psychic operatives. But she wasn't wellborn like the other members of the Order of the M.U.S.E. Honestly, sometimes the business of learning to read, and the even harder task of learning to carry herself like a lady, ground her down to a nub. Meg needed a few moments to refresh herself. Nothing was better than flitting above the streets of London. She reveled in a God's eye view of its residents, darting about with the speed of thought and passing through bricks and mortar as if they were water.

Since Meg didn't have anything in particular she was seeking during this *Finding* session, she decided to pop into the neighbor's house to have a look about. The family who'd occupied that residence during the Season had left London the week before, escaping to the country as the full heat of late summer and the Thames' low tides turned the city into a miasma of foul scents and even fouler tempers. When that happened, Meg was grateful that she couldn't smell a thing while she was disembodied.

All the furniture in the front parlor was draped with sheets to guard against dust. Even the paintings had been hung with linen, but the maids had neglected to cover the large mirror at the base of the stairs in the foyer. Meg drifted by it.

No one had ever claimed to have seen her when she was in this state, but she could see herself in mirrors. Not clearly, of course. Her image was translucent, as if she'd been scraped thin enough to allow light to shine through her. She grinned at her spectral reflection. When she was like this, with the glory of pure spirit radiating from every bit of her, she wasn't as plain as she thought.

Then she heard repeated thumps coming from above her. She shot upward through the painted ceiling and floor joists to the first floor. Meg was glad that she could make no sound in her present form, because what she saw made her want to scream.

There were two men, sweating and swearing as they tried to work a wall safe from its hiding place amid lathe and plaster. They evidently couldn't crack it, so they'd decided to take the whole thing away with them. Seeing a burglary in process was bad enough, but what really startled Meg was that she recognized the pair as her Uncle Rowney and Cousin Oswald—the two people in all the world she'd hoped never to see again.

Meg shivered. She thought she'd left them behind when she had run away and hid herself in the city, taking a position as a lady's maid. Then when her psychic gift had brought her to the Duke of Camden's attention, she'd felt doubly safe from her past. But it couldn't be a coincidence that Rowney and Oswald were trying to burgle the house next to the one she'd called home for all these months. They were looking for her. She floated closer to listen.

"You sure this is worth the trouble?" Oswald grunted with effort as he leaned his considerable bulk on the crowbar. The safe didn't budge.

"I'm tellin' you, I was walking out with Mrs. Tesh, the cook what worked here till the family moved away, and she swore his lordship left any number of things behind in the safe on account of them not havin' one at the country house." Rowney crossed his arms over his chest, content to watch the younger man do all the work.

Some things never change, Meg thought.

Oswald adjusted the angle of the bar and tried again. "What kind of things?"

"His mistress' jewels, for instance. Don't do to let the wife stumble across those, do it? And a bit of blunt for emergencies. A good bit, I'm told," Rowney said. "According to Mrs. Tesh, his lordship don't exactly trust banks."

"And why should we trust Mrs. Tesh? Peaching on your employer is never a good idea."

"She's got no call to be loyal. His Nibs gave her the sack when they left. Said they already had a cook at their place in Sussex. Couldn't be bothered to keep two on. He gave her a reference, but since she can't read, she's afraid to use the blasted thing. Who knows what lies Quality folk might take into their heads to write about them what work for a livin'? Ain't one of 'em worth spit."

The Quality folk Meg had fallen in with were worth a good deal more than spit. Lady Easton, the Duke of

Camden's sister, worked tirelessly with her, trying to educate her well enough to pass as a lady. And if there was a single soul in the world whom Meg wanted to make proud of her, it was the duke himself.

"This'd be a lot easier if we still had Meggie with us. She'd be able to poke in there and tell us for sure was it worth me bustin' my spleen over." Oswald reared back and brought the crook of the crowbar down on the hinges with all his strength. The steel was unforgiving and the shock seemed to reverberate up his arms. Spouting a long string of profanity, Oswald threw the bar across the room. Wood splintered under the sheeting when it struck the covered highboy.

Meg shuddered. Even though she knew her cousin couldn't see her, his nearness made her feel prickly all over.

"Never you fret over that, my boy," Rowney said. "I've had my eye on the high and mighty 'Miss Anthony' for weeks now. She's close. Right next door, in fact. The Duke of Camden has her cozied up in his place. She don't venture out lest she's in some pretty high-toned company, but she'll get lazy about it one of these days. And then we'll pinch her right off the street."

Panic gripped her with both hands and squeezed. Rowney was right. If they nabbed her, her uncle and cousin would force her back into their life of drawing latches and picking pockets. She had to be extra careful every day to stay free. They only had to get lucky once.

"You and Meggie will be tyin' the knot before you know it," Rowney went on.

She couldn't listen to more. The thought of marrying Oswald made her want to start shrieking and never stop.

But she couldn't so long as she floated outside of her body.

So long... How long has it been?

Another kind of panic seized her. What if she'd stayed away too long? Quick as thought, she zipped through the walls shared by this town house and His Grace's, then up another story to the chamber that had been assigned to her.

Her body was slumped in the comfortable wing chair near her cold fireplace, but a candle burned on the low table before her. She preferred to have someone lay their hands on her shoulders to help anchor her to earth during a *Finding*. Failing that, she'd discovered that the light of a candle also served to ease her re-entry into her house of flesh.

But her body wasn't alone. Gaston LeGrand was standing over her still form, a frown on his face. He reached a hand toward her shoulder and then drew it back, clearly undecided about whether touching her would help or hinder her return at this point, since he hadn't been with her from the beginning of her dash into the spirit realm.

Meg hovered over her body. She almost didn't recognize herself.

It was as if that body in the chair belonged to someone else. The waxy pallor, the dead stillness, the chained-to-earth heaviness—how could it house something as light and heaven-born as her breathless essence? But she slipped back into it, anchoring her spirit to the body that became hers once more.

A deep lungful of air hissed over her teeth. Her heart lurched from its nearly stopped state into a galloping rhythm. Meg tingled all over as her freshly animated skin sent frantic messages to her brain. She was suddenly aware of the scratchy lace on her petticoat beneath her muslin gown and the feel of old leather on the arms of the chair beneath her fingertips. As if she were a hedgehog waking after its long winter sleep, her eyelids fluttered open. She looked up into LeGrand's scowling face.

"His Grace, he will not be amused." And neither was LeGrand. When it came to Meg's safety, he was like the disapproving older brother she'd never had. "What is so important that you would risk his noble wrath?"

She hadn't intended to tell. In truth, she wanted to forget that Rowney and Oswald were only a few walls away, but she had to give LeGrand something. The duke was deeply concerned about the risk she ran each time she used her gift to *Find* objects or people who had gone missing. If she admitted that she just wanted to lark about without her skin for a while, it would upset His Grace out of all knowing. So she let the fact that the neighbor's empty house was being burgled spill out of her.

"Should we send for a Runner?" she asked. His Grace had a number of Bow Street Runners in his pay who could be relied upon to clean up any criminal activity the Order of the M.U.S.E. stumbled upon in the course of their work.

"If the thieves, they are there now, they will be gone by the time Runners arrive," the wiry Frenchman said. "Some of the servants I will take and make to apprehend these miscreants."

As he turned to go, Meg grasped his arm. "Be careful. They're dangerous."

"And you will be knowing this, how?"

She could have kicked herself, but LeGrand needed the warning. "Because I know *them*."

That evening, the Duke of Camden summoned the members of the Order of the M.U.S.E. to his study. M.U.S.E. stood for Metaphysical Union of Sensory Extraordinaires. Never mind knowing what it meant, Meg could barely pronounce it when His Grace had first discovered her unusual ability to *Find* and brought her into his psychic fold. She was the only *Finder* in the group.

But the others had gifts of their own. For example, Garret Sterling, Lord Stanstead, possessed the ability to *Send* a thought into another's mind so thoroughly, they believed the *Sending* more than their own senses. Pierce Langdon, Lord Westfall, had been his psychic opposite, being able to hear the thoughts rolling around in the heads around him. After he suffered a clout on his head during a recent mission for the Order, the voices of other minds had been silent for a while. Then, before he left for an extended honeymoon in Scotland with his non-Extraordinaire bride, the voices had returned. Only now, Westfall was able to control which voice he chose to listen to so that they only intruded into his head one at a time.

There were three elementals in the Order—magical persons with an affinity for one of the four ancient elements. Gaston LeGrand was a water mage, able to bend liquid of any sort to his will. Lady Stanstead, *née* Cassandra Darkin, was a fire mage, as was Vesta LaMotte, a witty courtesan who often provided the Order with an entrée into the Prince Regent's intimate circle. This was useful since the express purpose of the group was to protect the royal family from psychically-charged objects intended to harm them. The Duke of Camden blamed himself for King George III's occasional bouts with madness. His Grace was convinced that something malignant had slipped through his gauntlet and was playing fast and loose with His Majesty's mind.

"Well, Miss Anthony," the duke said as he paced the perimeter of the chamber. "What have you to say for yourself?"

"I'm most terribly sorry, I'm sure." She was. Terribly. Especially when she glanced at the mottled bruise blooming around LeGrand's left eye.

Uncle Rowney and Cousin Oswald's burglary had been thwarted. According to the Frenchman, the older fellow was limping when the thieves tore down the back alley behind the row of town houses, but the pair got in a few good licks before they ran off. In addition to LeGrand's black eye, His Grace's handsome footman James was missing one of his front teeth. This was a disaster of biblical proportions for one in his position, because above average height and a pleasing face were the foremost qualifications for a footman. In any other establishment, James might have been given the sack since his looks had been spoiled, but the duke had promised that as long as James' work continued to be excellent, a lost tooth was of no consequence to the dignity of the Camden table.

He seemed to be less forgiving of Meg. "Being sorry does not change matters."

"Oh, Camden, stop it. You're frightening the girl," Vesta said. She was the only one of the group who dared reprimand His Grace. And she excelled at it through constant practice.

"She should be frightened. She disobeyed a direct order. I expressly forbade her to use her gift until we are assured she may exercise it safely," Camden said to Vesta before turning back to Meg. "Do you not understand that the use of your *Finding* ability could result in your death?"

No one knew that better than she, but Meg decided silence was the best course. She nodded mutely.

"In a way, it's a good thing she disobeyed," Lady Stanstead said. "Otherwise we'd never have known her uncle and cousin were so close and that they still plan to abduct her."

"What's this?" Camden demanded.

When LeGrand had given his account of the afternoon's events to the duke, he'd tactfully left out Meg's connection with the thieves. Evidently, he'd felt no need to do so when he shared his exploits with the rest of the Order.

"We thought you were aware of the threat, Your Grace." Lady Stanstead sent Meg an apologetic grimace. "You'd better tell him, Miss Anthony."

Meg sighed. The members of the Order knew she'd been engaged in some shady dealings before she became a lady's maid because her skills as a pickpocket had been put to good use once or twice. When she tried to teach Lady Stanstead some sleight of hand, she'd confided in her about her horrible family.

Now Meg launched into the sorry tale for everyone's ears.

Her Uncle Rowney wanted her back under his thumb, she explained, so he could use her ability to *Find* as they roamed from town to town "looking for the main chance." The gang's usual plan was to discover somebody who'd lost someone or something of value and then convince them that Meg could retrieve the item or loved one...for a price. She didn't mind *Finding* objects so much. But it was gut-wrenching to watch people give all they had for the least bit of news about a missing person. Often, the person was either dead or had abandoned their family willingly. Meg hated delivering either of those outcomes. It was part of why she'd run away.

The other part was Rowney's plan to marry her to Oswald. She had to admit it was the best way to assure her compliance. She'd have no choice but to be obedient and outwardly grateful to the men who held power over her. As a married woman, she'd be considered little better than a child or an imbecile by the courts and have no say in where she went or what she was forced to do.

No matter what that might be.

It was hard to keep secrets in a group of psychics, but Meg had managed it. His Grace would be understandably upset. After she finished with her story, Meg folded her hands on her lap to hide their tremble as she waited for the duke's anger to fall on her. Why hadn't she trusted him with everything from the beginning?

The duke didn't say anything for the space of several heartbeats. Then he sank into his wing chair and crossed his legs. "Well, this alters matters."

Meg's heart sank to the pit of her stomach. It was just as she'd feared. He was going to ban her from the Order. She knew it.

He considered her through half-lowered lids for a moment, and then looked away.

"Is Lord Badewyn still in residence at Faencaern?" His Grace directed this query to his steward, Mr. Bernard, who was busy taking scrupulous notes of the Order's business. Meg released the breath she'd been holding. The duke was moving on to other issues. A small candle of hope fluttered to life within her.

"I should think so. His lordship didn't come by his reputation as a recluse dishonestly. London hasn't seen Lord Badewyn in years," Mr. Bernard said with a shake of his head that set his ponderous jowls a quiver. "He'll not have left the castle, I'll be bound."

"Good. Pack your bags, Miss Anthony."

"What?" That small candle of hope guttered completely. He was giving her the boot after all. "Please, Your Grace, give me another chance. I'll not keep anything from you ever again. Don't make me leave the Order."

"Leave the Order? Of course not. You are merely leaving London. You're bound for Wales on the morrow."

"Wales? But it's so wild and lonely there," Lady Easton said with dismay. She was the one member of the Order who possessed no psychic ability of any kind, but her sense of refinement and social niceties smoothed the way for the others as they moved through the *ton*. "Well, I suppose it can't be helped. It's certainly remote enough for our purposes. Miss Anthony will be safe there. I shall have my abigail begin packing immediately."

"No, sister, you will not be accompanying her," Camden said.

"But this is wholly unacceptable." Lady Easton set her mouth in a prim line. "Lord Badewyn is an unmarried gentleman. If Miss Anthony is to stay at Faencaern Castle, she *must* have a chaperone. Otherwise her reputation will be ruined before she makes her first appearance in society."

"She'd only need a chaperone if anyone knew she was there. I intend that no one shall discover her whereabouts. As far as Polite Society is concerned, Miss Anthony is about to disappear," the duke rose and began his habitual prowling of the room. "Her nefarious relatives have evidently been watching the comings and goings of this house. They expect her to be surrounded by my associates, so she certainly cannot be seen in your company, sister. To further confound her uncle and cousin, she will not be traveling in my carriage. Miss Anthony will go by public coach instead."

Meg hated to interrupt His Grace, especially when he was on a tear with new plans, but there was no help for it. "But…I don't know the way to Wales."

"Of course you don't," Camden said agreeably. "Especially not to the part of Wales to which I'll send you. Few civilized people do. Mr. Bernard, however, is one of those few. He will accompany you to Faencaern Castle."

"Very good, Your Grace," the steward said, as unflappably as if the duke had asked him to ring for tea instead of set off across the country with a fugitive *Finder* in tow. "With Miss Anthony's permission, I will pose as her grandfather for the duration of our travels."

Meg sent the steward a tremulous smile. With all her heart, she wished that the kindly fellow was her grandfather in truth, but only the good were gifted with family like that. She supposed Rowney and Oswald were no more than she deserved.

"Capital suggestion, Bernard. Off with you now, Miss Anthony, and see that you pack lightly. You'll have to manage your own luggage for this trip," the duke said. "And nothing fashionable, if you wish to pass as Mr. Bernard's granddaughter. Plain leaves no lasting impression."

"You're being unkind to the girl, Camden. Miss Anthony has a number of lovely gowns and it would be a shame for her to have to wear the same thing day and day out. Even in Wales." Vesta sent Meg a conspiratorial smile. "I'll make sure he sends the rest of your wardrobe later."

Meg nodded her thanks to Vesta and rose, grateful that she was still counted one of His Grace's Extraordinaires. But being whisked off to Wales still felt very much like banishment. "What if something happens and the Order needs me to *Find* something?"

"In that unlikely event, be assured I will send for you post haste," the duke said. "However, there is nothing pressing at the moment. There seems to be a psychic lull. I've detected no malevolent objects making their way toward the royals. Perhaps during this respite, I can study the problem of how to make the use of your gift less dangerous."

"Thank you, Your Grace," Meg said with a deferential nod. "But when will I be able to return?"

"When we are certain your relations no longer pose a threat," he said kindly. Then his expression turned stern. "And when you have learned to obey a direct order. No more *Finding* on your own. Not until we have discovered a way for you to do it in safety."

"Yes, Your Grace." She'd have agreed to travel to Wales on her knees if it meant she was still part of the duke's Order. Dropping a low curtsy, Meg turned to go. On her way to the door, she overheard Mr. Bernard ask if he should send word to Lord Badewyn in Wales that he was about to receive visitors.

"No need," Camden said. "He'll know you're on your way before you leave London."

I've heard it said the best gift a man can have is a noble friend. Failing that, the second best gift is a noble enemy. I have no friends and my enemy is my father. Alas, he is anything but noble.

~ from the journal of Samuel Templeton, Lord Badewyn

Chapter Two

Samuel pored over the star chart. The vellum was in remarkable repair considering that the map was at least eight hundred years old. The dye used to colorize the chart had probably been added later, possibly as early as the 1600's, but even so, the embellishments were impressive. The constellations wheeled in a celestial circle, fanciful creatures and ordinary beasts chasing each other across a flat sky. The chart was an important find.

"Where did Ingfeldt get this?" he asked, scarcely able to contain his excitement.

"Some monastery outside of Milan," came the bored response. Grigori had no use for star charts. He much preferred to experience the night sky directly, as he did most things. Samuel's intense scholarship—his "bookishness," Grigori called it—irritated him no end. Samuel didn't commit to his studies solely to annoy him, but it was a nice side benefit. "So, it's not a forgery?"

"No, it's genuine. A real relic," Samuel assured him. He

set a felt-bottomed paperweight gently on one corner of the chart to keep it from curling. "And the oldest one I've ever seen."

Grigori brushed his dark hair back off his forehead so it wouldn't hide his pale gray eyes. Women found the stark contrast appealing, irresistible even. Many had been captivated by the juxtaposition of light and dark, of hard chiseled features and the seductive smile that softened them. Grigori was undeniably handsome, but Samuel would never admit it. Except for a few bars of silver at Grigori's temples, his striking appearance and coloring too closely mirrored Samuel's own.

"Please," Grigori said with a sneer, "unless you think that piece of calfskin has been around for a couple of millennia or so, don't talk to me about old."

He was always difficult to impress. Samuel decided to take a different tack. "All right. How about this? Even though this is hand drawn, the proportions within the constellations are roughly the same as current charts."

"Meaning what?"

"Meaning after all these years, the stars still whirl in the same orbits, as orderly a progression as a Mozart symphony. They don't change."

"They change. You just aren't able to see it from here." Grigori hefted himself up onto the thirty inch deep ledge before the arch-shaped window in the gray weathered stone. His broad-shouldered frame filled the space. It was a good sixty feet down from Samuel's study in the topmost tower of Faencaern Castle to the floor of the bailey below, but when Grigori looked over his shoulder at the long drop, he just yawned.

"'Canst thou bind the sweet influences of Pleiades?'" Grigori quoted from Job. "Those stars are bound together by a gravitational force but every second, they're moving farther away from Earth in tandem. They do change. Trust me."

Well, he'd know. Samuel was rarely disposed to trust him about anything, but he'd give him this one. Grigori's faults were legion, but he knew two things backward and forward—the heavens and the Bible. He was dogmatically truthful about the night sky but, as any consummate theologian, he wasn't above twisting scripture to suit his purposes.

"You seem more than usually disgruntled this fine day," Grigori said. "Do I detect a bit of regret over not bolting to the Village to partake of the Season? London's crop of debutantes featured a number of true beauties."

"No, I'm not sorry to have missed it. Once was definitely enough. All that infernal mucking about in one crowded parlor after another, listening to banal conversations, and pretending to take interest in them." And the underlying subtext of all those conversations was that every young miss was frantic to snag any eligible gent in the Marriage Mart before they were all taken. There was no respect. No meeting of the minds. Merely a joining of ledgers and titles, the marital unions that came out of the Season struck him as degrading on all sides. Of course, Samuel had his own reason for shunning marriage. "I'd rather have my entrails roasted before my own eyes."

Grigori laughed. "The parson's mousetrap isn't as bad as all that."

"You never wed."

"Yes, I did. Once." His tone was so different, Samuel's

head jerked up to find his father in a rare moment of reflection. If melancholy had a face, it was the one Grigori wore. Then just as quickly, he shook it off. "After that time, I never needed to marry again," he said with a falsely bright grin. "But you need to face facts. It's high time you wed."

"Is this about the business of getting an heir again?"

"Getting an heir isn't as automatic a process as you seem to think. Depending upon how fertile the young lady is, it may take some time," Grigori said. "So this is also about finding something for you to do besides rattling around in Faencaern by yourself. A wife offers all sorts of diversion — in and out of the bedchamber. It would be good for you. Bring you out of hiding a bit."

Samuel doubted Grigori had his best interests at heart, but he was right about one thing. Samuel was hiding. That's what monsters did, wasn't it? If they weren't disposed to terrorize the populace, they burrowed themselves away, only appearing when the moon was full, cloaked in legend and half-truths.

"If a pretty face doesn't move you, perhaps a bluestocking would be to your taste," Grigori went on. "Lady Winifred, the Earl of Chalcroft's daughter, is more than able to keep up with your intellectual pursuits."

"I'm not looking to rescue a wallflower from spinster-hood."

"If I didn't know better, I'd suspect you were a molly."

Samuel glared at him. He liked women very much, but he wasn't about to become leg-shackled to one just to please Grigori.

"Contrary to what you appear to think, you cannot incinerate me with a look," Grigori said, turning sideways and folding his long legs up onto the window ledge. Most people would be terrified at being so close to a precipitous edge like that, but Grigori seemed perfectly comfortable. "But back to wedded bliss. It is the lot of mortals. Since the Garden, people have been going through life two by two. Why on earth do you resist marriage so strongly?"

"You know why." Samuel narrowed his eyes at him.

Grigori rolled his, clearly unaffected by Samuel's displeasure. "Well, the whole matter may be settled before you know it."

"What makes you say that?"

"If you'd take a few moments from your study of that old calfskin and think back to the last time you exercised your gift with a scrying basin, you'd remember that the Duke of Camden is sending one of his wards to you, a certain Miss Meg Anthony."

Samuel had *Seen* the approach of the young lady and her companion more than a week ago. His ability to view distant events was one of the few things in which he bested Grigori. Samuel's scrying vision was much clearer and he seemed to possess something of a psychic cloak for himself. Try as he might, Grigori had never been able to view Samuel's activities in a still surface. But though Samuel had *Seen* Camden's ward on her way to Faencaern, he couldn't divine why the duke had ordered the lady to travel to Wales. "I wonder what she's done to deserve banishment."

This part of Wales wasn't the least fashionable. No wellborn miss who was used to the bustle of London would relish spending time here.

"She's not being punished. I sense it's for the lady's protection."

It was hard to argue with Grigori's intuition. He was rarely wrong. "Protection from what?"

"Does it matter? The duke needs a favor. You ought to be more than pleased over a chance to put a gentleman as powerful as Camden in your debt."

If a lady needed protection, Samuel was willing to offer it without entangling her guardian in anything as distasteful as obligation. Goodness was supposed to be its own reward, though it seldom turned out that way. "Very well. She can stay."

"Good," Grigori said. "As I said, this turn of events might well settle our problem, too. Two birds with one stone and all that. The best way to protect a lady is to marry her. Then thanks to the strength and reach of the Badewyn name, no matter who is threatening her, no one could touch her."

"No one but you, you mean."

Grigori laughed. "That's right. No one but me."

The anger that perpetually simmered inside Samuel boiled into quiet rage. There was nothing he could do about his situation, so he forced his attention back to the star chart. If only he were as cool and distant as the stars, it wouldn't matter. But he was flesh and blood, and hot blood at that. So it did matter. It mattered very much. A muscle ticked in his cheek as he willed himself not to rant, not to lash out at the pitiable hand fate had dealt him.

Grigori would only find it amusing.

When Samuel finally mastered himself enough to look up at the window ledge again, it was empty.

While traveling with Uncle Rowney and Cousin Oswald, Meg had seen the seedy underbelly of London, the crowded markets and gaming hells. When the gang had roved through the countryside, they'd slept in cattle byres and had stolen eggs from under sitting hens for their breakfast. Her belly had knocked against her backbone more often than not. Under the Duke of Camden's protection, she'd been introduced to the finest of everything, from His Grace's elegant homes to the delights of his table to the astonishing new wardrobe he'd provided for her. She'd wanted for nothing while she bided under his care.

Her journey to Wales with Mr. Bernard introduced her to life among the middling class. The public coach in which they traveled was fairly clean, but when they approached steep grades, the passengers often had to disembark and walk up the hill to spare the horses, who were decidedly long in the tooth. Each evening, she and Mr. Bernard stayed at coaching inns, eating thick stews and barley bread for their suppers with their fellow travelers. They slept on benches in the common rooms, because the duke had thought it might occasion comment if they were to show sufficient funds to be able to afford a private room for Meg.

The goal was to blend in, to hide in plain sight.

Meg couldn't have felt more invisible if she'd been exercising her gift. Then when she caught her first glimpse of Faencaern Castle in the distance, she wished she really could disappear. Forbidding didn't begin to describe it.

They'd been walking since mid-morning. The coach had reached the end of its route and dumped them in a village whose name Meg couldn't pronounce. The way from there wound steadily up, through a forest of oaks, birches, and mountain ash. Then the trees gave way to rolling moorlands. Barren peaks rose around them and finally Meg found herself trudging up one.

She had seen a few castles perched on high places. This was the first one up close. Situated on a barren crag, Faencaern seemed to have sprouted up from the rock itself, instead of being built by human hands. Its spires stabbed at a leaden sky. With no sense of softness or ease in its battlements, it was fashioned strictly for defense. When she and Mr. Bernard drew near enough to see that there were armed servants manning the turrets and patrolling the curtain wall, it struck her as more of a prison than a safe haven.

"How does His Grace know Lord Badewyn?" she murmured as she and Bernard were waved through the portcullis and into the bailey by an unsmiling guard. The iron grill clanged shut behind them.

"Lord Badewyn is one of His Grace's most trusted sources of information."

"He's a spy?"

"No, no. Nothing like that. He is more like…a Watcher."

"A what?"

"I confess I know little more than that," Mr. Bernard said. "Like Lady Easton, I may be associated with the Order of the M.U.S.E, but I have no unusual qualities."

"That's not true." Meg squeezed the old fellow's forearm. "You are unfailingly dependable and kind. Believe me. Those qualities are quite unusual."

Mr. Bernard smiled down at her as he lifted the heavy knocker that would gain them admittance to the great hall. "I only know that when Lord Badewyn warns of something, the duke takes notice. He trusts his lordship implicitly. If His Grace sent you here, you may well believe it is in your best interests."

The heavy oak swung open to reveal a rough-hewn fellow. He was dressed in nothing resembling a livery. His waistcoat was a faded shade of red, covered by a full-skirted knee-length jacket of somber gray wool. A neckerchief, which looked as though it had never seen a bit of starch, was knotted carelessly beneath his Adam's apple and he wore breeches instead of trousers. The porter's clothing might have belonged to the previous century, but the fellow himself displayed none of that era's exquisite manners.

"Well?" the man said. "Who might you be?"

Meg had been surrounded by genteel folk for so many months, the porter's bluntness shocked her to her toes. Bernard, however, was totally unperturbed.

"I am Mr. Bernard, steward to the Duke of Camden and this is Miss Anthony, His Grace's ward. We present ourselves here at Faencaern Castle at the duke's behest." When the fellow didn't respond, Mr. Bernard added, "I believe Lord Badewyn is expecting us."

"He's expecting someone," the surly fellow admitted. "But we've naught but your say-so that you twain are the ones he's looking for."

Meg dug through her reticule and came up with a letter embossed with the duke's seal. "I have a letter of introduction from His Grace."

"Well, that's something, I guess." The porter took the missive and shoved it into his waistcoat pocket. Then he waved them in. He screwed his mouth into what passed for a smile if one wasn't too picky about it. "Mr. Bernard, you'll take yourself across the bailey to the common house. That's where us servants sleep. A room has been prepared for you, I'll warrant." The fellow cast a jaundiced eye at Bernard. Like Meg, the steward had dressed down for their travels, but his apparel was still several notches up from the porter's tired ensemble. "'Tis not so fancy as you're used to, I'll be bound, but you'll find it clean and dry."

For accommodations in Wales, that was evidently high praise.

The porter looked down his crooked nose at Meg. "You'll be waiting here for his lordship then. I'll be telling him where to find you." And with no further comment, he turned on his heel and left her gaping after him. She'd become accustomed to the duke's beautifully run household. None of His Grace's servants would be so rude to a guest.

"I apparently must go, too," Mr. Bernard said to Meg. "And if you have any correspondence you'd like me to deliver, please write it tonight. I will begin traveling back to London on the morrow."

"So soon?" She'd hoped to have Mr. Bernard near her for the duration of her stay. His familiar sagging face was such a comfort. Panic began to gnaw her nerves.

"My duties require my presence elsewhere, but I urge you not to fear. Remember, His Grace trusts Lord Badewyn with your safety. That means we should as well." He gave her a quick bow, as if she really was a lady, and took his leave.

Meg was alone in the long hall and feeling very small indeed. She cast about in her mind, trying to remember what Lady Easton had taught her.

A lady is always confident, but she never pushes herself forward.

Meg was feeling anything but confident and there was no one around to push herself forward to. Still, she needed to do something to screw up her courage. Setting down her valise, she decided to explore a bit. The hard leather soles of her practical traveling boots clacked on the flagstone floor. The sound echoed off the stone walls as she wandered farther into the great hall.

Pennants wavered from the high beamed ceiling, adrift in meandering air currents. Along one wall about midway in the space, there was an enormous fireplace with a spit large enough to roast an ox whole. At intervals, small niches had been carved in the stone walls. In one, there was a sculpture she recognized as some Greek or Roman god or other. He was clad in only a well-placed leaf or two. Little wings sprouted from his ankles. A real lady would be able to name him. She scolded herself for not attending more closely when Lady Easton had taken her to the art museum a few weeks ago.

A brilliantly colored triptych, featuring the Madonna and Child in the center panel, filled another niche. She couldn't say who the figures in the side panels might have been, but they were dressed in far richer clothing than the Holy Family could have afforded.

Then she came across a tapestry that covered so much of the gray stone she had to stand with her spine pressed against the opposite wall in order to see it all. The work had dulled with time so that the colors tended toward muted blues and faded greens. There were so many figures in the scene, it took her a while to puzzle it out. Usually, tapestries depicted great battles or triumphal processions, but that didn't seem to be the case here. There were no knights in armor or war horses with hooves raised to strike.

In the foreground, people cowered in distress. Their mouths gaped in fear, their hands clasped importunately toward heaven. In one corner, a lone woman stood, her belly swollen with child. She shielded her eyes from something hurling toward her, but did not stoop low like the others. The something tumbling from the threadbare sky seemed to be a man.

At least, Meg thought it was a man at first. A pair of wings with a span wider than that of the swans at Kensington Garden fell with him. She moved closer to the tapestry and stretched out her hand toward the ancient threads.

"Don't touch that!"

Guiltily, Meg thrust her hands behind her and turned to look up into the face of the most terrifyingly beautiful man she'd ever seen.

I beheld Satan as lightning fall from heaven.

~ Luke 10:18, King James Bible

Chapter Three

Meg supposed it wasn't right to think a man beautiful, but this one was. Of course, his clothing was only slightly less out of date than his servant's had been, but Meg spared little thought for that oddity. The man himself was so astounding, it didn't matter how he was dressed. His features were more regular and well-formed than any Greek statue ever thought about being. His dark hair was too long for fashion, but if he made an appearance in London, Meg laid odds that every dandy in town would desert his barber, trying to copy this man's style. It might have been a trick of light, but he almost seemed to have an inner source of illumination that gave him a slight glow in the dim hall.

Her insides wavered a bit, as if she'd accidently swallowed a drunken faery.

And then there were his eyes.

His pupils were fully dilated, so at first she thought they were as black as a lump of coal and smoldering with as much tightly contained heat. But then she noticed the thin circle of palest gray around the edge of his irises. In normal light, when his pupils relaxed, the effect of those pale eyes would be almost feral, like a wolf in the woods whose eyes glinted soullessly in the dark.

Could this be Lord Badewyn?

There was something larger than life about him. He moved with the sturdy grace of a military man, but his brow seemed to belong to a poet or dreamer. Even so, the deep crease in that brow betrayed the fact that he was a bit uncomfortable, as though the flesh that housed his spirit was a devilishly tight fit.

Meg knew better than to trust appearances. Lord Badewyn's jaw-dropping outsides might turn feminine heads from here to Brighton, but his insides might be cruel and selfish. She pressed a gloved hand to her chest. It wouldn't do to let *her* insides continue to flutter over him until she knew him better.

A *Watcher*, Mr. Bernard had named him. Since she'd joined the Order of the M.U.S.E., she'd learned that she was not alone in possession of an unusual ability. She accepted that there were any number of people in the world whose gifts marked them as different. But what on earth might a *Watcher* be?

"Step back," he said in a softer tone. It was no less an order than his previous thundered one.

"I didn't touch it." Meg took a step back. Lady Easton would be proud of her for not pushing herself forward.

"You were about to. That tapestry is old beyond reckoning. Sometimes I think just looking at it will cause it to disintegrate." He squared his shoulders and gave her a curt bow from the neck. "You will pardon me, I hope. I don't normally greet guests with a shout."

"Only the ones who are about to commit a grave sin."

His mouth twitched in a half smile that disappeared so quickly Meg thought she might have imagined it. "I doubt you know much about grave sins."

You might be surprised. Meg was dressed like a lady of modest means and, thanks to Lady Easton's training, she could do a fair imitation of one, but she'd been raised as common riffraff. A wellborn miss could afford the luxury of fine manners and a clean soul. A hungry one only knows her belly needs filling and will do anything to ease the dull ache.

"You must be Miss Anthony," he said.

"Were you expecting any other stray women to turn up on your doorstep?" The words slipped out of her mouth before she could contain them. Lady Easton would be aghast. One of the first lessons on how to be a lady involved not saying everything that popped into her head. Unless she was in the Duke of Camden's presence, and feeling thoroughly overawed by His Grace, minding her tongue was one of the hardest rules for Meg to follow.

"No, we are expecting only you. We actually don't receive many visitors." He glanced around the barren hall. "I can't imagine why."

"I can. Not everyone finds charm in cold stone, you know." *Oh, piffle! I've done it again.* She needed to change the subject quickly before she offended him further. Meg started to extend her hand for him to shake, but then remembered that wasn't proper either and drew it back in haste. Botheration! There were so many rules to remember, it was hard to keep them all straight.

"So you must be called Lord Badewyn." Stating the obvious didn't require a response, and since silence yawned between them, she added, "Probably because Prince Charming is already taken."

She clamped a hand over her mouth. At least his looks matched Meg's imaginings of the fairytale hero, even if his abrupt manner didn't. When Lady Easton first discovered Meg was illiterate, she'd begun teaching her to read by reading aloud together. Fairytales had caught Meg's fancy and she'd worked hard to puzzle the words out for herself. She was half in love with the heroes in those stories. Now she faced the embodiment of them and, judging from the way her insides quivered, she must be three-quarters in love with him already.

This will never do. Lady Easton would have a fit if Meg discarded all her training simply because the man was handsome enough to tempt a gaggle of nuns! Meg drew a deep breath to settle herself lest she grovel at his feet in a quivering puddle.

His mouth was curved with amusement.

He's probably used to quivering puddles.

But Lord Badewyn was too polite to laugh at her. Or say aloud whatever popped into *his* head.

Heat crept up her neck. She forced her gaze away from the breathtaking lord and back to the tapestry. Pointing to the figure tumbling from the clouds, she asked, "Who is that supposed to be?"

His brows arched in surprise. "Most people assume it is Lucifer, falling from heaven."

"Oh." Meg had attended church regularly with Lady Easton since she joined the Duke of Camden's household.

It was the done-thing for upper and lower classes alike. But when Meg had been growing up rough with Uncle Rowney, her sacred education had suffered as badly as her secular one. There were plenty of holes in her knowledge.

"However, this tapestry does not depict the fall of the Prince of Darkness," Lord Badewyn said. "People tend to forget that when Satan was cast from heaven, he took a third of the angels with him."

"Oh. And this is one of those angels. I should have known by the wings."

He shook his head. "Actually, that is a common error. Most angels do not have wings. The maker of this tapestry was taking a bit of poetic license."

Surely that was wrong. Meg had seen enough stained glass windows decorated with angels to know they had beautiful wings. "If they don't have wings, how do they fly?"

He stiffened, as if she'd asked a question that was too personal for so short an acquaintance. "Not being an angel, I'm sure I don't know. Perhaps they merely think about being somewhere else and there they are."

Meg cringed inwardly. That seemed personal, too, because it pretty much described how she operated when her spirit left her body to go *Finding*. For the first time in her life, someone had an inkling of what she experienced, even if it was only a guess about some other sort of being entirely. He was the most devastatingly handsome thing in trousers she'd ever seen, and she dearly hoped he lived out the whole "handsome is as handsome does" adage. She was more than willing to try to find out, but she wasn't sure she wanted this man to have such an open window to her soul.

At least, not until she was sure he was willing to accept

what he might find there.

"You have a number of lovely things on display," she said as she wandered away from the tapestry and toward the next niche. It was occupied by something that didn't seem to be an object of art. The circle of brass was etched with all sorts of lines and symbols. A second smaller circle was situated on top of part of the larger one. A lever allowed the smaller circle to be moved. The device was pretty enough to be merely decorative, but Meg doubted it. The thing was pregnant with mystery and purpose. Meg reached up, intending to move the lever to see what it would do.

Before she could touch it, Lord Badewyn picked it up and brought it down for her to examine more closely. By doing so, he also kept her fingertips from making contact with it. He didn't shout this time, but by not allowing her to handle it herself, he made her feel as if she were an urchin with her nose smashed against the bakery window, unworthy to touch, to sniff, to even be in the same space with such delights.

"I didn't touch that either," she said defensively. "And even if I had, how could I harm it, whatever it is?"

"*It* is an astrolabe and if you don't know what it is, how can you be sure you won't break it?"

"Very well. Instruct me." She crossed her arms over her chest. "What does an astrolabe do?"

"Nothing. Unless one knows how to use it."

"No one is born knowing how to use such a thing, are they?" she said testily. Meg was terribly travel-worn and he was terribly arrogant about his superior knowledge. "Perhaps I was hasty in assigning you Prince Charming status."

Again, that amused smile. She wished she could swipe it off his smugly handsome face.

"My apologies," he said. "Here." He held the device closer so she could examine it. The brass glinted brightly as she squinted at the markings. She'd hoped to be able to show him she could read, but she could make no sense of the indecipherable squiggles here and there.

"There's not a smidge of English on it," she finally said.

"No, it's Persian."

"And I suppose you can read Persian." If he claimed he could, she had no way to prove him wrong, but the only language Lords Stanstead and Westfall ever complained about having to learn during their school years was Latin.

"I don't read it well enough to appreciate their poetry, but I'm sufficiently fluent to use this instrument." Lord Badewyn turned the lever and the smaller circle glided around the larger one, as she had suspected it would. "An astrolabe gives us a way to solve problems relating to time and the movement of the heavens."

"I see." She almost did. When she was younger, she'd slept under an open sky often enough to know the stars wheeled in a great circle. If she ignored the Persian squiggles, she recognized a few of the constellations gouged into the brass. "You use this to predict where certain heavenly bodies will be at certain times."

"Yes," he said, clearly pleased that she'd grasped that much. Then he replaced it into its niche with something akin to reverence.

"If it's so useful, why do you keep it here?"

"Where else should I keep it?"

"Close to where you use it, of course." Sometimes, the

most educated of folk hadn't a lick of common sense.

"I never use this one. I have another astrolabe for my work," he said. Now his tone was a little testy.

"So this one is just for show?"

"I wouldn't say that. It's fully functional," he explained. "It's simply too dear for constant use."

"Do you mean to say you own something that's too good for you?"

"No, but—"

"Oh! I think I understand. You must have a son you wish to leave this fine instrument to."

His face darkened like a storm brooding over Mount Snowdon. She had no idea how she'd offended him. It seemed a perfectly natural conclusion that he might be saving the dear astrolabe for his heir. But her words had clearly upset him and if she could have stuffed them back into her mouth, she'd have gobbled them up posthaste.

"Is that your artless way of trying to discover whether or not I'm married?" Samuel knew it wasn't the polite thing to say, but he wasn't accustomed to polite discourse. Miss Anthony would simply have to deal with his plain-spoken ways.

Of course, he had a few things to deal with as well. Miss Anthony wasn't at all what he'd expected when he'd seen flickering images in his scrying basin about the Duke of Camden sending his ward to Faencaern. For one thing, she wasn't as young as he'd predicted. This lady was closer to twenty than fifteen. For another, her manner was off. If she were attached to the duke's household, she ought to show a bit more restraint, more refinement.

And where had she come by that singularly plain traveling ensemble? A duke's ward ought to be wearing his station a good bit more than this miss was.

"No, of course I'm not trying to discover if you're married," she protested. "It doesn't matter a smidge to me if you are or not. You might have half a dozen wives stashed in a place as remote as this and it wouldn't signify in the slightest."

"I'd have to be Persian myself to do that." Samuel snorted at the unlikely scenario of having multiple wives. He was doing his best to avoid having one. "Besides, I believe followers of the Prophet are only allowed four wives, not half a dozen."

"Well, even if you had a full dozen, it would make no difference to me," she said. At first sight, he'd thought her as plain as her dark blue gown, but when she colored up, the blush rendered her pretty in a windswept sort of way. "I'm only here because…the Duke of Camden sent me to escape…an unpleasant situation."

"Ah," he said with sudden understanding. "You have become embroiled in a scandal."

"Where would I be able to get into one of those? Lady Easton and I only go out to make calls on her friends. They're all forty if they're a day and far too old for scandals. Or else we visit museums or go shopping. Trust me, there is nothing the least scandalous about staring at Egyptian mummies or buying Brussels lace."

She rolled her eyes at him. He couldn't tell if they were blue or green. Hazel, he decided.

"I've actually not been presented, you see, so I've been to no balls or attended dinner parties or done any of the usual things one expects in a London Season," she explained. "The chance of getting myself *embroiled* in anything as interesting as a scandal is slim to none."

He could almost hear her silently added, *More's the pity*. Perhaps having Miss Anthony around was going to be less trouble than he thought. She had a quick mind. She was amusing without intending to be, and more to the point, she wasn't the breathtakingly attractive sort Grigori usually favored.

"But back to your beautiful astrolabe," she said. "I'll never understand why people have fine things if they don't allow themselves the pleasure of using them. We none of us know how many days we have on this earth. What are we saving things for? Why eat off pewter if there's china in your cupboard?"

"I take your point." Evidently, the duke's ward had a healthy respect for herself, despite her pedestrian wardrobe. "I shall tell Malachai to use the best settings for supper this evening in your honor."

"No, I didn't mean for me," she said, exasperation fairly leaking out her ears. "I meant for you."

Actually, Samuel rarely bothered with the dining hall. He didn't need the fuss of a formal meal in that echoing chamber. It was simpler to take a tray in his room. But before he could explain that his household was a small one and not accustomed to extravagant dining, she was wandering back over to the tapestry again. This time, she stopped near the corner where the lone woman stood.

"She doesn't seem to be afraid like the others, does

she?" Miss Anthony said.

"She's not." *Though she should have been.*

"Why not? Seems to me that watching an angel fall would be a pretty terrifying thing. Who is she?"

Samuel shifted uncomfortably. He was wrong. Having Miss Anthony in residence was going to be difficult after all. She was the inquisitive sort, which made her high class trouble in work-a-day boots. "Have you never read that Augustine believed that before God created the heavens, He fashioned hell for the curious?"

She cut her gaze quickly to him, clearly aghast. "No, and I don't want to read anything of the sort. What a horrid thing to think. If God didn't want us to be curious, He'd have given us pudding where our brains should be."

She stared at the woman in the tapestry again as if she might divine her identity with her concentrated gaze. Samuel wished he'd asked Grigori if Camden's ward was also one of his Extraordinaires.

"But since you brought up reading," Miss Anthony said, "have you a library here?"

"Yes. However I doubt we have anything you'd enjoy."

"Why? Is it all by that Augustine chap?"

Samuel snorted. He doubted anyone had ever referred to the saint as "that Augustine chap" before. "No."

"Then I'm sure I'll find something better than his stuff. And now, will you kindly ring for someone to show me to my room?" she said with a sigh. "I've been traveling a good long while and I'm in desperate need of a bath."

Miss Anthony's hand flew to her mouth. Evidently, speaking her mind before she fully considered her words was her main vice.

Samuel's was a vivid imagination. It coursed into ramming speed as an image of Miss Anthony in a copper hipbath filled with bubbles bloomed in his mind. She might be wearing the most unfortunate traveling gown ever, but despite the stiff bombazine, he saw signs of pleasing curves beneath it.

"I beg your pardon, my lord," she said. "I didn't mean… that is to say…I apologize for being indelicate."

"No need. If an apology is in order, it should come from me for keeping you from your chamber after such a long journey." Samuel tugged at a nearby bell pull.

He really ought to be thanking her. Usually, he subjugated his body and all its urges, but imagining Miss Anthony in the tub wearing nothing but her blushing skin reminded him how pleasantly male he could feel. How empowered.

He just hoped the cut of his trousers disguised how very empowered he was at the moment.

Fortunately, the maid arrived just then, though for the life of him, he couldn't recall her name. All the help looked alike to him.

"Afternoon, miss." The girl executed a flurry of bobbing curtseys and launched into a running stream of idle chatter about the vagaries of travel and how lovely Miss Anthony must find it to finally stop moving. She collected Miss Anthony's valise by the door and urged Samuel's guest to "Follow me, Miss, if it so please you."

Miss Anthony trailed her to the winding stairs in the far corner, but stopped when she reached the foot of them. She turned back to look at him.

"Will there be a dressing gong?"

"A what?"

"The signal that we have only an hour before dinner," Miss Anthony said with a puzzled frown. "So we'll know when it's time to change for the evening meal."

Samuel hadn't followed that sort of rigid schedule since his last tutor had been dismissed years ago. Once he dressed each morning, with very little assistance from his valet, he wore the same clothing until he retired for the night. When he became hungry, he rang for food which always appeared with near miraculous speed. If he wanted to ride, he had a horse saddled and rode. If he wanted to read, he spent the whole day in the library. If he wished to observe a celestial event that kept him on the roof all night and left him sleeping the next day away, he did so with no compunction. The lack of regular order in his life hadn't troubled him one jot.

Until now.

"The gong will ring at seven," Samuel assured her. He hoped the servants could scare one up in the lumber room. "We dine at eight."

At least they would this evening.

She flashed a smile at him then. The expression made her eyes sparkle and lit up her face, rendering her surprisingly lovely. Her smile revealed her soul and it was exquisite— curious, open and trusting. Miss Anthony was a beauty, after all.

Why had he thought her plain?

Samuel watched until she disappeared up the staircase. His scalp prickled and he knew, without knowing how, that Grigori was behind him. He'd probably been eavesdropping on the entire conversation from around the corner.

"Not a pattern sort of debutante, is she?" Samuel said. He was glad of it. Grigori lived for the biddable ones he could seduce with a smile and a few sweet words.

"No, but then you're not a typical lord, either."

Samuel needed no reminder.

"So, we're dining at eight, are we?" Grigori said.

"Miss Anthony and I are, yes."

"I believe I'll join you."

"Why?" This was a departure from the plan. Grigori had made no bones about the fact that since Samuel had no interest in choosing a wife for himself, he considered Miss Anthony a prime candidate for the role of Lady Badewyn. But Grigori had also told him he didn't intend to meet the woman Samuel wed until well after the vows had been spoken.

"Let us just say that even I feel time nipping at my heels on occasion. I want to help," Grigori said laconically.

"I don't need help."

"From what I was able to overhear, you certainly do. The girl is right. Charm doesn't seem to be in your repertoire. It would be a pity to lose this one because of your boorish behavior. Your Miss Anthony seems like a rippingly unconventional find."

"She is not *my* Miss Anthony."

"Maybe not yet, but she will be."

Samuel's gut churned. He wouldn't wish that on anyone. Least of all the young woman he'd just met. Miss Anthony had come to Faencaern Castle for sanctuary from some unnamed danger. She had no idea she'd stumbled into a situation fraught with far more peril than she was likely to encounter among the *ton* of London.

So long as Samuel didn't become involved with her, she'd be safe until the Duke of Camden recalled her. But when Grigori made pronouncements about the future, he was usually right.

My Miss Anthony.

He'd found her surprisingly attractive and he'd enjoyed talking with her more than he could have imagined. Her ideas were fresh, not the canned, careful conversation a debutante learned to make at finishing school. But Samuel would have to be careful. He'd have to steel himself against her, to be polite and nothing more. Hands awash in innocent blood never came clean.

My Dear Lady Easton,

As you know, I've never written a letter before but Mr. Bernard seems to want something to deliver to you, so I'll give it my best effort. I won't tell you we arrived safely because it's obvious we must have since I'm writing to you. Dear me, my words are chasing their own tails, aren't they?

Faencaern Castle isn't at all what I expected and neither is Lord Badewyn. I know His Grace thought I'd be safer here, but in truth, my belly hasn't stopped jittering since we arrived. If only I could poke about a bit I might discover what's afoot here, but no, I promised His Grace I wouldn't Find *without his say-so. I understand that the duke wants to protect me, but the thing is, don't all the Extraordinaires run into danger when they serve the Order sometimes?*

Why should I be different?
Yours ever so truly,
Meg

~a letter to Lady Easton from Miss Meg Anthony

Chapter Four

Meg knew perfectly well why she was different. She was His Grace's pet project, his proving ground for the idea that the upper class held no monopoly on psychic powers. He so wanted her to succeed, to rise above her humble beginnings, and if she was to be useful to the Order she needed to be able to move in aristocratic circles as one of them. So far, she'd been a dismal failure in that department.

Meg cleaned off the quill and replaced it in the small escritoire. There had been just enough light from the setting sun streaming through the arrow loop that served as a window in her chamber. It was growing too dim to write even if she had anything else to say.

"Oh, Miss, this gown is ever so smart." The maid shook out Meg's blue satin and held it up to admire it further. Her given name was Bronwen, Meg had learned, but as a lady's maid she was entitled to be called by her surname, which was a mouthful—Cadwallader. The girl hadn't stopped talking since she'd drawn Meg's bath. Now that Meg was clean and dressed in her softly draping afternoon gown, Cadwallader was busy as a sparrow, unpacking Meg's valise and stowing her few things in the large oak wardrobe. "Is this what they're wearin' in London these days?"

Cadwallader held the pale blue gown before herself and glanced in the nearby mirror, a not-so-subtle way of trying it on without actually slipping into it. Lady Easton had deemed the gown worthy of a dinner party, once Meg herself was worthy of attending one.

Worthy or not, I'm wearing it tonight.

"They wouldn't be wearing it in London 'these days.' That gown isn't for day wear. The fabric and the ornamentation are too fine. It's only for evening," Meg explained, pleased. She thought she sounded very like Lady Easton at her instructive best.

"'Struth, that's what it is to be a lady, I warrant. Even your clothes have curfews. Oh, my stars, would you look at these stockings!" The girl went on to exclaim over every scrap of lace or cunning embroidery on the undergarments Meg had brought. This was only the smallest part of Meg's wardrobe. Once the rest of her things arrived, Cadwallader would likely have an apoplectic fit over the column dresses with their matching pelisses and the sweet little slippers that went with each outfit. She'd probably faint dead away over Meg's collection of bonnets, caps, and hats. The duke hadn't stinted a bit in seeing her tricked out like a proper lady.

"Oh, dear, I don't see a corset here among your things," the maid said.

"I don't wear one. Just short stays."

"Oh, well, I suppose with the way your gown is nipped

in just below your breasts and doesn't show your waist, you wouldn't need a corset then, would you?" Cadwallader spread the blue satin on the bed and smoothed out the wrinkles with her hand. "Well, just you wait. All the women in the castle will get one look at your lovely things and out will come the shears and thread. We'll be remaking our clothes to the new fashions right enough. We may be out of the way here in Faencaern, but we take to new things whenever we can, just like ducks to water, indeed we do."

Judging from Cadwallader's attire, no new female clothing had been seen in the castle in several decades. The maid wore a snug bodice that cinched in her waist over a long sleeved shirt. It probably concealed a heavy whalebone corset since she'd asked about one. Her skirt was full with multiple petticoats under it and a long white apron over it. Her carrot red hair was tucked untidily under a mobcap.

"How did you come to work here?" Meg asked.

"Oh, I was born here. My mother was lady's maid to the previous chatelaine and her mother before her and so on time out of mind. Of course, there's never been a chatelaine here at the castle for very long. Still, we Cadwalladers stand at the ready when our time for service comes. I'm ever so grateful to have you to practice on, miss, before a new Lady Badewyn takes up the keys to the castle." She clapped both hands on her mouth. "Oh dear, that didn't come out right. I'm ever so sorry."

"Never mind. I take no offense." Whether Cadwallader knew it or not, Meg was practicing on her, too. This was a good test of how ladylike she could be. She decided she liked her maid. Compared to Cadwallader, Meg was the model of sophistication. "It's hard to believe you were born here though. You don't sound as if you're from Wales."

When Mr. Bernard had asked for directions to Faencaern at a nearby farm, Meg hadn't understood one word in three.

"That's because his lordship isn't exactly Welsh, you see. Not with a family name like Templeton. When this bit of rock was claimed, the first Lord Badewyn weren't Welsh either. We're guessing he were English," Cadwallader explained. "So when his lordship goes traveling, he sends a teacher. Some years past, Mr. Ingfeldt came to us, to make sure we was up to snuff. As I understand it, folks' ways of speechifying change over the years. My old mam said his lordship's father before him sent a tutor for everyone in the castle too, so's we'd be able to understand him once he finished his traveling."

The baron had mentioned spending time in Persia, which seemed an odd place to visit to Meg. But Cadwallader made it sound as if Lord Badewyn's outlandish wanderings were expected, almost required. "His traveling?"

"Oh, yes, you see, all the Lord Badewyn's down through the years have spent a good bit of their lives somewheres else. They're born here, o' course, and after they finish their schooling, they venture abroad in the wide world to seek a wife." Cadwallader sighed wistfully. "That's the shining time, my mam tells me, when young Lord Badewyn brings home his bride."

"And this Lord Badewyn hasn't done that yet?" The little flutter in her belly was disconcerting. Why should she care if he had claimed a bride or not?

"Well, he did the traveling, but he didn't come back with a Lady Badewyn. He'll need to go courting again unless happens he don't see a need to. After all, you're here, ain't you?" She winked conspiratorially at Meg, but then her face crumpled in a frown. "But mayhap you wouldn't fancy becoming our chatelaine. After all, there's the curse to deal with."

"The curse?"

"Oh, I shouldn't have said that." Cadwallader wrung her apron in her hands. "I don't know as it's really a curse, but it seems as if all the Lady Badewyn's die in childbed. Ain't that the saddest thing? I mean, you can see why his lordship would want to take his bairn and travel away from the heartache after that. They all do it, regular as clockwork, I'm told. Then after a time, once the boy is grown—and it's always a boy, never a girl—the old lord dies in a far country and the young lord comes back, indeed he does."

If Lord Badewyn had spent all his growing up years traveling, Meg wondered what else he'd learned besides Persian. He certainly didn't seem at ease around her, what with his long silences interspersed with imperious commands. "So how long has the current lord been home?"

"Oh, nigh onto ten years or so. Long enough for us to get comfortable with his ways," Cadwallader said. "Only since he didn't bring home a bride, we expect him to go traveling again any day now."

Meg hoped not. She'd been treated like a sister by the male members of the Order of the M.U.S.E. and she thought of them as the brothers she'd never had. Westfall or Stanstead never made her belly jitter or her mouth go dry. But when Lord Badewyn had simply looked at her, she'd felt her cheeks heat. Either she was coming down with the ague, or she didn't feel the least sisterly toward him. Those feelings made no sense, but there was no denying them.

They simply *were.*

Though Lady Easton had tried to teach her many things, Meg's education in flirting was spotty at best. However, she'd seen it done and taken note. It would be interesting to see if she could flirt Lord Badewyn into feeling less than brotherly toward her. "And what happened to his lordship's father?"

"The old lord died at some place called Ankara, or so Malachai tells us. But his lordship wasn't alone in his sorrow. Young Lord Badewyn's uncle joined up with them somewheres along the way because he came home to Faencaern Castle with his lordship and has been here ever since," the maid said. "Mostly."

Something was definitely off about Cadwallader's story, but the maid didn't seem to see it. Meg rose and paced the room, an unconscious echo of the Duke of Camden when he was trying to puzzle something out. "Since the old lord was dead, and the new one had been gone since he was a babe in arms, how could you know for certain it was he when he returned?"

"Oh, that's easy. All the Lord Badewyn's have a definite look about them, indeed they do. Cut from the same bolt of cloth and no mistake. Handsome as the devil, every single one. When you visit the gallery, you'll see it for yourself." Cadwallader's expression turned pensive. "Then there's the birthmark."

"What birthmark?"

"Yes, a truly unusual one. All the Badewyn's right-wise born bear it." She took Meg's hand and traced a pentagram on her palm. "'Tis a red five-pointed star on their...well, in an unmentionable place, but Malachai checked and his lordship has one right enough."

Meg's cheeks burned, wondering what unmentionable place Cadwallader meant. Her imagination flitted to several, but she tamped it down. *No good can come from imagining a man's unmentionables.* "You've brought up this Malachai several times. Who is he?"

"Oh, you've met him, miss. It's him what let you in. Not that he usually serves as a porter, you understand. Malachai is the steward here at Faencaern. It was a mark of favor that he opened the door to you and your man-servant, indeed it was."

Meg didn't like the idea of people believing Mr. Bernard was her servant. As they'd traveled together, she'd enjoyed thinking of him as her grandfather far too much. It was hard to equate the scruffy, surly Malachai with the always correct and kind Mr. Bernard, yet they both held the same highly responsible post on their respective estates.

The deep sound of a gong resonated through the castle.

Cadwallader's eyes grew round. "What's that?"

"The dressing gong, I collect," Meg said. Clearly, the maid had never heard one before. "It means I have one hour to dress for dinner."

"No, it means I have one hour to dress you," Cadwallader said brightly. The idea of dressing for dinner might be new to her, but she was quick to embrace the custom. "Now then, miss, sit you down and let me see what can be done with your hair. My old mam taught me a few things, indeed she did."

Meg surrendered to her capable hands, trying to settle the nervous flutters in her belly. She'd dined at Lord Albemarle's country house, which might have been considered a dinner party, but Lady Easton had been near to make sure Meg didn't put a foot wrong. This would be her first formal dinner without any help, her first chance to show she could pass as a lady. The first chance for Lord Badewyn to see her in such a setting. Perhaps she'd be able to undo any damage her bedraggled entrance might have caused.

Meg hoped she'd remember all the rules. She hoped she'd be able to figure out how to flirt without being obvious about it. As Cadwallader might say, indeed, she did.

"Well, Miss Anthony's arrival has produced one good thing," Grigori said as he lounged, one shoulder against the doorjamb that led from the great hall that could accommodate everyone in the castle to the more intimate chamber that was used when the number of diners was small.

"What's that?" Samuel tugged at the sleeves of his dark jacket. He wasn't sure, but he suspected too much of his cuffs were showing. He wouldn't normally care about such things, but Miss Anthony had been living in a duke's household. And something in her smile made him not want to disappoint her on her first night with them.

"You've abandoned that old frock coat of yours for something that might fit into this century. I salute you, son."

"I didn't do it for you." When it was only him rattling around the castle, it didn't matter to Samuel what he wore. Faencaern was very nearly its own little world, with none coming or going. Only Grigori popped down to London from time to time and tried to bring back news of fashionable trends. Samuel couldn't care less. So long as his clothing kept him decently covered and warm in winter, he was content. And if donning hopelessly out-of-date attire irritated Grigori, so much the better. But now that Miss Anthony was here, Samuel felt honor bound to present a more *au courant* face to the world. "And don't call me 'son.' You're supposed to be my uncle, remember."

"Uncles are so stodgy. Wouldn't you rather I show myself to Miss Anthony like this?" For a blink, Grigori's form shimmered and he reappeared as a gangly youth with the first wisps of a mustache along his upper lip. Coltishly handsome, he was still recognizable as himself, but seemed to be only about fifteen years old. "I can be your long lost nephew."

His voice even cracked as if on cue.

"Stop it," Samuel said through clenched teeth. "You'll upset the help if any of them see you like that."

Only Malachai knew the whole truth about the strange doings at Faencaern Castle. With the ward of the Duke of Camden in residence, the last thing Samuel needed was for his footmen and maids to fly into hysterical fits over Grigori's transformations.

"Oh, all right." Grigori faded out for a moment and then came back as a distinguished, hawkishly handsome gentleman in the final years of his prime, his usual manifestation. "I can see you're going to be no fun at dinner at all. But here comes someone who promises to be a feast."

Miss Anthony appeared on the winding stairs and began to descend. She was a vision in pale blue, a bit of softness the old castle hadn't seen in years. Samuel's mouth went dry at the sight of her, but before he could stir himself to action, Grigori strode across the open space to meet her at the foot of the staircase.

"Good evening," he said, sweeping a deep courtly bow. "You must be the duke's ward, Miss Anthony. I've heard so much about you."

"Good things, I hope." She glanced from Grigori to Samuel and back again.

Probably noting how alike we are. Looking at Grigori was like seeing his own face fifteen or twenty years hence.

"Why good things?" Grigori asked with a waggle of his brows. "Wicked things are so much more interesting, don't you think?"

Instead of being offended, she rewarded him with a sweet smile. "I'm sure I wouldn't know from experience, but I have heard rumors to that effect."

She extended her hand to him, palm down, and he brushed her gloved knuckles with his lips. Her gloves were thin, lacy confections, with more skin showing through them than was covered.

Why did women wear such tempting things? Samuel's insides did a slow burn, but his feet seemed rooted to the spot.

"You must be Lord Badewyn's uncle. I've heard about you, too."

"Wicked things, I hope," Grigori said, almost parroting back her response.

"Not yet," she said with a laugh, "but I haven't been here long."

Her pointed glance in Samuel's direction invited him into the conversation and pulled him toward her. He wondered if he'd have ever unstuck his feet if she hadn't sent that look of entreaty his way.

"A debutante who doesn't feign shock over a bit of light-hearted silliness. Isn't she charming, Badewyn?" Grigori turned back to her and bowed sharply from the neck. "Since my nephew seems to have lost the power of speech, allow me to introduce myself. I am Grigori Templeton, at your service."

He still hadn't released her hand, blast him.

"There now, didn't that sound nice?" Grigori was saying. "Actually, I make it a point of honor not to be in servitude to anyone. It's my one virtue."

Miss Anthony smiled again, a dimple carving a sweet indentation in her left cheek. "There are those who might argue your one virtue is a vice," she said teasingly.

"None whose opinion matters to me," Grigori cut a swift look at Samuel and then back to Miss Anthony. "However, I'll toss aside my scruples and offer my services to you, my dear. May I escort you into the dining room?"

Samuel found his tongue. "As Miss Anthony's host, that's my job." Holding out his arm, he stepped between them, demanding wordlessly that she take it. He knew he was skirting the edge of boorishness, but he couldn't bear to see Grigori flirting with her a moment longer. Wasn't there the least instinct for self-preservation in her, some inner warning bell that should have alerted her to what he was? Since she showed no sign of recognizing the danger, Samuel would have to step in. "Shall we?"

The kitchen staff outdid themselves for dinner. The white soup could have easily graced a duke's table. Samuel had no cause for complaint over the veal, or the mutton, or the braised chicken. He even liked the Cauliflower a la Flammond. Cook had prepared dozens of dainties and sweetmeats, as well. Even the footmen, who had no practice serving at table most of the time, made a creditable job of serving the dinner.

Miss Anthony was a gracious guest, making approving comments, seeming to enjoy herself immensely.

The only problem was she was enjoying herself with Grigori.

Samuel supposed he couldn't blame her. He tried to think of something amusing to say, some topic to introduce that would engage her, but whenever he looked into those changeable blue-gray-green eyes of hers, his mind went blank as a starless night.

Grigori was more than up to filling the void.

Even that might not have been so bad if not for the topics with which he filled it.

"Oh, he was a proper scamp, let me tell you. Samuel positively scandalized the housemaids in Milan by running naked through the villa when he was younger."

"Good heavens!" Wide-eyed, she stared at Samuel. "Er... How much younger?"

Grigori laughed. "Much younger than you're obviously thinking. Our Samuel's no libertine, more's the pity. He was only five. He slipped out of his clothes because he claimed his 'skin wanted to breathe.'"

"I can understand that." Meg shot Samuel a sympathetic glance. "We all feel constrained at times. I know I do."

Even as a child, Samuel had recognized how odd his situation was and how desperately he needed to keep that strangeness a secret. Finally! Someone who might understand what it was like for him to live such a buttoned-up lie all the time. He could have kissed her.

Grigori's thoughts, as usual, took a different path. "Don't let us stop you if you feel the need to dash about the castle in naught but your skin, Miss Anthony." He waggled his brows suggestively. "Anything to accommodate a guest."

Her cheeks pinked up prettily. "Oh, no. I didn't mean that."

"Of course not," Grigori said. "But an old man can dream, can't he?"

This time, she laughed. She flicked her fan on Grigori's forearm and told him he wasn't at all old. "Ladies grow old, I'm afraid. Gentlemen just become more interesting."

Even when he was being outrageous, Samuel's father could charm anything in a skirt.

How does he do it?

Then Grigori launched into the story about when he took Samuel backstage at the Parisian Opera. Samuel had climbed up onto the diva's lap and proposed to her because she had the "most beautimous voice in the world." He'd been all of six that time.

"As you can see, Samuel started early as a lady's man," Grigori explained with a laugh.

"I consider myself forewarned." Miss Anthony's eyes sparked with fun when she turned toward him. "But tell me, my lord. How is it you've remained unmarried when you began proposing at six?"

"I believe it has something to do with the fact that women are smarter than we credit them." Samuel buried his nose in his wine goblet, hoping to blot out the embarrassing stories, but Grigori went on and on. Finally, the last course of desserts came and went and Samuel decided to end his father's infuriating stroll down memory lane.

"Allow me to escort you back to your chamber, Miss Anthony," he said in a voice that brooked no refusal. "The corridors are dark and it would be easy for you to lose your way."

He might have been rushing the end of the evening a bit, but he wanted to beat Grigori to the punch. The last thing he needed was for his father to spend time with her in a dim hallway. However, even arm-in-arm with a candle to light their way, Samuel could think of nothing memorable to say to the first woman he'd actually wanted to talk to in years.

Miss Anthony seemed able to pick up where Grigori left off. She chattered about how lovely the meal was, about her trip to Faencaern, about how pleasant she found her accommodations at the castle.

"I can only surmise you aren't well traveled," he said at that. "Faencaern isn't the most welcoming of places."

"Rather takes its cue from its lord, I think."

"I apologize if I have made you feel unwelcome. That is not my intent." Of course, if she didn't feel welcome, perhaps she'd go back to the duke to face whatever unpleasantness she was fleeing. Whatever it was would be safer for her than remaining here.

He opened the door to her chamber and held the candle aloft while she stepped lightly across the threshold. She moved gracefully, as if her feet didn't deign to touch the floor. As she turned back to face him, he caught a whiff of her perfume, the heady scent of violets, the fresh breath of a summer day. Her little pink tongue swept her bottom lip and his knees nearly buckled. He so wanted to capture that lip between his and suckle it.

The sudden urge shocked him to his toes.

Samuel prided himself on extreme self-control where the fair sex was concerned. He had to keep that part of himself under tight rein, so he was unprepared for the rush of lust that washed over him. He wanted things. Desperate, impossible things from the alluring young miss in front of him.

But at that moment, he wanted more than anything to kiss Miss Anthony.

"If, by your long silences, you don't mean to make me feel unwelcome," she said, "may I ask just what *is* your intent, my lord?"

Samuel closed his eyes. If he got the kiss he wanted, it wouldn't be enough. Once his lips touched hers, he'd want to sweep into her chamber and seduce her thoroughly. A jumble of conflicting desires warred inside him. He could lose himself in her.

And maybe find himself as well.

He opened his eyes to discover her looking up at him, head cocked to one side.

"I mean no disrespect. I simply need long silences to compose my thoughts."

"Oh! Very wise. Speaking too quickly gets me into trouble more often than not. So please, by all means, go ahead. I shall be happy to wait here in the drafty doorway while you think."

He suspected she was being sarcastic, but he thanked her in any case and closed his eyes again. Even if there was a bit of snippiness in her tone, something within her still called to him.

When he and Grigori had traveled the capitals of Europe, he'd met countless women, but he'd never teetered on the edge of losing control with one before. There was something different about her. She understood him, at least a little bit. She knew how it felt to be constrained, how hard he tried to hold in secrets and how, even as a boy, he'd had to break free once in a while lest they consume him.

No one else ever had.

Her artless way of saying the unexpected even seemed to keep Grigori a little off balance.

Is Grigori behind this?

Had his father had a hand in putting this temptation before him? If Samuel ruined Miss Anthony, not only would he be betraying the Duke of Camden, a powerful ally who would make an even more powerful enemy, he'd have to make things right by marrying her. And that would condemn her to far more than the loss of innocence.

He opened his eyes. She was gazing up at him, her arms crossed over her chest, her toe tapping. How long had he been standing there, his light side struggling with the dark?

What must she think of me?

"My intent," —he raised her hand to his lips and settled for a kiss on her knuckles, grateful for how thin those lacy gloves were —"is to bid you goodnight."

He handed her the candle and stalked away in the dark. It didn't matter. He could navigate the twists and turns of Faencaern blindfolded. Desperate for a chance to quiet the urges that still raged in him, he decided some time alone on the roof of his tower gazing at the stars would help.

When Samuel reached the roof, he didn't find the

solitude he sought. Grigori was already there. Standing on the edge of the parapet, his father was looking steadily upward. Samuel couldn't blame him. It was a rare moonless night with no clouds scudding across the sky.

"You're welcome, son," Grigori said without glancing his way.

"For what? Telling all those stories and making me seem a buffoon?"

"No, for making you seem human. You're so stoic and stern and deucedly awkward. I thought if Miss Anthony got a chance to imagine you as a child, she'd be more kindly disposed toward you. So, as I said, you're welcome."

For once, it seemed Grigori's motives were pure even if he wasn't. Samuel still wouldn't give him the satisfaction of a thank you. It would only encourage him to further meddling.

The heavens were ink-black, as perfect a foil for the spangle of stars as black velvet was for displaying diamonds. The Northern lights danced at the far horizon, wavering greens and splotches of red. The Milky Way spilled across the dark vault.

"'The heavens declare the glory of God,'" Grigori quoted in a whisper.

And this was only a small part of the heavens, Samuel knew. There was much more than could be seen with the naked eye. Even his telescope could only reach so far, yet the heavens went on and on without end. "If the night sky we can see is this magnificent, it makes one wonder, doesn't it?"

"Spit it out, son. What do you wonder?"

"It stands to reason the heaven we can't see is even more glorious than the one we can."

"It is." Grigori's chin dropped to his chest.

Samuel had been very young, even before his naked romp in Milan, when Grigori first instructed him about the War in Heaven, about how Lucifer, the brightest and most beautiful of all God's angels had rebelled and convinced others to follow him.

"I've always wondered about Lucifer's troops. They knew full well what they might be giving up," Samuel said. "Why risk losing all that?"

"Oh, that's easy," his father said with a sad smile. "We thought we'd win."

When I was younger, I longed for a way to escape Uncle Rowney and the crowds he drew, by using my unusual ability. I thought I'd be swallowed up by all those pressing bodies, those desperate demands for me to Find *their loved ones or their lost heirlooms. Now, in the loneliness of Faencaern Castle, I could do with a bit of a crowd. Being alone is all it's cracked down to be.*

~ from a letter to Lady Easton that Meg Anthony will never send

Chapter Five

Meg knelt to pull up a cankerwort in the garden just off the castle's kitchen. After a few rainy days had kept her cooped up in Faencaern Castle, her color starved eyes were desperate for the sight of something besides gray stone. Once the sun peeped from behind the curtain of clouds, she was delighted to find a patch of green within the walls.

It was a small space with an overgrown, crushed gravel path wandering through it and bounded on every side by more gray stone in the form of waist high walls. But it was enough land for the cook to grow herbs for her kitchen. In the absence of a chatelaine, the housekeeper cultivated healing plants to tend the illnesses and injuries of the inhabitants.

But there were no blossoms. No spots of color. Meg's young years had been so bereft of the luxury of beauty for its own sake, she was all the more enchanted by flowers now. She stooped to yank up another weed.

"By working in the garden, you are taking someone's

livelihood," came a rumbling voice from behind her.

Meg recognized it as Lord Badewyn's without the need to turn around to make sure. His voice had been invading her dreams since she arrived. She never remembered anything he said. Just the shivery way the deep tones made her feel. She didn't know what that meant exactly, only that she woke with a blush of confused pleasure.

"Surely your gardener won't care if I pull a weed or two," she said.

Badewyn chuckled. "I have it on good authority that old Mr. Priddy doesn't consider cankerworts to be weeds. In fact, he ferments them into something he claims is wine, though I've yet to be convinced."

Meg rose and faced him, still holding the incriminating long stem. She thrust her hands behind her guiltily. "I'm ever so sorry."

"Don't be. How could you know? To most of the world, it *is* a weed."

Meg sighed. "Lord Westfall is right. Plants are like people. Some are useful and some are merely pretty. Some are neither, but all are part of God's creation." She let the cankerwort stem slip from her fingers. "We shouldn't judge."

"Who is Lord Westfall?"

"Really?" Meg blinked in surprise. "That's all you gleaned from what, if I do say so myself, was a remarkably well-spoken sentiment?"

"Who is he?"

As singleminded as he is handsome. "Lord Westfall is a particular friend of the Duke of Camden. And, not that it's any of your concern, I count him a friend of mine, too."

"He wouldn't be the reason you've run away from

London, would he?"

"What? No. Westfall is newly married and I'm delighted for the happy couple." She frowned at him, wishing that while he was irritating her with rude questions he didn't also make her wonder what it would be like if he were to try to kiss her. Lady Easton would be aghast if she knew how jumbled Meg's insides were over it. "And besides, what makes you think I'm running away?"

"Aren't you?"

"I've already told you that scandal has not driven me from London." Then she mumbled under her breath. "I'm not that lucky."

A scandal would have been child's play compared to the threat posed by her uncle and cousin. Meg walked over and plopped down on the stone bench at one end of the garden. To her surprise, Badewyn followed her. Granted, she'd not been in many social situations, not many proper ones at any rate, but it was still a source of amazement that someone as striking as this Welsh lord would take any notice of her at all.

"My apologies," he said with apparent sincerity. "A gentleman should not pry into a lady's affairs."

"Especially when the lady has no affairs." Meg crossed her arms over her chest.

Lady Easton would certainly not sanction this topic of conversation, but it wasn't Meg's fault. *He* started it.

After the awkward beginning, she wondered how he intended to end it.

He ought to leave her to ripping up old Priddy's plants. He ought to pack her off, put her on the next stage and send her back to His Grace. He certainly ought not to spend a minute more than necessary with her and yet…he couldn't bring himself to leave.

Being with Miss Anthony was the only way he could be sure Grigori was not.

His father had always told him he didn't have anything to do with his son's wives until after the wedding, but he wasn't running to type now. Grigori had set himself to be charming to Miss Anthony. Samuel didn't trust him not to try to seduce the girl. If she were already fleeing a scandal of some sort, it would mean she was the sort to be easily duped by a man.

But the way she was frowning at him made it seem as if she didn't particularly trust men. Or even like them.

Or maybe it was just him. Lord knew, he'd had little enough practice with the fair sex.

"May I join you?" he finally asked to fill the yawning silence.

She slid over. "It's your garden."

He sat beside her, careful not to be close enough for even their clothing to touch. He wasn't sure why that was important, but he needed to keep that small bubble of air around himself. He'd allowed so few people inside it, he wasn't sure how he'd react if he were any closer to Miss Anthony. And now that he was in a position to have a conversation with her, his mind became a blank slate. Finally, Miss Anthony broke the silence.

"I notice no one has called since I arrived. Do you have no near neighbors?"

"Not really. A few, I suppose, but they are more than a day's ride away. We don't entertain much here."

"Cadwallader says you're expected to go traveling again any day."

"Who is Cadwallader?"

"The maid you lent me. She is a bubbling caldron of information."

"Oh." He really ought to get to know the help better since they undoubtedly knew a good deal about him. "Why does she think I'm leaving?"

"To seek a wife, of course. If you have no near neighbors with marriageable daughters, it would not be surprising for you to go to London next Season."

"Now you sound like my f—my uncle."

"Mr. Templeton undoubtedly wants what's best for you."

"That's debateable." Grigori wanted what was best for himself. Always and only.

Miss Anthony cocked her head at him. "But perhaps you aren't meant to marry."

Samuel straightened in surprise. When he'd gone to London years ago, it seemed every matron in town was pushing their darling daughters toward him. And the young ladies themselves had assumed that simply because he danced a quadrille with them or fetched them a cup of punch, he must be working up to a proposal of some sort. There was no question that a gentleman of title and wealth would—and should!—take a wife.

"Since the Garden, people have been going through life two by two," Samuel said. "Why would you think I'm different?"

"It comes back to plants again," Meg said. "My friend

Westfall says some people are like birches and some are like oaks."

"I don't understand." Even if that Westfall chap was married, she still quoted him far too often for Samuel's liking.

"Birches grow in clumps, so close together even their roots become entangled. They are incomplete if they are alone. An oak on the other hand can only thrive when its roots aren't crowded. They must be solitary. So which are you, my lord? A birch or an oak?"

Miss Anthony turned toward him. Her changeable eyes were definitely blue today, a clear bracing hue that seemed to welcome him to dive in. Samuel looked away. He was probably an oak. He didn't need, or want, to become entangled with anyone. And yet...

He stood and extended a hand toward her. "Come with me."

To his surprise, she rose and took it. "Where are we going?"

"To see something your Lord Westfall hasn't imagined."

Samuel led her out a small gate that was nearly hidden by vines. Once beyond the opening, the path was so close to the rocky mountain face, they had to walk single file. It was little more than a goat track leading downward, so he kept hold of her hand as they edged along. When they neared the tree line, Samuel was pleased to see that last winter hadn't changed anything in the sparse forest since he was there last. On the edge of the wood stood two trees. Each had sturdy trunks and spreading limbs.

"Here in Wales we have sessile oaks. Like your English oaks, the trunk is massive and solitary. But these two trees are different. Their branches have grown so close, over the years they have grafted to each other in places, here and there." He pointed to several spots where the two entities had grown together. "So you see, one doesn't have to be a clinging birch. Even an oak can reach out and join with another."

Even as he said it, he realized he still had her hand in his.

It felt so good, those slim fingers entwined with his. Sort of like the oaks. Both of them still themselves, still unique in their only-ness and yet not alone. It was a new sensation for him.

One that he ought not to have.

He released her hand. "We need to get back."

"Why? Have you a pressing appointment?"

"No." He couldn't explain why. She likely wouldn't believe him in any case. But every moment he spent with her put her in danger from his father and his plans. So, Samuel took the coward's way. "I have come to the conclusion that your Lord Westfall is right. Our sessiles are an anomaly. I am an oak. A solitary one."

The loneliest star is Fomalhaut. Why lonely, some would ask? I believe it's because the autumn star's brilliance might be dulled by a brighter companion. It would surely overwhelm a dimmer one.
For some, solitude is the only choice.

~ from the journal of Samuel Templeton, Lord Badewyn

Chapter Six

Meg squinted at the ornate script, trying to make sense of it. The treatise on the stars was an old one, with unusual spellings for a number of words. The scribe seemed to have had a curious disregard for the letter "J," substituting an "I" for it every time. Mr. Ingfeldt, the odd little keeper of the library who had blinked like a mole in bright sunlight when she first approached him, had recommended this particular codex to her when she asked for something about the heavens. He didn't often make suggestions to those who visited his library, he explained. His main job in Faencaern was to oversee the library's upkeep and curate its new acquisitions.

After a quarter hour with the codex, Meg decided Mr. Ingfeldt's real job was picking books that would most exasperate people.

Still, she bent her head and tackled the next page. After the conversation she'd had with Lord Badewyn about the astrolabe, she knew he was keen on stars. The man was so very taciturn, she reasoned that if she studied about them, she'd be able to use her new knowledge to draw him out in conversation the next time they happened upon each other. Every time she thought of Lord Badewyn, her insides tingled. It was a curious enough sensation when he was nowhere near. Meg wanted to see if the feeling grew stronger in his presence.

However, the likelihood of that happy accident seemed slim. Granted, the castle was a large place, but she had expected that they would stumble across each other with some regularity. Instead, wherever she happened to be over the past week, it seemed his lordship had just left. He even sent his regrets and claimed work kept him from the dinner table. It had been several days since she'd even seen the handsome lord.

He couldn't have avoided her more thoroughly if he tried.

She had no idea why. She'd been a perfect lady since she arrived. Well, almost. She'd committed a few minor faux pas—the wrong fork used here, an unladylike sprint up the stairs with her hem hiked to mid-calf there—but even Lady Easton would admit her lapses had been small and easy to overlook.

Perhaps that was just what Lord Badewyn thought of her—small and easy to overlook.

"I don't know why I bother," Meg muttered to herself as she drew her lap rug more snuggly around herself. Castles might be all the crack for defense, but when it came to warmth, even in the last days of summer, they left a good deal to be desired. Her fingernails had a definite bluish tinge.

She blew on her fingertips and then struggled on with the book. The description of how to use an astrolabe almost made her admit defeat. Then she turned the page.

Spread before her was a two-page layout of the night sky. The star chart reminded her of the etchings on the astrolabe. Now that she could see the embellished versions of the constellations, their human and animal images superimposed over the stars, it became easier for her to puzzle out their names. She was so engrossed in the book that she didn't hear the soft footfalls approaching the curtained alcove where she was reading.

The curtains parted and she looked up to meet the gray-eyed gaze of Lord Badewyn. He was dressed in his shirtsleeves covered by an unbelted dressing gown—a scandalous state of affairs had they been in London. A man was considered nearly naked without a jacket, but it seemed natural to Meg that he'd make himself comfortable in his own rather drafty home. Then too, they were alone in the library since Mr. Ingfeldt had left to unpack a new shipment of exotic codices and maps. Being found with Lord Badewyn without a chaperone in this cozy little alcove would be enough to ruin her in London.

But they weren't in London.

"My apologies, Miss Anthony." He started to turn away. "I didn't know you were here."

Obviously. It occurred to her that in order to avoid her so completely, he would have to have taken an inordinate interest in her whereabouts. The thought pleased her more than it should. "Have I taken your favorite reading spot?"

He paused. "Yes, but please don't stir. I can go elsewhere."

"Why should you since there is room for two?" She

patted the cushion beside her. He might think her shockingly fast, so she cast about for a practical reason for him to stay. "It would be far warmer with two."

"I wouldn't wish to impose."

"How can you impose if I invite you to join me?" Honestly, the man was harder to be near than her friend Lord Westfall's favorite cactus. "Have I offended you in some way, my lord?"

He shook his head.

"Then please, sit."

He settled gingerly beside her. Though the small nook was a tight fit, she noticed he took care not to let his thigh touch hers. Still, the warmth of him radiated toward her.

Yes, indeed, those little tingles in my belly are having a party.

She forced herself to breathe normally. It was a wonder Lord Badewyn couldn't sense how unruly her insides were.

"I see you've met Mr. Ingfeldt," he said.

She looked up into Lord Badewyn's handsome face. He was almost enough to snatch her breath away, but she managed to ask, "How can you know that?"

"You're reading the Chaucer Treatise."

"Trying to read it, is more like," she admitted.

"That was my first experience with it, as well." That lightning smile of his sped across his features and then disappeared just as quickly. "Don't feel you have to stick with it. Ingfeldt likes to bedevil people with the thing. I believe he considers it a test of character."

"If that's the case, I'm failing miserably."

"No, you haven't. Not until you admit defeat and ask him to explain it to you."

"Well, then there's hope for me. Perhaps you can explain it so I won't have to ask him for help."

"Wouldn't that be cheating?"

"As you said, a test of character, but only you and I will know mine is a bit shady," she said with a grin. "Now, what am I to make of this? Clearly, that Chaucer fellow didn't put this illustration in among his oddly-spelled waffling on, but I'm ever so glad someone decided to add it." She pointed to the two page spread of constellations.

They spent the next quarter of an hour poring over the star chart. When the topic was the night sky, his lordship's tongue was loose enough. Lord Badewyn pointed out the most important stars and better known constellations.

"I don't understand why one would need an astrolabe if one possesses an accurate star chart," Meg said. "If I had this beside me on your roof some night, I should be able to find and name all the heavenly bodies for you."

"Not all." He shook his head. "The stars are orderly, but they aren't static. They parade across the heavens in accordance with the times and seasons. Some aren't even visible here in Wales at certain times of the year. Take *Fomalhaut*, for example." He pointed to a fairly bright star that was shown on the chart situated off by itself near the southern horizon. "It only appears during the autumn months."

"So it's not here yet."

"Probably not. The end of August is pushing the edge of its viewing time, though perhaps with luck and a clear night—"

"Then there's a chance, however small," she said. "Do you think the sky will be clear tonight?"

He blinked at her. "It has been surprisingly clear of late, but that's no surety those conditions will continue."

"So even though the sky's been clear, you haven't seen it this year?"

"I wasn't looking for it."

"Well, we shall have to take our chances, won't we?" Meg closed the Chaucer and rose to her feet. "What time shall we meet?"

If she'd bitten him, he couldn't have looked more surprised. What was the matter with the man? Oh, all right, perhaps if they'd been in London, he'd be right to be scandalized by her suggestion, but they weren't in London. She meant nothing wrong by it. The tingles in her belly aside, surely there was no harm in a little innocent star-gazing.

"We shall have to go up to the roof of my tower around the time for the dressing gong," he finally said. "This early in the season, that's when Fomalhaut reaches its culmination."

"Its culmi-what?"

"It'll be highest in the sky then," he explained, not meeting her gaze. "Are you sure you wish to do this? It may make us late for dinner."

"Hang dinner," she said inelegantly. "Why don't you ask your cook to fix a picnic supper for us and we can eat on the roof while we star-gaze?"

He looked at her as if she'd just suggested they fly off the battlements together. Then his rare smile made a quick reappearance. "You'll have to dress warmly. Once the sun sets, at this elevation, a clear night is chilly."

The fire glowing in her belly would be enough, but just in case, she'd bring along one of the blankets from her bed. "I'll expect you to collect me at seven then." She pulled back the curtain that hid the alcove and started to leave.

Lord Badewyn caught her by the wrist. "Don't tell anyone we're doing this, will you?"

"Of course, I won't." What a sweet thing to say. Even in this remote corner of Wales, he had a care for her reputation. "But I shall have to tell Cadwallader. She'll wonder when I insist on dressing for warmth instead of fine dining."

"Very well, but no one else. And swear your maid to secrecy."

"All right. Until this evening, then, my lord." Meg dropped a shallow curtsy and hurried away before he could change his mind.

She skittered out of the library and up the long stairs, sure her kid soles were barely skimming the old indented stones. Even when she was *Finding*, Meg had never felt so light, so giddy. She was going to spend an evening under the stars with arguably the most handsome man in the kingdom.

A secret evening.

Why secret? At first she'd been flattered that he was aware of the risk to her good name, but now she realized that couldn't be his motivation. No one in London, other than the members of the Order, knew she was here, much less planning a roof-top tryst. There were no other guests in residence at Faencaern who might carry tales, so the stringent rules governing her behavior in the city hardly signified here. Besides the help, the only person who might learn of her assignation with his lordship was his Uncle Grigori.

Why did Lord Badewyn wish to hide his time spent with her from Mr. Templeton?

Some of the lightness floated away and Meg suddenly felt

very chained to Earth. Men hid time spent with mistresses or game girls, women they didn't have good intentions toward.

Meg lifted her chin in determination. She'd show his lordship. Perhaps she didn't have good intentions toward *him*.

With a deferential bow of his gray pate, Mr. Bernard put the letter from Lord Badewyn into the Duke of Camden's hand. "Will there be anything else, Your Grace?"

Camden shook his head. "Seek your bed, Bernard. It's a long way to Wales and back. Once again, you've gone above and beyond your duty to this house. You have my thanks."

"It is ever my desire to serve Your Grace, and in any case, the journey was no trouble," the steward said. "If I was of some small assistance to Miss Anthony, that is thanks enough."

"She *is* special, isn't she?" Camden said, glad his steward seemed to sense it, too.

"I thought all the members of your Order were special," Vesta LaMotte said dryly. She lounged on the chaise in his study, but the candle in the wall sconce nearest Camden flared white-hot for a moment. "Hence the appellation, Extraordinaires."

Vesta had stayed on after the brief meeting of the Order. There still seemed to be a psychic lull surrounding the royal family. Camden had sensed no object of malicious intent being directed toward the Prince Regent or His Majesty, so no business pressed them. Not that Vesta ever let anything press her, even when they were engrossed in M.U.S.E.

intrigues. She was always as serene as a swan. Only Camden knew she was paddling furiously beneath the surface. Their psychic forays on behalf of the royals were a game to her, as much an entertainment as her theatre-going and endless parties.

Or her lovers.

"Of course, you're all special," Camden said as Bernard made good his exit. Like Camden, the steward probably sensed fire beneath the smoke of Vesta's comment. "It's just that Miss Anthony has risen from such humble beginnings. And of all my Extraordinaires, she is the first one to fall under my care who was already in full possession of her psychic gift."

"And you believe your role is to help her use it safely."

"Exactly."

"Has it occurred to you that Miss Anthony may not want safety? For some, the spice of danger is much to be desired." Vesta's lovely eyes were hooded and all the candles in the room suddenly blazed up and then settled to flicker dimly. "Necessary, even."

"So if you didn't possess an affinity for flames, you'd still play with fire," Camden said.

"You're right. Risk is the only thing that makes a game worth playing. However, I'm not the only one. We all have a personal opiate that calls to us."

"And what, pray, is mine?" He expected her to say *she* was his own brand of laudanum. Heaven knew, her body called to his in the language of lust with regularity and his responded in kind.

"You, my dear duke, are addicted to control."

He swallowed back his surprise. "That comes with the

title, I suppose."

"No, it comes from you, Camden. Had you been born a chimney sweep, you'd still feel the need to direct the lives of others."

He glanced up at his dead wife's portrait hanging above his mantel. Had Mercedes felt stifled by his need to assure her safety and well-being by carefully monitoring her activities and associations? Had he driven her to disobey him? Surely she had known it was only because he loved her that he cosseted and protected her. Again, he wished he could talk to her.

Once would be enough.

Camden sank into the wing chair and tore open the missive from Lord Badewyn. As he read, he sat forward, the words on the parchment raising him up.

"Well?" Vesta LaMotte said from her lounging position on the chaise. "What does your mysterious *Watcher* have to say for himself?"

"Badewyn says he's *Seen* a medium worthy of the name a day or so distant from Faencaern. In a village called Gryffydd, to be precise," Camden said, carefully refolding the missive and secreting it in his waistcoat pocket. He needed to reduce his expectations. All the other mediums he'd tried had proven charlatans of the worst sort, preying on the grieving. "His lordship has extended an invitation to stay with him if I wish to investigate."

"So if only we'd waited a while, we could have accompanied Meg to Wales."

"We? No, that would have never done. The whole point of sending Miss Anthony to Faencaern Castle secretly was to distance her from her nefarious relatives. If members of my household had gone to Wales *en masse*, her relations surely would have taken notice and assumed she was with us."

Vesta examined her expertly lacquered nails and then smiled with sweetness at him. Deceptive sweetness, if Camden was any judge.

"I am not a member of your household," she reminded him.

She wasn't now. Vesta kept her own house in a quiet but fashionable street near St. James Park. But there had been a time when she'd been the center of his lustful world. His dear wife and infant son had been gone for some time, but Camden was still wild with grief. During that horrible period, when he had struggled for the will to rise each morning, Vesta had burst into his life and seduced him into a white-hot affair. She had helped him forget…for a while.

"Are you going to Wales, then?" she asked.

"Yes," Camden decided on the moment. He'd been desperately seeking the reason for Mercedes' death for years. A medium seemed the only way to answer his questions. If Lord Badewyn had located someone he believed was legitimate, it was worth Camden's time to see if the Welsh medium could truly converse with the dead.

Something like hope stirred in his chest.

"You'll need company," Vesta said.

"As I said before, we dare not risk exposing Miss Anthony's whereabouts by having the Order travel to Faencaern."

"I wasn't suggesting the entire Order should go," Vesta said. "Westfall and his bride have yet to return from Scotland. Lord and Lady Stanstead are busy cooing over the new addition to their nursery. You'll need to leave someone in London, so LeGrand can hold down the fort here. What a pity Paschal can't be trusted to help him."

"You know, as well as I, that we are unable to release the time thief at this juncture." Down in the sub-basement of Camden's fashionable town house, a being with the ability to siphon years of life from others was held prisoner. Andre-Simon Paschal was an old soul, and a fascinating conversationalist, provided he was safely behind bars. Camden often spent a quiet evening of chess with the fellow. He provided Paschal with books, a harpsichord upon which to exercise his prodigious musical talent, and plenty of food and drink. He respected the time thief's intellect and hoped one day to be able to release him, provided a guard who was immune to Paschal's power could be found. But for now, Camden didn't trust him farther than he could throw him.

"That means you and I are the only ones available. We are overdue for an adventure," Vesta went on. "So I shall accompany you to Wales."

"But you loathe travel."

"I do," she admitted. "It's inconvenient and tedious and ever so time consuming, but it so happens that I care more about you than I despise jolting along in your coach for all those miles."

Even more than the travel, Camden dreaded what he might find at the end of this journey. Lord Badewyn could be wrong. This medium might not be able to reach Mercedes either.

"Thank you for offering to accompany me," he began. "But—"

"It wasn't an offer. I was merely stating a fact. If you go to Wales, so shall I." Fire danced in her eyes. "Granted, it would be more pleasant to travel together, but if I must, I shall hire a conveyance and fol—"

Camden rose and crossed over to her chaise. He knelt and silenced her with two fingers against her lips. "There will be no need for you to hire a coach. We will go together."

She removed his fingertips from her mouth and held his hand between her two soft ones. "Good. That's settled then. Now, there is one more item to be agreed upon."

"And that is?" he asked. All warmth and softness, Vesta's fingers twined with his. He'd forgotten how good it felt to hold a woman's hand.

"We must go to Wales by way of Bath."

"But that's very much out of the way."

"It is," she agreed. "It will be far enough out of the way to deter anyone from following us long enough to arrive at Faencaern Castle and discover Miss Anthony's whereabouts."

"Brilliant."

For once, she seemed disposed not to dispute his word.

"I think it important for London to see us together," she went on. "That way it will occasion no undo comment when we shake off the dust of the city and go cavorting about the countryside with each other. To that end, I propose that you escort me to the opera this evening, where we may see and be seen."

Camden squeezed his eyes closed. The opera would turn into a screaming fest between a soprano who'd put him in the mind of a cat in heat and a tenor who sounded as if his balls were caught in a vise. "Very well. If we must."

"Good, and for the rest of the week, we shall make the rounds of various parties and routs."

That sounded marginally better, so Camden nodded his

assent. "Then when we leave a few days hence, everyone will assume you are my mistress." He raised her to her feet and drew her into his arms. "I see only one flaw in that plan."

"And that is?"

"Why should we pretend?"

"You've made it abundantly clear that you do not wish to renew our liaison. I took you at your word. Now you must take me at mine. I am accompanying you to Wales because I care about you and want to be there to offer my support when, and if, you learn what befell your family. Nothing more, Edward."

Camden swallowed hard. When she called him by his Christian name, it made him yearn for the intimacy they used to enjoy. It hadn't been just physical. He'd told her things. Secret things he'd confided in no one else. They'd laughed together and she'd made him forget he was a bloody duke and peer of the realm. She'd given him a holiday from himself.

But Vesta was right. He did like control. Obviously, he lost it completely where she was concerned.

He thrust his hands behind him so he wouldn't be tempted to reach out and take her. "I respect your decision, of course."

"Of course, you do. You are nothing if not a gentleman. Until this evening, then." Vesta swanned across the room, her hips swaying with each step. She stopped at the doorway. "And wear that gold brocade waistcoat, would you? It suits you so very well."

He nodded. "Because you wish it."

She gave him a feline smile that reduced him to the status of a cat toy. She was definitely not done with him yet.

Please, God.

Astrologers would have us believe our Fate is written in the stars. If it is, in what quadrant of the sky will I discover what will happen once I betray Miss Anthony's trust? I do not say if I betray her. By agreeing to meet with her secretly, I fear I already have.

~ from the journal of Samuel Templeton, Lord Badewyn

Chapter Seven

"Leave the jug," Rowney said to the barmaid who plopped down two mugs, neither of them terribly clean, before him and Oswald. The slatternly wench filled them only half way.

"That'll be another tuppence if I leave you the rest," she said, a cheeky, purse-lipped smile tightening her very red mouth. It was as if she knew he didn't have any more blunt.

He whipped out his hand and reached into her low bodice. The maneuver was performed with only a fraction of the speed he used to have when he was at the height of his pick-pocketing days, but he still managed to surprise her and was in and out before any of the nearby bar patrons was the wiser. Instead of fondling her ample bosom, he'd pulled a coin out of the stash of tips hidden behind the busk sewn into her stays. The maid covered her cleavage with one hand and whacked him over the head with the other. Mildly chastised, he handed the coin back to her.

"Take our tuppence out of this one, there's a love," he wheedled. "We'll pay you back with a spot of interest. You know Oswald and me is good for it."

"I don't know anything of the kind, Rowney Jackson." She ripped the coin out of his hand and stuffed it back down the front of her gown. "Don't you be taking advantage of an honest working girl."

"Honest since you stopped kicking up your heels behind the Brass Monkey, you mean," Oswald said, his eyes narrowing. Rowney's nephew looked a bit like an angry boar when he did that, but it seemed to put the fear of God into the maid. "The man what pays you to serve his ale don't know you used to be a common tart, do he, Lil?"

Her glance shifted sideways to the tavern owner, an affable, respectable sort who was pulling pints behind the bar.

"I'll take that for a no and be taking this for my silence." Oswald tugged the jug from her grasp and she let it go without a whimper of protest. Rowney grinned wolfishly at her as he scooped up the mugs. He and his nephew carried their booty to the booth in a dark corner.

"Don't suppose there's any chance of getting shepherd's pie the same way," Oswald groused.

"Not unless you can pull sommat more out of your pockets than a handful of fingers. Threatening Lil got us more than I thought it would." Rowney slid into the hard bench, glad for a place to sit and rest his bones. They'd covered a lot of ground that day, looking for an opportunity to line their pockets. None had presented itself. "Be grateful for half a loaf, I always say."

"And I always say half a loaf is never enough." Oswald took a long pull of his ale and then swiped his mouth with a greasy sleeve. "Never went this hungry when we had Meggie with us. She could always *Find* where there was a drawn latch or a window what was left open."

"Well, we don't got her with us, do we? So shut your face about it." Rowney would have happily traded ten Oswalds for one Meg. At least she'd been quiet-like so he could drink in peace, especially after he'd give her a bruise or two where it wouldn't show. It had been several years since he could risk cuffing his nephew in more than jest. The big lug had a temper and his fists were even harder than his head.

They nursed their ale in silence after that. Rowney divided the contents of the jug more or less evenly between them.

"Make it last," Rowney advised. "Ain't no telling when our stomachs will see anything else."

He wished the tavern wasn't rich with the scent of yeasty bread and thick stew. It made him all the hungrier. It'd been a day and a half since they'd wolfed down a stolen songbird pasty. Then just as Rowney was about to upend his mug and leave, a fresh-faced young man burst into the tavern. He was hailed all around by its patrons.

"Well, would you look at that?" a nearby fellow said. "Here's young James Goodbody back from the duke's service to grace us salt-of-the-earth folk with his presence. Hey, Jimmy! Will ye be havin' some of Lil's stew? I see ye have a soup strainer now."

Sure enough, the young man's smile was ruined by a missing front tooth.

"I recognize that blighter," Oswald said in a furious whisper. "He was one of them what run us off that night in Mayfair."

"Shut it, lest he recognize you, too." Rowney turned up his collar and sank lower into the booth's bench. Servants borrowed their status from their employers. If a bloke in a duke's service were to finger him and Oswald as burglars, no magistrate in the world would believe them over him.

The barkeep himself came around from behind the counter and showed James Goodbody to an empty booth, where both food and drink were brought without so much as a shilling changing hands. Clearly, this Jimmy fellow was a favorite at the tavern.

It was just Rowney's rotten luck that the newcomer had settled into the booth right behind him. He slumped lower in his seat.

"Sorry about your tooth, lad. Now tell me true," the barkeep said. "Is the duke at least going to give you a good reference?"

"I'll not need one. I'm not losing my position," James said. "His Grace isn't the sort to be put off by a lost tooth. Especially since the accident happened in his service."

T'weren't no accident. T'were Oswald's left jab.

Rowney smiled. Served the pretty boy footman right for interfering with blokes who were just trying to make an honest living by a bit of burgling.

"Well, His Grace is a true gentleman and no mistake." The barkeep raised his voice so all could hear him. "The Duke of Camden ain't going to sack my grandson on account of his lost chopper. That calls for ale all around so's we can toast His Grace's very good health."

So the footman was the tavern owner's grandson. No wonder he got a steaming bowl of stew without paying so much as a farthing.

Rowney clapped his disreputable hat on his head and pulled the brim low, but he held out his mug for the free ale being offered. After cheers for the duke rang through the taproom, the barkeep must have taken a seat in the booth with Jimmy because the two of them continued to jabber on behind Rowney.

"No, I've no cause to fear," James said. "In fact, I may not be a footman much longer. I'm being elevated to valet."

"Valet? Now there's grand news and no mistake," his grandsire said.

"Not permanent like, you understand. The Duke of Camden is planning a long journey and old Dabney—he's His Grace's usual valet—well, the duffer is a poor traveler. The duke has a care for his servants' comfort, you see. 'Specially them as have been with him a long time."

"Makes him a bit odd, don't it? Him minding whether or not the old feller wants to go."

"Oh, Dabney wants to go, make no mistake. But what with the rheumatism and the way his knee gives out sometimes, he's not much use even when His Grace is at home," James said. "The duke figures Dabney can give his knee a rest and I can learn some new skills in the bargain."

Rowney figured the duke didn't want a bloke with a missing tooth serving at his fine table. No one saw much of a valet except the gentleman he served.

Oswald poked Rowney and whispered, "Did you hear that? No one's going to be at the Duke of Camden's house but an old crippled-up fellow."

Rowney held a finger to his lips to shush Oswald, staring daggers at him. He'd been thinking along those very lines, or would have, if Oswald had given him half a minute. It stood to reason that the silver alone in Camden House would set them up pretty for a good long while, but a fellow ought not to talk about a job when there were so many ears about.

"Where's the duke going, if I may ask?" the barkeep said.

"Well, we're off to Bath. Seems His Grace has a new mistress who's keen on taking the water there," James told his grandfather. Then he dropped his voice to a whisper. "But that's not the real reason for the trip. After Bath, we'll head north. The duke is after seeing someone in Wales. I don't know who exactly."

Rowney leaned back so he wouldn't miss a word.

"We'll be staying at Faencaern Castle so's we can visit a village called Gryffydd, grandsire," James said. "A real honest-to-God castle. Don't that sound grand?"

"Don't sound grand to me, Jimmy. I've enough Welsh to know Faencaern means Devil's Rock and I don't like it that you'll be faring there, not by half. What's so important that the duke would take you to such an ill-named place?"

"Surely it can't be as bad as all that. After all, he sent his ward there. You know the one. I told you about Miss Anthony. A very kind, unassuming lady, she is."

Lady? Ha! Makes me want to puke. The duke's ward, is that how she styles herself? She'll have to learn her place all over again once she's back with us. But if Meg's been packed off to Wales, no wonder we couldn't catch wind of her hereabouts.

"Watch yourself, lad. That's all I'm sayin'. The castle sounds chancy. Places earn their reputations just like people. I don't want you discovering for yourself why Faencaern earned its name." The barkeep raised his voice to be heard over the rumble of conversations all over the taproom. "Lil! Bring my grandson some more stew." Then he returned to a normal tone. "Need to weatherboard you up if you're about to go traveling. You'll miss a few meals on the road, like as not."

When Lil arrived with another steaming bowl, Rowney used the distraction to slide out of the booth and head for the door. If young Jimmy's attention was diverted by both food and Lil's tits, he wasn't likely to mark Rowney and Oswald as the fellows responsible for his gap-toothed smile.

As soon as they were out the tavern door, Oswald said, "So we're headed to Faencaern Castle, eh?"

Rowney risked smacking his nephew on the back of the head. "Not until we've some traveling money, idgit. Do you want to walk to Wales?"

"We can try a few pulls in Leicester Square," Oswald suggested. "If we wait till the taverns close and the dandies are drunk, we might make off with a couple of fat purses."

They hadn't had much luck with pick-pocketing lately. Drunk dandies had usually squandered whatever wealth they might have started the evening with, leaving precious little for enterprising thieves. Besides, Oswald's thick fingers had never been very deft and Rowney's had grown too slow. They needed Meg. On top of that trick of finding things, she had lovely light fingers. A mark could walk all the way home after Meg had been in his pocket and never know his wallet had gone missing until he took off his clothes.

"We'll try the Square, but that'll only keep us a day or so. The real score will be when we hit the Duke of Camden's town house. We only need to watch and mark when the duke and his new lady-bird leaves." Rowney clapped his hands together. "Then once we make off with the Camden House silver, we go to Wales, my lad. And we'll be going in style."

Samuel felt seven times a fool, treading down the dim corridor with a basket of food in one hand and a lantern in the other. He ought not to be doing this. It played right into Grigori's hand. Yet, he couldn't pass up the opportunity to spend some time alone with Miss Anthony. He wasn't sure why she drew him so strongly. Granted, he'd not had much experience entertaining members of the fair sex. But his one Season in London had taught him the difference between a coquette and a genuine person.

Miss Anthony was as genuine as they came.

He set down the lantern to rap softly on her chamber door. She opened it almost immediately.

"There you are. Finally," she said, peeping from around the thick oak. "The dressing gong sounded half an hour ago. I thought you'd forgotten about me."

He'd thought of little else since they'd parted company in the library.

"I didn't wish to arrive while you were still…" He'd started down this execrable sentence, so he might as well finish it. *Make that eight times a fool.* "…still dressing."

A vision of Miss Anthony in the midst of her toilette, dressed in only frothy lace and clocked stockings rose in his mind. She opened the door a bit wider. He was glad to see she had donned that horrible traveling ensemble she'd arrived in. It made her a little less tempting.

But only a little.

"Oh, I've been ready for some time. Cadwallader is nothing if not efficient," she said. "Oughtn't we to hurry now if we're to see that star of yours?"

"We may not be able to see it, remember," he warned. "It's just now twilight, so the sky may not be dark enough before it disappears. If we catch a glimpse of Fomalhaut at all, it'll be the luckiest of chances."

"Then it's a good thing I'm feeling lucky this night," she said, draping a blanket from her bed over one arm. Clearly, she intended to spend more time on the roof than viewing the elusive autumn star would require. "Lead on, my lord."

He offered Miss Anthony his arm. Grigori would have laughed at him, taking orders from a mere slip of a girl, but Samuel didn't care what his father thought. In fact, the fewer of Grigori's thoughts that entered Samuel's head, the better. When Miss Anthony slipped her hand into the crook of his elbow, pressing her softness against his forearm, Grigori might as well have been on another planet. She made Samuel feel protective and strong and slightly bewildered because of his reactions to her. They walked the long corridor and down the curving staircase to the great hall. Samuel had heard that women could so meddle with a man's mind that he couldn't think straight. He was beginning to believe it.

He led her across the bailey to his tower where the portal was locked fast and he pulled out his key.

"As difficult as it is to enter the castle, what with the guards and portcullis and all, you still keep your tower locked?"

"I do," he said. "I don't fear theft, you understand. The keep is locked to protect my work from prying eyes. I apologize ahead of time for the condition of my study. You'll find it terribly dusty."

"That's surprising. The rest of the castle is spotless." The enterprising servants were always sweeping or polishing something.

"There are a number of delicate instruments and rare charts in my study." Plus evidence of his investigations into matters philosophical. Those were even more private to him. "I let the maids in once a year and then only under my watch."

"In that case, I'm honored to be allowed into your study." She smiled up at him, a hopeful, almost coy expression that had him kicking himself for ever agreeing to this lark. She had no idea what sort of danger she was flirting with.

If she *were* flirting. It was hard to be sure.

"You have to be allowed in. It's the only way to the roof." As soon as the words left his mouth, he realized they were vaguely insulting. "I didn't mean it like that."

Instead of being offended, she laughed. "Oh, I'm so glad not to be the only one who speaks first and thinks later."

"I think all the time." Now she was insulting *him*.

"But you don't speak often." She laid a hand on his forearm. "It's all right. I expect it's because you've chosen to be alone so much. To be honest, it makes me feel I can trust what comes out of your mouth when you do."

But she shouldn't trust him. She really shouldn't. He just couldn't find the words to explain why. If he told her the truth, she'd think him mad.

He pushed the door open and held his lantern aloft to illuminate the narrow stairs hugging the curved walls.

"Those stairs seem rather dangerous," she said doubtfully. "No railing."

He began leading the way up the steps. "As I understand

it, they are better than what used to be here. This keep is the oldest tower in the castle. It was built by the first Lord Badewyn as a final line of defense. Back then, instead of stairs, the upper floors were reached only by means of ladders which could be pulled up by defenders."

"On second thought, the staircase is lovely."

He glanced behind him as he ascended. She followed closely, careful to stay near the gray stone walls.

In the flickering light of his lantern, each of the successive floors was revealed to be littered with crates that used to hold the books and items he kept in his study on the top floor. Seeing it afresh through Miss Anthony's eyes, he decided he ought to bring order to the lower levels of the tower. It was quickly becoming a boar's nest. At least, barring the dust, his study was well-organized.

But once they reached it, he realized allowing her into this space was a little like inviting her to tour his mind. In addition to the books in his private collection, she'd see the articulated skeletons of animals he'd assembled when he was making a study of comparative anatomy. On the shelves ringing the room, there were hookahs and swords, ivory carvings and brass protractors, oddments from every land he and Grigori had visited during their extended travels. And of course, his precious star charts and well-used astrolabe.

Everything that meant anything to him was in plain view.

She strolled over to his desk and ran a fingertip along the edge as her sharp-eyed gaze lingered on the books he'd left open. *Sons of Anak. The Book of Enoch. Annunaki from the Epic of Gilgamesh.* He doubted she was acquainted with any of those titles, but their topic cut far too close to the bone for his comfort.

"We need to hurry or we'll miss any chance to see Fomalhaut." With a firm hand under her elbow, he guided her to the final set of stairs and then led the way up them so he could open the hatch to the crenellated roof of the keep.

Once he handed her through the opening, he closed the hatch behind them. The last thing he needed was for the Duke of Camden's ward to take a tumble down an open stairwell.

He extinguished the lantern so their eyes would adjust to the dark. Then he set down the basket that held their cold supper. Twilight had fallen hard enough to paint the sky gunmetal gray. Only the brightest stars broke through the steel curtain.

"After all those curving stairs, I'm terribly turned about. Which way is south?" Miss Anthony asked.

He pointed to the North Star. "There's Polaris, so"—he traced a finger across the sky in the opposite direction—"south is over there."

She dropped the blanket and hurried to the edge of the parapet, peering at the southern horizon. There, winking at the edge of the earth's curve, was a solitary star.

"Is that it?" she asked breathlessly.

He nodded, inordinately pleased that he could show it to her. "That's Fomalhaut, the Lonely One. Seventeenth brightest object in the night sky."

She looked up at him, her expression shrewd. "This star is special to you, isn't it?"

He'd always felt an affinity for the Lonely One, but it wasn't as if that information was tattooed on his brow. "How can you know that?"

"It's like you." She seemed to see right through him.

"Set apart. In hiding for a good deal of the time."

"I'm not in hiding."

"When was the last time you were in the company of anyone besides your uncle?"

"Not counting you?"

"Not counting me."

"It's been a while." Before he and Grigori had returned to Faencaern, they'd spent a Season in London where he'd been in more company than any mortal man should be forced to endure, but that had been ten years ago. She didn't need to know that. It rather proved her point. He decided no further response was the best course and turned back to view Fomalhaut. As they watched in surprisingly companionable silence, the Loneliest Star sank beneath the southern horizon.

"What do you suppose Fomalhaut does when it's gone from our view? Does it have friends in the southern sky that we can never see from here? A lover, perhaps?" she mused, leaning her elbows on the parapet. "Maybe that's why it doesn't stay up north for long, why it doesn't seek the company of others here."

"If that's your way of asking if I have a lover hidden somewhere, the answer is no."

"I would never ask such a thing!" Obviously affronted, Miss Anthony took a short side step away from him. "A lady wouldn't even think it."

"I ask your pardon." Samuel ducked his head in a quick bow.

"Lady Easton would say that's far too personal a conversation for an acquaintance as young as ours."

"And she'd be right, of course."

"Then it's a good thing I'm not terribly ladylike." Meg

turned and smiled impishly up at him. "Because I'm glad to know you don't have a lover."

Then her smile changed. It went all soft and trusting. A smile that warmed his chest and made his heart gallop. A smile that made him want to open a vein to protect her. Why didn't she recognize what a danger he was to her?

She cocked her head. "But truly, I was only speaking about why the star is so alone."

"Maybe," he said in a growling tone, "the Loneliest Star keeps to itself because it's a monster and would hurt anyone who got too close to it."

Even as he spoke, he found himself gathering her in his arms. It was almost as if he watched himself from outside his own body, unable to control his own actions. Yet he was achingly aware of everything about her, from the neat way her softness fit against his hardness to the faintest whiff of her sweet scent.

If he was offending her, she didn't show it. Miss Anthony draped her hands over his shoulders and tipped up her chin so she could meet his gaze.

"I'll never believe a star would be so cowardly. If there was danger, which I doubt, a fiery power like that wouldn't allow harm to come to someone else, even from itself."

He didn't plan what happened next. Truly he didn't. But he bent his head down so that the warmth of her breath feathered over his lips. God help him, she tempted him sore. "The star might not wish to cause harm, but—"

"The star should trust in his wish. I do." Her eyelids fluttered closed. "No harm will come."

He covered her mouth with his.

God help us both.

My dear Lady Easton,

I doubt I will ever send this letter. For one thing, I don't know who would bear it to you since no one ever seems to come or go here. And for another thing, I would be embarrassed to have you know the events of this evening, but I need to get it all out, even if no one ever reads it.

Never think this is your fault. You could not have foreseen such a thing. I am sure I did not. After all, I am only a commoner playing at being a wellborn lady. The thought that I would actually pull off the ruse well enough to fool Lord Badewyn never entered my mind. Or perhaps he did realize what I am and that is why he felt free to take liberties.

Please do not see this as a criticism of you or your teaching. I would never dare such a thing. But I do wish, sometime in all your lessons, you had taught me what a proper lady is to do after a gentleman kisses her.

As Cadwallader, my abigail, might say, "Indeed, I do."

Yours ever so guiltily,
Meg

~ a letter to Lady Easton from Miss Meg Anthony that was never sent

Chapter Eight

Oh, good heavens! How did I allow this to happen?

Meg had imagined being kissed in the chaste, foolish way young girls do. But that was only because she had no idea how powerful the force that draws a man and a woman together is and how irresistible its pull can be. Then when she grew older and her cousin Oswald began to pester her, she'd pushed away all thought of kissing. She'd stuffed it into the corner of her mind that held distasteful things like casting up one's accounts after eating rancid beef.

Once she went to live at Camden House, she'd never imagined that a kiss might happen to her. She was far too cosseted and protected for anything as interesting as a kiss to befall her, so there was no point in considering it. But when she'd arrived at Faencaern Castle and seen Lord Badewyn for the first time, thoughts of kissing had leaped back into the forefront of her mind.

Of course, a real lady might not allow him to kiss her,

but Meg was no lady. She wasn't about to waste such an opportunity. She'd be pleased to allow it. Just once, mind you. Enough to say it had happened. A memory she could hug to herself in the cold winter of old age.

There. Do you see? I did that. I kissed a Welsh lord. I kissed him thoroughly and lived to tell the tale with my virtue intact.

Would it be so terrible?

Yes, she decided, now that his lips were pressed to hers. She'd never be satisfied with just one kiss.

Lord Badewyn's kiss made her feel things. She suspected they were things that a lady ought not to feel. First, it was a yearning, empty sort of feeling. Then her insides became all jumbled and achy. Her skin prickled with the awareness of every scrap of lace against it under her stiff bombazine gown, every bit of pressure from his hot male body. She wanted him to touch her, not just his hands palming her cheeks as they were now, but all over. If only he'd smooth those thick capable fingers over her needy places. His kiss was beyond delicious, but she wanted so much more.

But even more than she wanted to receive from him, Meg ached to give.

She wanted to convince him he wasn't that lonely star. He didn't need to be alone. She accepted him. That's what she wanted her kiss to say. She would be with him. Surely her lips were telling him that without the need for words.

But that sort of thing ought not to be left to chance. She wasn't like Lord Stanstead, who could broadcast his thoughts into the minds of others. Lord Badewyn might be a man of few words, but she had rarely been at a loss for them. If she didn't speak, he might mistake the message in her kiss.

"You aren't like the Lonely One," she murmured when he released her mouth and began kissing along her jaw line and then down her neck. Delightful little tingles trailed in his wake. She arched into him. "Not when you have me."

Instead of drawing him closer to her, the words had the opposite effect. He pulled back, staring down at her as if he couldn't believe what they'd done. Then he released her from his arms.

He retreated a step or two as if he'd suddenly discovered she carried the pox. "Forgive me, Miss Anthony."

What had he done wrong? What had she? "There's nothing to forgive. I wanted you to kiss me."

"Please. I beg you to forget what happened." He held up a hand that brooked no argument. "We will not speak of it. We must not."

She realized her mouth was gaping like a cod. Quickly, Meg clamped her lips shut. Had her kiss been that awful to him? No, his breathing was still ragged. He'd been as moved as she. She was sure of it.

"Naturally, you will wish to return to your chamber now and—"

"Naturally, I will wish to do nothing of the sort," Meg said in her haughtiest imitation of Lady Easton when she was on her high horse. It was a small shield for the hurt churning in her belly, but it was all she had. Meg picked up the discarded blanket and spread it on the flat roof. What was wrong with that kiss? It was easily the loveliest thing that had ever happened in all her life. "We have not yet had our picnic supper and even if Fomalhaut has disappeared for the night, there are undoubtedly a number of other stars you can point out for me."

When he didn't move, she added, "Or is Welsh hospitality so strained that a guest's wishes are ignored?"

With obvious reluctance, he sat on the far corner of the blanket, folding himself up, knees raised, arms clasped around them, while Meg unpacked the meal. Lord Badewyn wouldn't even look at her.

Merciful heavens, what's the matter with the man?

If he could act as if their kiss had never happened, she could, too.

"Perhaps you'd care to make yourself useful instead of merely ornamental. Kindly light the lantern so we can see to eat." If he was intent on behaving so oddly, she felt no guilt over chiding him. He didn't seem to take offense at her words and, pulling flint and tinder from his pocket, had the lantern flickering again in a few moments. The homely chore seemed to steady him and he began to behave as he had before the kiss, distant but not unfriendly though he still seemed interested in her—in the same way a kestrel seems interested in the field mouse he intends to have for supper.

Meg pushed that disquieting image aside, blaming her empty stomach.

Lord Badewyn's cook had done him proud. There was a pleasant selection of cold meat—sliced mutton, beef, and ham—cucumber sandwiches, a savory pasty for each of them and a variety of sweetmeats. To wash it all down, there was a jug of ale for his lordship and a container of cool buttermilk for Meg.

She'd rather have ale, too, but she sipped at the buttermilk dutifully.

"Have you always been interested in the stars?" she asked to fill the silence that yawned between them.

"For as long as I can remember."

"Did your father teach you?"

A guarded look passed over his features. "It was Grigori who taught me."

Well, that made sense. Lord Badewyn and his uncle had an unusually close relationship, even if it didn't seem a terribly cordial one. He blew out the lantern and began to show her the same constellations in the heavens that they'd seen when they were looking at the star chart in the library. As he spoke, he relaxed, stretching out his long legs. Meg leaned back on her palms, letting his words, the deep rumble of his voice, and the beauty of the night sky wash over her.

"It's ever so much better to see the stars for real instead of on a flat parchment," she said. "They seem almost alive, don't they? All twinkling and merry?"

"It's strange to hear you say so. When I was a child, I used to imagine that stars were somehow like people. That they had loves and hates and could be good or evil," he said softly. "It's rubbish, of course. The stuff of bad poetry and far too fanciful an idea to share with anyone."

"Yet you shared it with me."

"So I did, Miss Anthony." He smiled briefly for the first time since they'd kissed.

"In that case, perhaps it's time you stopped referring to me as Miss Anthony." After all, their mouths had touched. They'd shared a breath. He ought to call her familiar. "My name is Meg. I'd appreciate it if you'd use it."

He shook his head. "It wouldn't be proper."

"Nothing about this evening has been proper, come to that," she agreed. "This time spent together is our secret. The names we call each other could be, too. Who would be scandalized if you were to use my Christian name when we are alone?"

"No one, I suppose…Meg," he added, his low tone shivering over her. Her simple name had never sounded so good. "I am called Samuel."

"It suits you." She cast about for something that would keep this taciturn man talking. Mr. Bernard had told her that Lord Badewyn was something called a *Watcher*. It sounded as if he would fit into the duke's Order easily. "I suppose you know about the Duke of Camden's Order of the M.U.S.E."

He nodded. "I do, but I am not a member. I cannot bear being in London long enough to be useful to Camden."

"You wouldn't have to be in the city. There are cells of the Order in other places. I should think your abilities more than qualify you to be one of his Extraordinaires wherever you choose to live." She wondered why the duke had not recruited him. "His Grace trusts your warnings implicitly. You could be *his* Watcher."

"I am a Watcher for many people, not only for the duke. I *Watch* whether I want to or not. Then if it's appropriate, I warn of what I see."

"Of course." Samuel was the sort who'd never do anything that would be deemed inappropriate. *More's the pity.* "How do you do that, the *Watching*, I mean?"

"In any still, shining surface, I see images of such things as I am allowed to see."

"Things you're *allowed*? So you can't control your visions?"

"It's best just to let things come. Sometimes, if I concentrate on a particular person, the images will be about them, but the clearest information comes when I don't try to force it." He sat up straight and turned his gaze toward the heavens. "I am able to see things from afar, things past, things present, and things to come. It makes me an object of fear, especially when I see the future. People always claim they want to know what's waiting beyond the next corner, but that's not true."

"They only want to know about the good things," Meg said.

"That's right." Samuel's gaze cut to her sharply. "Most people don't understand that."

"But I do." How often had she *Found* something that should have remained lost? Families had been destroyed because they couldn't agree on who should have possession of a recovered object. However dear, a thing was just a thing, something that would eventually be dust, but things often had the power to upend lives and relationships forever. However, she refused to feel guilty over it or guilt was all she'd ever feel. "When you have a gift, you are only responsible for its use. You aren't responsible for what happens after you use it."

"Sometimes *Watching* doesn't feel like a gift."

She put a consoling hand on his forearm. "I know."

"You do? I thought you were His Grace's ward. Are you also one of his Extraordinaires?"

"One of his lesser ones."

He cocked a questioning brow. "Are you an elemental?"

"No, nothing so powerful." Meg was in awe of Vesta and her mastery over fire. Even though she'd never seen LeGrand use his gift, as a water mage, he had similar control over liquids. "For want of a better word, I'm a *Finder*. When something is lost, all I need is a description of the item and I can usually recover it."

"Sounds very useful. Can you do the same with people?"

"Yes, but in that case, a description isn't enough. I need their name, not necessarily their given name, but the name they are known by. People don't generally realize how powerful their names are." It was connected to their essence. It was why she was so glad to be able to call Samuel by his Christian name instead of his title. "Once, using just a name, I located a little girl who'd wandered away from a village fair and was about to tumble into a river."

Of all her *Findings*, that was her proudest moment.

"Your *Finding* sounds much more useful than my *Watching*."

"Not always." When she had worked for her Uncle Rowney, she'd had no shining times to remember. Either he'd been wringing an exorbitant fee from people who were desperate to find something they'd lost or she'd been forced to *Find* places for Rowney and Oswald to burgle more easily.

She shivered.

"The night has turned chill." Samuel rose and extended a hand to her. She slipped hers into it. His hand was warm. "We need to get you back to your chamber before your absence is marked."

"No one will miss me," Meg said. Since she'd arrived at Faencaern, Samuel had often sent his regrets for dinner. She frequently ended up eating the evening meal only with his uncle. She hadn't wanted to pique Mr. Templeton's curiosity over her absence at table this evening, so she had made sure Cadwallader delivered the message to Samuel's uncle that she was fatigued. She'd been trying to make sense of the Chaucer treatise and would dine in her room that evening. Grigori Templeton shouldn't question that a bit.

Chaucer would weary anyone.

"I would miss you," Samuel admitted. "I *did* miss you on those evenings when I didn't come down for dinner."

"So why didn't you?"

"It's complicated, Meg."

He sounded so very lonely. Perhaps he *was* like Fomalhaut. "Tell me," she said. "Maybe together we can make it simple."

Samuel shook his head and began packing up the remains of their supper. "I will not allow my problems to become yours."

Meg wanted to argue but Samuel wasn't the sort of man to argue with if one didn't have all the facts, so she simply folded up the blanket in silence.

After he opened the hatch door, she shot a parting glance at the night sky. Some of their evening together had been as magical as the heavens and some of it was just as frankly bewildering. Meg headed down the steep stairs to his study. Then in silence, they made their way down the long curving steps of the keep, across the bailey and through the great hall again.

By the time they reached the foot of the stairs that led up to the guest rooms, Meg decided castles were built to confuse people with all their ups and downs and twists and turns. Perhaps like the ladders used in the old keep, everything was about confounding an enemy. The entire place had a defensive posture. Samuel Templeton couldn't have chosen a home that more closely reflected his guarded personality.

Without exchanging a word, they climbed up to the floor where her chamber was. She stopped at the door with a hand upon the latch. "Thank you, Samuel."

"I'm pleased to have been able to show you Fomalhaut."
He inclined his head slightly, but the rest of him was ram-rod
straight.

"You showed me more than that."

"The night sky is splendid. I was happy to be your guide."

He'd been her guide for more than star-gazing. Her lips
still tingled. "No, I mean you showed me a little of who you
are. At the risk of not seeming very lady-like once again, I
would like to know more."

If it were possible, he seemed to stiffen even further.
"Miss Anthony, I cannot conceive of a world where you are
less than a lady."

You might be surprised.

Meg was more than a little surprised that he'd stopped
calling her by her Christian name so quickly. Had their kiss
meant so little to him? Surely she wasn't the only one who
sensed what might be a connection between them?

His face gave away nothing. He might have been carved
of granite.

But Meg wouldn't be swayed by the mask he tried to
hide behind. They'd had a moment together—a splendid
time when the world seemed to spin a little slower and
nothing beyond the circle of Samuel's arms meant a thing.
He must have felt it, too.

Whether he had or not, Meg wasn't about to act as if it
hadn't happened. She stood on tiptoe and gave him a peck on
the cheek. "Good night, Samuel. We'll talk more tomorrow."

Then she hurried into her chamber and closed the door
behind her. She leaned against it, aghast at her audacity.
She'd not only let a man kiss her this evening, she had kissed
him. And with no encouragement on his part at all. Lady

Easton would have a conniption if she learned of it.

She covered her face with her hands, her cheeks heating with embarrassment.

Then she heard something. It was the soft, but unmistakable shifting of booted feet on the stone corridor. Lord Badewyn was still there on the other side of her door. She crouched down to peer through the keyhole. Lamplight illuminated the corridor, but he was too close to the door for her to see above his waist. She pressed her ear to the door. He seemed to be just standing there. Then she heard the tramp of his footfalls as he walked away, but before he left, she heard something else.

"Good night, Meg."

She clasped her hands to her chest. He'd called her by name. It wasn't much, but it was a start.

Meg Anthony was wrong.

Someone had missed her. When Samuel reached the great hall, he saw that the smaller dining chamber adjoining it was still flickering with the light of dozens of dear beeswax candles. He strode into the room.

His father was seated at the head of the long table. Partially empty platters and serving dishes were spread over the white linen. Globs of gravy stained the cloth. Grigori had hitched one leg over the arm of his chair. He'd discarded his jacket, untied his cravat, and unbuttoned his waistcoat. He looked a proper rogue, an image reinforced when he dispensed with a goblet and drank straight from a bottle of the best Riesling in Samuel's cellar.

"There you are, son. Welcome to my very empty table."

"I sent my regrets."

"So did our Miss Anthony. I can only surmise the two of you were together."

It was pointless to lie to Grigori. His father was too good a liar not to smell untruths in others.

"I was showing Fomalhaut to her," Samuel said.

"Brilliant. A rare star this time of year. A rare man as can find it. Hope you showed her something else, too. A man of your endowment shouldn't be shy." His brows waggled suggestively. "I can only assume she was properly impressed. You are my son, after all." His words slurred together. If Samuel didn't know better, he'd say his father was bosky. "You see, son, courting a female is not all that difficult."

"I'm not courting her."

"The devil you aren't."

"I thought you said he didn't like you to swear by him."

"Unlike the Almighty, the Prince of Darkness is not omniscient." Grigori took a long pull on the Riesling. "What Lucifer doesn't know won't hurt me."

Samuel sat down at the far end of the table. In addition to the congealing food, there were several bottles of whisky lying on their sides amid the epicurean squalor. "I gather you sent the servants on to bed."

"I did. No point in having them stand around. Can't have a decent conversation with any of them. Or an indecent one, come to that." Grigori knocked back the bottle and then growled in frustration because it was empty. Flinging it into the nearby fireplace, he shattered the bottle into thousands of glistening shards. "Well, maybe Malachai. He's a good listener at least, but that's the whole of it."

Samuel had known Grigori to consume copious

quantities of alcohol before, but never once had he shown the least sign of being in his cups.

"You're drunk," Samuel accused.

"As a lord." Grigori put a fist to his chest in an effort to stifle a belch but he wasn't successful.

"Why get so jug-bitten?"

"It's tradition." Grigori pointed his forefinger skyward. "Each time a son of mine goes courting, the Grand Cycle begins again. It would be a sin not to mark the occasion."

"You have odd notions about what constitutes a sin, but I suppose that's to be expected," Samuel said. "Besides, there will be no cycle this time, grand or otherwise. I will break it."

"You won't." Grigori shook his head slowly. "Do you think you're the first to have tried?"

"I'll succeed."

"Ballocks. There's no point in resisting. This is the way of things and there's no changing. I'll prove it to you." He stalked the length of the table, popped the cork on another bottle, and upended the last of the Riesling into an empty silver tray near Samuel. The golden liquid lapped at the edges of the dish and then settled into a still translucent pool.

"There you are, my *Watcher*. Look for yourself." He grasped Samuel by the neck and forced him to stare at the clear surface. "Tell me what you see for our Miss Anthony."

Samuel was a big man. He was stronger than most, yet he couldn't match Grigori for brute strength and he knew it. Closing his eyes would be pointless. If thwarted, Grigori would only grow more violent. All Samuel could control was his own mind. He forced any thought of Meg away lest he trigger an image of her in the shimmering liquid. Instead, he bore down on thoughts of his father. The surface of the Riesling flickered.

The world around him faded.

Samuel heard rippling water. And feminine laughter. The air was heavy with the breath of green growing things. He pushed forward, shoving aside the undergrowth to reveal a hidden pool. A group of young women, wrapped in white linen, disappeared into the woods, leaving one of their number behind. She was still hip-deep in the water, turned away from him. Her dark hair hung down her back, but it didn't disguise her slender waist or the graceful flare of her hips. What he could see of her olive skin was flawless.

"Atara." Samuel recognized the voice as Grigori's.

The girl turned and seemed to look right at him. Samuel was seeing the girl through his father's eyes, he realized. His muscles twitched under his skin at the thought of inhabiting Grigori for even the short span of a Watching. But he still had a firm sense of himself, so he made no effort to cut off the vision.

The girl's dark eyes were wide-set and lovely, a trifle alarmed if the whites that showed around them were any measure. Her features were delicate, a pure expression of the Golden Mean. In bone structure, it was an ancient face, everything in exact proportion, as stylized a beauty as any Grecian sculptor ever conceived. It was a face of such symmetry and balance, Samuel's chest constricted. Beauty always moved him, which was part of why the night sky so often held him captive.

The girl's mouth turned up in a timid smile.

"Atara." This time the voice belonged to one of the women who'd already left the pool. "Where are you?"

"I'm home," Atara murmured and began to swim toward him. "Home with you, Grigori."

She rose from the pool, water sloughing from her skin, leaving her glistening and—

As he closed his eyes, the vision was abruptly cut off. "Atara," Samuel said. "I saw Atara."

Grigori released Samuel's neck and backed away, a stricken look on his face. Then he grabbed his own ears and bent double. He erupted with a sound that was a cross between a bellow and a roar. The noise went on and on. Everyone in the castle would shiver in their beds, clutch their blankets a little tighter and pray, hoping the horrific sound was just a trick of the wind howling through the mountain passes.

Samuel knew that whatever else the noise was, it was the sound of a creature in grave distress.

Grigori finally ran out of air. Then, he bolted from the chamber.

And it came to pass, when men began to multiply on the face of the earth, and daughters were born unto them, that the sons of God saw the daughters of men that they were fair; and they took them wives of all which they chose.

~ Genesis 6:1-2, King James Bible

Chapter Nine

Samuel found Grigori slumped in a ball before the faded tapestry in the great hall. He was pounding his fist on the unforgiving stone floor.

"Stop it," Samuel said. "Or—"

"Or what? Are you afraid I'll hurt myself? Do you think I haven't tried?" Grigori laughed mirthlessly as he substituted his forehead for his fist and continued to pound. Finally, when he couldn't even raise a bruise, he gave up and sat upright. "I am reserved for judgment. It appears I don't get to punish myself."

"What's the matter with you?"

"Do you think only humans know how to grieve? She was my wife, Samuel. My only wife." Grigori rose haltingly and put a hand on the frail tapestry, caressing the lone standing woman's figure. "I loved Atara. With every fiber of my being, I loved her. She was all I knew of Woman. All I ever wanted to know. So lovely. So…trusting. Together, we made a whole world. How could I not give up everything for her?"

Samuel's gaze flicked to the portion of the tapestry where the angelic figure was tumbling from heaven. When Meg had studied it that first day, she'd had no idea she was looking at his family's history.

Grigori's grief dissolved from rage into alcohol-sodden tears. He sobbed as if his heart would break.

As if he has a heart.

Samuel had no comfort to give him. Even if Grigori had acted impulsively or in ignorance, his private hell was of his own making. Now that Samuel's father knew better, he was still intent on inflicting the same pain over and over, on each of his offspring from one generation to the next.

The sins of the father.

Grigori collapsed to his knees. "I didn't know what would happen to her. You have to believe that I didn't know."

"I'm willing to believe you didn't know the first time."

"How could I?" he snarled. "Women give birth all the time on this pismire planet."

"And some of them die doing it."

"But not all of them." Grigori loosed a string of profanity, breathtaking in both its crudity and its eloquence. Then he fell into sobs again. "Why must all mine?"

"Maybe because you can't mix angel with human and not create a monster."

"You are not a monster, son. You are Nephilim. Be proud of it." Grigori narrowed his eyes. "You are part of a mighty race, 'men of renown,' according to scripture. Would you argue with holy writ?"

"You certainly did." Samuel folded his arms over his

chest. Normally, he didn't like to tangle with Grigori on the Good Book, but he was sure he had the high ground this time. "What about 'Thou shalt have no other gods before me?'"

"Lucifer isn't my god. He's my general. There's a difference. He may want to be God, but trust me, he doesn't have the character for the position." Grigori untucked his shirt from the waist of his trousers and used the tail end to wipe his face. "Besides, don't go quoting the commandments to me. There is a different set of rules for angels."

"You have free will as humans do."

"Yes, to my sorrow, we do have that," Grigori said, sounding more sober by the minute. "But no hope of redemption."

Meg pulled off the tired old bombazine gown to get ready for bed. There were only a few things to commend the ensemble. First, the stiff fabric wore like iron. It would last far longer than the prettier, more fragile dresses in her wardrobe. And secondly, the gown was designed so that Meg could get into and out of it without needing a maid's help. While Cadwallader would have been eager to hear about the evening's events, Meg wasn't ready to share them with anyone. Not even her gregarious maid.

He kissed me.

Even if the kiss had ended strangely, she still hugged that little secret to herself. Lord Badewyn had kissed her.

And he'd called her by her Christian name. Sometimes even married people didn't do that. Or if they did, it was only in private. Just like the agreement she and Samuel had made about it.

He was a very closed-off man, but in several ways, he'd opened to her tonight. She longed to dive into him, to discover who he really was. She was sure it would be worth the effort. Even if it only led to one more kiss. Of course, it might lead to…other things, the kind of things Meg had been warned against all her life.

Ladies were expected to remain pure, of course, but if their dowries were large enough, a future husband might wink at an indiscretion. Low-born women knew they had only one chip in the game. Give it up and a girl may as well start kicking up her heels for pay. Meg had guarded her virginity as if it were her last hoarded coin.

But Samuel's kiss had made her want. He'd made her realize it would be easy to give herself to him.

This flirting business was a dangerous game.

Meg was stripped down to just her chemise and stays when the horrific howling began. She ran to the arrow slit that served as a window, thinking it was the wind, but there was no trace of a breeze. The sound, whatever it was, came from inside the castle. It was a noise filled with excruciating pain.

Suddenly she needed to know where Samuel was. Every bit of her ached to be certain he was safe.

"I'm ever so sorry, Your Grace, but this is an emergency," she muttered as she lit a spill from the banked fire and transferred the flame to a candle. She placed the candle on the small table next to the only chair in the chamber. At least if she was going to disobey her mentor and use her gift without permission, she'd be as careful as she could about it. The candle would help her spirit return to her body. It was no guarantee of safety, but it was better than going without a friendly light to guide her home. As the roaring went on and on, she settled into the chair and emptied her mind of everything but one name.

"Samuel Templeton, Lord Badewyn."

Then between one breath and the next, she was hovering near the ceiling, gazing down at her empty body. Usually, she was happy to fly free of it, but tonight, her body had shown her it was capable of some amazingly pleasant and frustrating sensations. She definitely had more to learn in that department. Then she realized that the awful sound had stopped, cut off like a thread snipped by a pair of shears.

The silence lit a fire under her. She had to *Find* Samuel. Zipping through stone and mortar, she homed in on his essence like a pigeon coming to roost. He was in the great hall with his Uncle Grigori who seemed to be pounding his own forehead on the unforgiving floor.

Why he didn't collapse or, at the very least, bleed profusely, was a wonder.

With relief, she saw that Samuel seemed fine and was in no immediate danger. Meg knew she should whisk back to her body, but she burned to know more about this very strange encounter between the two men. It wasn't polite to eavesdrop and Lady Easton had drummed that point home with thoroughness.

But as Vesta says, "Sometimes, it's the only way to learn anything worth knowing."

She strained to listen, but try as she might, she could only hear Samuel's side of the conversation. Grigori's lips moved. Surely he was speaking, but in her present spirit form, she could hear nothing coming from his mouth. She was used to not being able to discern smells, but this was the first time she'd been unable to hear someone speak while she was *Finding*. Judging from Samuel's words, he and his uncle were deep in a theological discussion, which certainly didn't explain why Grigori was trying to bash his own head in. Or why he erupted in a fit of tears.

"You may not be able to redeem yourself," Samuel said, "but you can stop this blasted cycle you started."

Grigori gestured wildly, clearly impassioned, but Meg couldn't make out a single word.

"No, I'm not ungrateful," Samuel said. "I'm fully aware it has taken hundreds of years for you to amass the wealth that allows me to live in this castle—"

Hundreds of years? Grigori wasn't that old. Judging from the sprinkling of gray at his temples, he'd seen perhaps forty-some winters. Surely he was no older than the Duke of Camden and His Grace wasn't counted a graybeard at all. And besides that, what did Mr. Templeton have to do with the estate? Meg knew enough about how titles and lands passed from one generation to the next to know Faencaern Castle must have belonged to Samuel's father before him, not his uncle.

Grigori seemed to have interrupted, because Samuel raised his hands in the timeworn gesture of surrender.

"... yes, yes and study the stars and whatever else piques my interest. But what else can I fill my days with? You have made a mule of me."

Meg had heard men refer to each other as jackasses, but she'd never encountered one who called *himself* a mule. What could he mean by it?

"No, you're mistaken. I don't care about her. Not in that

way. But I do care about her safety," Samuel said, his fingers curling into fists. "Someone has to."

Meg's heart sank. If he was speaking of her, it meant she wasn't special to him. The kiss that had all but upended her world meant nothing to him. She'd never felt ill when she went *Finding* before, but now her chest ached so badly, it was as if her spirit were still trapped in her body, caught up in all its sensations.

She wished she'd remembered Lady Easton's lessons and hadn't allowed him to kiss her. Anything not to hurt like this.

A half smile on his face, Grigori seemed more himself as he leaned against the tapestry. Samuel hadn't even let her touch it, as if she would damage the relic with a fingertip's brush, but Grigori might as well be wrapping himself in the threadbare work. He was talking a blue streak, but she still couldn't hear a word. She floated lower, hoping being closer would change matters.

"I won't let you use her," Samuel said.

How could Mr. Templeton use her? He'd only been a pleasant dinner companion to Meg. Maybe they were talking about someone else entirely.

Grigori seemed to laugh for he threw his head back. Then he turned to look directly at her. His dark eyes narrowed and a sly smile curved his lips.

Surely he couldn't see her. No one ever had.

"I believe the expression is 'Speak of the devil and he will appear.' But apparently it works for Miss

Anthony as well. I am charmed," Grigori said with a bow to the apparition hovering over their heads. "You see her, don't you, son?"

"I see something." Samuel squinted in the direction his father was gazing. There seemed to be a hazy entity floating about ten feet below the rafters. This was not the first spirit being he'd encountered, but usually their features were clearer to him. "I can't tell who it is."

"She's very recognizable. Right there." Grigori pointed at the haze. "It's Miss Anthony and the little vixen is larking about the castle in naught but her chemise and stays. Quite fetching, I must say. The girl has a pleasing set of curves. This is going to be more fun than I expected."

Samuel reared back and punched Grigori in the face. He put all his weight behind the blow, yet his father didn't fall. Grigori did however rub his jaw and move it back and forth, testing to make sure the bones still articulated properly.

"Well, that stung," he admitted. "And here I thought you didn't care about her."

Samuel glared at him. "I'm warning you."

"What can you possibly threaten me with? Even though I'm totally foxed, you can't do something as simple as knock me down." Grigori chuckled, then all mirth left his features and he shot a fierce look at Samuel. "When one is already damned, precious little else matters. I will do as I will, as I always have, and you can't stop me."

Samuel roared with rage and laid into Grigori, pummeling him with both fists until his father finally collapsed to the floor.

Grigori sprawled on his back and laughed. He hiccupped a few times as he gasped for breath. "Not bad. A few of those blows actually got my attention. You've got some grit, son, I'll give you that."

Then Grigori leaped to his feet and threw a punch to Samuel's gut that lifted him from the floor and made him fly backward a good fifteen feet before landing on his arse. Grigori leaned over to peer down at him. "And I am not even at the top of my game. Watch yourself, son. After a certain point, you will be expendable. And that time might come sooner than you imagine."

Quick as thought, Meg zipped through the stone walls of the castle and back to her chamber. She paused a moment at the sight of her own body. She never thought she looked like herself when her eyes were rolled back in her head so only the whites showed. But the body was wearing her chemise and stays. She recognized the embroidered French knots along the edge of her bodice, so she slid into the house of flesh and drew a shuddering breath. She still hadn't discovered the source of that horrendous noise, but what she had learned was upsetting enough.

Meg trembled, as she always did when confronted with violence. It was part of why she had run away from Rowney and Oswald. The two of them had always tried to settle things with a fight.

She hadn't been able to hear enough of their conversation to understand why Samuel launched into a bare-fisted brawl with his uncle. He and Grigori Templeton were both solidly built men, but Samuel had youth on his side. Why hadn't he been able to best the older fellow handily? And, most disturbingly, why had Samuel's uncle been able to see her in her disembodied state?

Clearly there was more to Grigori Templeton than met the eye.

There was nothing she could do tonight to unravel these mysteries so Meg shoved her questions aside, took several steadying deep breaths, and continued to undress. Then she donned her night rail and slid between the bed linens. As she tried to warm her feet by rubbing them together, the wondering returned with no answers in sight.

At least she didn't have to wonder about one thing. Samuel didn't care about her. Not in "that way." She'd heard it straight from his own lips.

Earlier that evening, Meg had started up to the roof with him with a light heart. She'd wanted to have a delightful time under the night sky, while they ate their picnic supper. Instead, there'd been precious little delight. Samuel had been distant as the stars most of the time. Even now, she couldn't remember exactly what had led to that spectacular kiss, which he'd broken off without explanation. He'd have ended their evening then and there if she hadn't coaxed him back to their meal and into conversation about the stars.

Meg released a shuddering sigh. Well, if Lord Badewyn didn't care about her in that way, then she wouldn't care about him, either. She'd simply experienced her first kiss. That's all.

Then why did her chest feel as if someone were piling bricks on it?

Before she could concoct an answer to that distressing question, someone rapped on her door. This night had been so full of oddities, she almost didn't wonder at the irregularity of a late-night visitor. Meg rose and shrugged on her wrapper, but before she reached the door, it opened as if by its own accord.

Samuel stood in her doorway, his expression forbidding in the dim light of her fireplace. "Get dressed."

"I beg your pardon."

"You're leaving. Tonight. Now."

She slammed the door in his face. "Of all the cheek!" Meg might not be a real lady, but she'd done nothing to deserve such ill-mannered treatment. The duke would be coldly furious when she told him about it.

Samuel pushed the door open again, even though she leaned against it with all her might. This time, he didn't remain in the dark corridor. Samuel strode into the room and relit her candle. He had changed into rough clothing, a coarse-cloth shirt, and woolen trousers topped by a serviceable jacket and oilskin cloak.

"Can you ride?" he asked bluntly.

"No."

"Not at all?"

"I've never sat a horse." Since becoming part of the duke's household, Meg had mastered a number of ladylike graces—how to serve a proper tea, which conversation topics were safe and which should be avoided like the plague, as well as slogging through how to read and write. She'd learned many things at Lady Easton's hands, but the equestrienne's art wasn't one of them.

Samuel began to pace before the fire, scrupulously ignoring her. "It can't be helped. We shall have to ride double then. Wear something appropriate."

Meg didn't have anything remotely resembling a riding

habit with her. And she wasn't about to embark on a journey in the dead of night on the strength of nothing more than his terse order. Crossing her arms over her chest, she tapped out her frustration with one stockinged foot.

"Why aren't you getting dressed?" he demanded when he finally looked her way again.

"Perhaps because there is a gentleman—and I use that word very loosely indeed—prowling around my chamber."

He turned to face the fireplace, bracing his hands on the mantel. "There. No more prowling. You have my solemn promise I won't look, but we must go quickly."

"Why?"

"Because your guardian sent you to Faencaern Castle for your safety. I cannot guarantee it here any longer."

The castle walls were still as stout as ever. No one could breech its defenses to harm her. "I don't understand."

"No, of course, you don't. How could you?" Despite his promise to remain staring at the fire, he turned and closed the distance between them. Samuel grasped her shoulders hard enough she was sure it would leave a bruise. She didn't think he meant to because his expression wasn't angry. He was clearly agitated and the cause of his concern seemed to be...

Me! Her insides churned with excitement, but she ordered them to quiet down. He wasn't making passionate love to her. He was only concerned for her safety and then only because of her association with the duke. She reminded herself that he didn't care about her in "that way."

"If you're afraid of infuriating His Grace in case something ill befalls me—"

He released her and resumed pacing. "I'm not afraid of

the Duke of Camden."

Clearly, he was afraid of something. Or someone. And on her account.

Maybe he does care. And in "that way," no matter what he said to his uncle.

"I promise I will explain all, but not here, not now. You must trust me, Meg."

When he said her name, he had her. She'd do anything for him if only he'd keep caressing that little syllable.

"Very well. Back to the fireplace with you, while I change." She fetched the awful bombazine back out of the wardrobe along with the right unmentionables to go with it. The ensemble wouldn't be attractive, but it was the most practical garment for travel she possessed. "It's Mr. Templeton you're worried about, isn't it?"

"We can't talk about it now." Ashen, he started to turn to face her again, but caught himself in time and glued his gaze back on the fire. "And don't say his name again. You, of all people, know the power of calling someone's name. For God's sake, hurry. We haven't much time."

There are rhythms built into the universe—morning and evening, seedtime and harvest, birth and death—cycles that are repeated because they perform a useful function. But I'll be damned before I become a party to Grigori's infernal "Grand Cycle."
And it may well come to that.

~ from the journal of Samuel Templeton, Lord Badewyn

Chapter Ten

Grigori's tongue tasted as if a whole band of gypsies had tramped through his mouth. After dancing through a cow yard. Barefoot. He opened one eye and surveyed his surroundings uncertainly.

He was sprawled on the stone floor under the long dining table. Something sticky under his cheek made it difficult to raise his head. The castle's footmen were tiptoeing around him, trying to clean up the mess from last night's supper without the least clink of any silverware on the plates.

How long had he lain there? He believed his fight with Samuel had taken place just last night, but since excessive drink had rendered him nearly comatose, he wasn't the best judge of how much time had actually passed. It had been several decades, maybe half a century, since he'd allowed himself to become that ape-drunk.

Gingerly, Grigori rolled out from under the table and sat up.

His head pounded. "A physical body is so frail sometimes," he said as he massaged his temples. "It is a curse unto itself." He cast a quick glare at the ceiling and launched one of his rare prayers heavenward. He was sure none of them reached high enough, but it was an old habit. Hard to break.

"Thank You very much. It's not enough for You that I'm banished to earth, caught in nearly human form like a bug trapped in amber. You had to make me susceptible to human weaknesses like feeling crapulous after a night of drinking, too. Words fail me in expressing my gratitude, O Beneficent One."

Grigori no longer heard that still small voice that meant the Almighty was speaking to him. In weaker moments, he'd admit he missed hearing it, but now, he didn't expect a reply. It was part of the whole damnation business—being cut off from the Source of All Joy forever and all that.

So instead of sitting in quiet contemplation waiting for a response to his admittedly impudent prayer, he struggled to his feet and started to bellow for a bath to be drawn in his chamber. The sound of his own voice made him feel as if his head were being cleaved in two. Tea and a breakfast tray were ordered in hushed tones. Then he trudged his way to the most opulently furnished chamber in the castle.

And why shouldn't I have the best?

It was all his in any case. Samuel was just the latest placeholder, as all his sons had been, stretching back some eight hundred years. Before he conceived of what he liked to call "The Grand Cycle," his life had been solitary and nomadic. If he'd wanted to tarry in a region, he had to create a new persona; but he could only remain so long before his longevity became a topic of curiosity and he'd been forced to move on. Now, since he was the power behind each Lord Badewyn, he'd been able to amass wealth in abundance, far beyond what might be acquired during the normal span of human years. Grigori provided positions for a grateful staff that could be counted upon to be discreet since part of the terms of their employment meant they remained at the castle their whole lives. He had a home to return to periodically and even some semblance of a family.

That's not too much to ask, is it? Considering how much I've lost.

Of all the pleasures he'd discovered during his time on earth, the sense of belonging to a family had surprised him. Grigori hated to admit how much he had enjoyed Samuel's early years, his halting steps, his first words, and his precocious intellect. Of all his offspring, Samuel was the only one with whom Grigori could converse about deep things, of philosophy and science, of mathematics and metaphysics. Samuel followed his logic perfectly and sometimes, even rushed ahead of Grigori. On occasion, this particular son had even led the old Fallen One to fresh conclusions, to ideas that had never occurred to him in the course of thousands of years of debate.

He tamped down any sense of paternal pride. It only made this part of the cycle harder.

Grigori stripped off his soiled clothing and sank into the steaming hipbath. One of the silent footmen came and went, depositing the breakfast tray and laying out the fresh suit of clothing Grigori had ordered. His valet cared for the upkeep of his wardrobe, but Grigori rarely saw the man. He always preferred to dress himself. No one needed to see his tattoo-like mark, the one that labeled him as fallen, or rejected, or whatever the Almighty wanted to call him. Besides, no one could have a better sense of style than he, so the argument in favor of a valet was moot.

Finally, as the bath water was just becoming tepid, Malachi arrived with a tumbler of whisky.

"The hair of the dog that bit you, sir," the steward said laconically.

"Actually, it was whisky *and* wine. Lots and lots of wine," Grigori said as he accepted the drink, "but this will do."

When he knocked back the tumbler, the amber liquid burned down his gullet. He loosed a prodigious belch and felt better for it. Then Grigori threw the empty glass across the room and enjoyed the sound of it shattering on the floor. Destruction, even on a small scale, was always satisfying.

"Where is Lord Badewyn?" he asked the steward who had dropped to his hands and knees to clean up the unnecessary mess. Malachai anticipated his master's proclivities and was never without a small whiskbroom and dustpan. Where he secreted those items on his person Grigori never discovered, but he applauded his servant's foresight none the less.

"I have not encountered his lordship this morning," Malachai answered. "He did not come down to breakfast and the maids say his bed was unused last night. The bedclothes had not been disturbed."

Grigori chuckled. Samuel might protest, but he was clearly taken with the duke's ward. Everything was proceeding according to plan. It was only a matter of time.

"What about Miss Anthony?" Grigori asked. "Wherever she is, Badewyn will be there, I warrant." He fell short of suggesting that his lordship was in the lady's bed, but a father could hope, couldn't he? Grigori never chastised his sons for anticipating their nuptials. He cultivated a rather loose regard for the rules and tried to instill the same in his progeny. Besides, they deserved some compensation for their contribution to the cycle.

Malachai shook his head and kept sweeping in short staccato bursts. "Miss Anthony seems to be missing as well. Her bed, however, was used."

I'll just bet it was. Grigori allowed himself a lascivious smile. He hoped Samuel would teach her a few things about pleasing a man. Inexperienced women were so very tedious. "No doubt they'll turn up when it's time for supper."

Slipping around to find a quiet place to copulate undisturbed in a well-populated castle became hungry business after a while.

"I doubt they'll present themselves this evening." Malachai finished sweeping and rose to his full lanky height. "His lordship's horse is gone, you see. And a good bit of Miss Anthony's things are missing as well."

"Why didn't you tell me that straight away?"

"You didn't ask."

Grigori glared at him.

Malachai bowed, careful not to spill any glass shards from the dustpan. "If there won't be anything else…"

Grigori waved him away, glaring at Malachai's retreating back. He wished he was still able to shoot lightning from his fingertips. It would be so gratifying to incinerate, if not a whole city, at least one taciturn servant from time to time.

Though the bath water was fast becoming too cool for comfort, he forced himself to sit perfectly still. The surface between his knees stopped wavering and he bent his will toward discovering the whereabouts of his son.

His effort went unrewarded.

Grigori had never been able to *See* Samuel at any distance, not even when he was a child. It was a source of real consternation. His other sons had been no trouble to track in any shining surface. Grigori had no idea why this one was so different.

How could a *Watcher* be so stymied?

"Very well, we'll go for the girl." He emptied his mind of all thoughts but those of Miss Anthony. She appeared briefly in flickers and disjointed images, but Grigori couldn't get a solid bead on her.

She must be with Samuel.

Whatever power shielded his son from Grigori's gaze was also hiding her. Swearing fluently, he rose from the bath and dressed in record time. It was time to roust some riders and loose the hounds.

Even if he couldn't follow Samuel and the chit by supernatural means, there were other ways to track one's prey.

Through the dark watches of the night, they took narrow paths through the mountains at a much faster pace than Meg thought prudent, but then, nothing about their headlong flight had seemed the least prudent. When they reached the first small village, Samuel traded his fine blooded Arabian for a sturdy hill pony. Giving the villager some extra coins, he ordered the man to ride north into Scotland. Samuel instructed the villager to trade for a new mount once he crossed the border and, if he valued his skin, to return home by a different way. Then Samuel and Meg turned south.

"Why did you do that?" Meg asked. The pony was sure-footed enough, but his gait wasn't nearly as smooth as the Arabian's had been. Since Meg's gown was too narrow for her to ride astride, she was seated in front of Samuel on the rough peasant saddle with her legs draped to one side and his arms around her to steady her. She clung to the pony's mane to keep from leaning back into Samuel any more than she had to. "You certainly made a poor bargain."

"On the contrary, with my horse and a few pence, I bought the most precious commodity on Earth—time. Anyone tracking us will follow the Arabian's trail, not ours."

"So you believe we're being followed?"

"I don't believe it. I know it." Samuel's arm around her waist tightened.

"Where are we going?"

"A little village called Gryffydd. I've *Seen* it in one of my *Watchings*. We'll be safe there for a while," he said. "Hush, now. Sound carries strangely in these hills. If you must talk at all, make it a whisper."

He'd all but told her to shut it. Meg felt like shouting just to spite him, but she clamped her lips shut. If someone as big and strong as Samuel was concerned for her safety, she supposed she ought to be, too. But still, it wouldn't hurt him to be a little more civil. No one had ordered her about so rudely since she'd run away from Uncle Rowney.

"You are a very strange man," she whispered.

The silence between them stretched for so long, she'd almost given up on a response, but then, his chest heaved and he said, "That's because I'm not a man. I am Nephilim."

"You're what?"

"The offspring of one of the sons of God and a daughter of men," he said into her ear. Despite his strange words, little tendrils of pleasure followed in the wake of his warm breath spilling down her neck. "You've read Genesis, haven't you?"

She'd tried, but all those begats and odd names had stopped her cold. Now she wished she'd tried a bit harder. "So you're saying that—"

"This is not the time or place for conversation," he interrupted. "Once we stop for the night, I will explain. I promise."

Her curiosity twitched like a cat's tail, but she was satisfied with his promise. What she couldn't be satisfied with was the idea that they weren't stopping until nightfall. They'd already ridden most of the previous night and even the rising of the sun hadn't raised her spirits. Samuel seemed to be taking a circuitous route now, turning off the path to trudge through shallow riverbeds whenever he could. Samuel produced a couple of crusty rolls and wedges of cheese from his saddle bag. They washed down their meal with clear water from the stream. Meg was forced to relieve herself behind an ancient sessile oak, festooned with lichen and ferns. Then she and Samuel remounted and moved on.

A son of God and a daughter of men. Her mind chased the idea around as they rode. The pony's determined plodding fell into a rhythm. Meg relaxed and let her head drift to Samuel's shoulder. Surrounded by his distinctive male scent and snugged under his woolen cloak, she was surprisingly warm, but not exactly comfortable. His thighs were too hard for that. And she was far too close to his male parts for her insides not to start turning back-flips. It was almost, but not quite, as exciting as his kiss had been. If she turned in his arms, maybe he'd be tempted to kiss her again.

Or maybe she'd slide off the horse.

She decided to stay still, safe within the circle of his arms and warm cloak. However unruly her insides were becoming, she was too tired to act on its urges. She let her eyelids close—only for a moment, mind!—and had no idea when she slipped from drowsy awareness into the hazy land of dreams.

Usually, she didn't remember her night-phantoms. As they rode along, shadowy images came together in her subconscious and then broke apart like storm clouds gathering and dispersing, as if they couldn't decide to go ahead and drop a deluge. Finally, one dream sliced through her mind with the startling clarity of a lightning bolt against a black sky.

Meg would remember it all her life.

Stars fell from heaven, tails of fire trailing them. She couldn't hear herself think over the shrieks of the pushing, scrambling crowd. Someone jabbed an elbow into her ribs, trying to muscle around her. Gasping for breath, she pressed her spine against a stone wall and let the mob stampede by. Fear was contagious. It reached out to grasp her throat with its bony claw.

There came a voice from heaven—a monstrous big voice, louder than the thunder of a waterfall, deeper than the ocean's depths—but the words it spoke were in a language she didn't understand. People fell to their knees. They buried their faces in the dirt. Something besides stars was falling now.

She shielded her eyes and looked up. And suddenly, she was unafraid.

The pony stumbled and Meg was jolted awake. A soft rain had been falling, but she hadn't been aware of it until that moment. She pulled the edges of the cloak tighter around her chin. Though she shivered, it wasn't from cold.

She hadn't been fearful at the end of her dream, but the eeriness of it sent a ripple of apprehension over her.

"Not far now," Samuel said as he kneed the pony into a trot.

Meg hoped it was far enough for her to stop the shakes that threatened to overtake her on the heels of that vivid dream. She'd seen the world of the tapestry with its cowering mob and the angel falling from the sky. She'd lived it.

And in her nightmare, the lone standing woman was *her*.

The only thing more difficult than not having a well thought-out plan is knowing what will happen if my spontaneous efforts fail.

~ from the journal of Samuel Templeton, Lord Badewyn

Chapter Eleven

Light spilled from the small window of a rustic inn. The thatched roof was patched in places, but seemed to be turning the rain. If it had been no more than a leaky hovel, Meg would still have been grateful to see it.

Samuel helped her dismount, took off the cloak they'd been sharing and draped it over her shoulders alone. It trailed the ground. Meg clutched the oilcloth garment tighter around herself while Samuel handed the pony's reins to a waiting hostler. He flipped an extra coin to the lad, ordering him to give the sturdy mount a thorough currying and some hot mash. Then he shouldered the saddlebag, picked up Meg, and carried her across the muddy yard between the stable and the inn's door.

Meg clung to his neck. Despite the foul weather and their headlong flight, his simple courtly gesture was too comforting for words. It made her want to trust herself to this man and trusting anyone was something she'd rarely done in her life.

"I know this place isn't up to your usual standards after living under the duke's care, but it's the best this part of Wales can offer," he murmured as they entered the low-ceilinged common room. Samuel stomped on the threshold to knock the mud off his knee boots.

The air in the inn was thick with the competing smells of ale, stew, smoke, and damp wool. Tipping back mugs, a few patrons huddled around a fireplace. Benches lined the walls and would serve as beds for travelers who couldn't afford a private room. Or for those who drank too much to trust their feet to find the way back to their own homes.

"Whatever I say," Samuel whispered, "do not contradict me."

Meg nodded. She would have to be able to think to do that and she was far too weary.

A balding fellow with florid cheeks stood behind an age-darkened bar, wiping the worn surface with a damp cloth. "What can I do for you, sir?"

He ought to have said "my lord," not "sir." Clearly, the innkeeper didn't recognize Samuel as the lord of Faencaern Castle. Meg realized this part of Wales was so isolated, its residents might not travel farther than five miles from their homes in their entire lives. Each little valley was its own small world.

Which meant strangers stood out. If someone were to come along asking about a man and a woman traveling through and gave Samuel and Meg's descriptions, they'd soon learn all they wished to know.

"A room for me and my wife, good man." Samuel slapped a handful of coins on the bar. "Bring us bread and some of that stew I'm smelling and you'll find there's more blunt where that came from. And more for the wise innkeeper who knows how to keep his own counsel."

Meg's jaw sagged. All that registered of Samuel's little speech was that he had claimed her as his wife. Then she remembered Samuel's warning about not contradicting him and clamped her lips together.

"So far as I can see, sir, you and the lady was never here," the innkeeper said, secreting Samuel's coins into his threadbare waistcoat's pocket and laying a finger alongside his nose in a sly gesture of collusion. Then he led them up a set of narrow stairs to the rooms above. They were shown to a surprisingly tidy chamber with sloping walls under the eaves. The single window was shuttered against the rain. There was a string bed laden with thick blankets, a small washstand, and commode with a privacy screen. A rocking chair stood by a cold fireplace. The innkeeper knelt and stirred the embers to life.

"That'll chase away the chill and get you dry on the outside," he said once the blaze flared up. "My missus has a way with the cooking, if I do say so myself. Her food'll warm up your insides right enough. I'll be back with a tray directly."

Once he closed the door behind him, Meg rounded on Samuel. "Why did you tell that man I'm your *wife*?"

"Because he likely wouldn't have rented us a room if he knew differently. Despite its humble appearance, this is a respectable inn. I've *Seen* it. The innkeeper is an honest man who doesn't have much because he gives a good deal of what he earns to those in need," Samuel said as he lifted the wet cloak from her shoulders and spread it over the spindled back of the rocking chair to dry. "If I'm to keep you safe, I need to keep you with me, so I told him you're my wife. It's a forgivable lie."

She retreated to a far corner, trying to put as much distance between them as possible. "If we are discovered here together, nothing will keep my reputation safe."

"Frankly, your reputation is the least of my worries," he said.

"So no matter what situation a gentleman leads a lady into, he bears no responsibility? There's a man's thinking for you." She crossed her arms over her chest as she remembered something odd he'd said during their headlong flight. "But then, you claim not to be a man, don't you?"

"That's right," he said, rubbing the bridge of his nose wearily. "Perhaps you'd better be seated if we're going to get into all that."

"I'll stand, thank you."

"Well, I'm going to sit. You may have nodded off in the saddle, but I didn't." He peeled out of his jacket, settled into the rocker, and leaned forward, resting his elbows on his knees. "If you won't sit, at least slip behind that screen and remove your damp things. You'll catch your death of cold, otherwise."

It was a prudent suggestion, if not a strictly proper one. Teeth starting to chatter, Meg decided to follow his advice. She took her dry afternoon gown and fresh undergarments from the oilskin saddlebag and carried them behind the privacy screen with her.

"You're trying to change the subject by having me change out of my clothes," she said. "Don't be fooled into thinking I'll let this go. What did you mean?" When he didn't respond, she peered at him over the screen. His head lolled to one side and his eyes were closed. If he hadn't drifted to sleep, he was doing a fair imitation of it. She raised her voice. "You promised to explain. I'm waiting."

He startled awake at her sharp tone and then dragged a hand over his face. "All right, but begin undressing or I'll come behind that screen and peel you out of that wretched gown myself."

"Wretched gown, indeed. What did you expect me to wear when you ordered me to come away with you in the dead of night? This bombazine might not be attractive, but I can wiggle out of it unassisted, thank you very much. And in any case, how dare you threaten to disrobe me!"

"I dare because you're not the only one who needs to get dry, though I'll wait until you're finished with the privacy screen. I assume a lady would rather I didn't start stripping out of my clothes here in front of God and everybody."

Meg tried to swallow, but her throat had gone suddenly dry. *Samuel Templeton, in nothing but his skin. Now that would be a sight.*

Then a disapproving Lady Easton rose in her mind. Meg felt mildly chastised but the image of a naked Samuel would not go away. She wondered again about where the unusual birthmark that proved he was the real Lord Badewyn was located. Cadwallader had said it was in an unmentionable place. Then she realized he'd tugged off his boots and was working on his stockings.

"No, you're right. Hold a moment." Thinking about him naked and actually seeing him that way were two very different things. Meg would never be able to keep up the pretense of being a lady under those circumstances. Her fingers flew down the line of pewter buttons that marched down her bodice. "I'll try to hurry."

"Good." Samuel stopped undressing after he peeled off his last stocking and stretched it across the hearth to dry.

Meg shed the bombazine in record time and shot him a pointed look over the screen. "Now, I'm ready for your explanation."

"I doubt that. It's such an odd tale, I wouldn't believe it myself if I hadn't lived the truth of it." He huffed out a breath. "As I told you before, I am one of the Nephilim, the offspring of a daughter of men and a son of God."

"I understand well enough what a daughter of men is, but what is *a* son of God?" Her theological understanding was woefully inadequate at times but she was certain he wasn't talking about *the* Son of God. "Do you mean an angel?"

"A fallen angel, to be precise."

"So your father was—"

"Is," he corrected. "A fallen angel. It's Grigori."

Well, that explained a great deal. No wonder Grigori had seemed to be able to see her when she was in her disembodied state. Having once been a creature of pure spirit, he was undoubtedly still sensitive to that realm.

"So you see, the generally accepted story is not true," he went on. "My father did not die in Ankara as everyone at the castle was told. That was my half-brother, the man who pretended to be my father. Grigori styles himself my uncle, but he's actually my sire. I was gotten on the wife of my very much older half-brother."

Despite Meg's determination to remain standing, her knees gave way and she sank to the floor behind the privacy screen. She'd been exposed to some odd doings since she became part of the Order of the M.U.S.E., but never anything as outrageous as this. If she didn't have such an odd gift herself, she'd have wondered whether Samuel had lost his wits to suggest such a strange thing were possible.

"I apologize if my bluntness offends you," he said. "There is no way to explain this tangled mess with delicacy."

She drew a deep breath and rose to look over the screen at him again. "Plain speech is better than delicacy if I'm to understand and, believe me, I want to understand." She cast about for some way to make sense of his claim as she continued to strip off her stays and chemise. "When I first came to Faencaern Castle, I was fascinated by that tapestry in the great hall. Does that fit into all this somehow?"

He sat back in the rocker and stared past her as if he could see through the sloping walls and into the craggy peaks they'd left behind. Then his gaze cut to hers and she felt pinned to the spot. "Like most tapestries, it commemorates an actual event. In the distant past, Grigori fell from heaven along with Lucifer. But unlike the Prince of Darkness, he claims he willingly left paradise for the love of a woman."

Meg's insides glowed with warmth. She knew who this woman was. She'd inhabited her skin, if for only a little while, in that strange dream. Even with calamity all around her, the woman had been soothed by the sight of her beloved tumbling from the sky. He wasn't falling. He was coming for her. They could face anything so long as they were together. "The woman standing alone. She's the one."

Samuel nodded. "Her name was Atara. Grigori says he didn't think twice about giving up heaven for her. She was his wife and his only love."

"That's so sad." Meg's chest constricted with sympathy

for the fallen angel. "And more than a little romantic."

"Don't be fooled by his self-serving version of the events. Grigori never does anything solely for someone else. He thought he'd picked the winning side in the War in Heaven, that's all. Finding a woman on earth whom he wanted to wed was just an extra strawberry in his new situation. Turns out, he was wrong about the War," Samuel said. "And Atara paid the price."

"How so?"

"When a daughter of men joins with a son of God, they may create a child together, but the woman never survives the birth."

That squared with what Cadwallader had told Meg about all the Lady Badewyn's dying in childbed.

"After he lost Atara, Grigori wandered for millennia. Then he came to Wales. As a fallen angel, he's a formidable warrior. It was easy for him to carve out the Badewyn fiefdom for himself, but since he's immortal, he couldn't hold it indefinitely without drawing unwanted attention. So he hit upon a plan to perpetuate the barony's lineage without having to marry again."

"Why didn't he wish to remarry?" Meg asked.

"He claims he lost his heart to Atara and had nothing to offer another wife, but I doubt the blighter ever had a heart to begin with."

"He did raise you, didn't he?" Meg pointed out. "He must care about you. That means he has a heart."

Samuel's jaw was set like granite, but Meg read pain in his eyes. "Grigori only cares about holding Faencaern 'in the family.' My existence helps him do that. It's the only reason I'm still breathing. Why are you defending him?"

"I'm not. I'm just trying to understand." This time Meg's heart ached for Samuel. Uncle Rowney had been no picnic, but she wouldn't trade her past for Samuel's if someone tied it up with a bow. Obviously Grigori Templeton wasn't the charming fellow he pretended to be. "How does it all work, this plan of your unc—I mean, your father's?"

"To understand you need a bit more of his history. After he claimed Badewyn for himself, he ventured into the Scottish Highlands, stole a chieftain's daughter, and got her with child. After she died bringing a son into the world, Grigori hired a wet nurse, threatened her into silence, and returned to Faencaern Castle with them, claiming he'd been widowed. Once his son came of age, the young man married. But"—his tone turned bitter—"a Naphil cannot father a child."

Meg felt as if someone had punched her in the gut. Was he unable to—no, it didn't bear thinking of. The idea that someone as wonderfully made as Samuel couldn't…well, just couldn't…

"Wipe that sorry expression from your face. You've no reason to pity me. Nephilim are fully capable of the act of love." He stood and pretended to warm his hands by the fire, but Meg sensed he was only trying to avoid meeting her gaze. "But we are unnatural beings. Like mules, we were never intended to exist. And like them, we are sterile." Resentment etched in every line of him, he swung around to face her. "Are you going to take all night back there?"

She quickly stripped out of her pantalets and stockings, draping her wet things over the top of the screen. When she glanced back at Samuel, his gaze was fixed on her but he no longer seemed sullen and angry. He was just as intense, but now the way he looked at her seemed hungry. Possessive.

"Now you see why I'm determined never to marry," he said softly. Somehow he managed to sound more seductive the softer he spoke. His voice touched a deep place inside her. Alarm bells jangled over her skin, but she had to fight the urge to come around the screen and give herself to him. Even if he couldn't marry her, was there a chance he might love her?

Stow that, Meg. He's never said a word about love and even if he had, what you're thinking is decidedly unladylike.

In a rush, she wiggled into her dry pantalets and chemise. Now that she was partially covered she expected to feel more in control of herself, but he still gazed at her as if he could see through the screen. Perhaps if she kept him talking, he'd stop looking at her as if she were the last biscuit on the plate.

"If you're concerned about not being able to father a child, you shouldn't be," she said, bending to roll up a stocking, which had the benefit of allowing her to avoid his gaze. "If a lady loves you, she won't care about that."

I wouldn't care about that. Meg was grateful that Samuel couldn't hear her thoughts. She'd come perilously close to thinking she loved him. If he were to snatch the last biscuit and gobble it up, would that be so bad?

Yes. In the eyes of the ton, *it's the Queen Mum of bad.*

"Not being able to sire children is not the problem," Samuel said. "Not all women are fixated on motherhood. I understand that. The problem is that once I wed, my wife won't have the option of remaining childless. When Grigori thinks my bride and I have enjoyed enough wedded bliss and a child needs to be added to the mix, he'll step in to do the honors by visiting his daughter-in-law by night."

Meg's eyes widened. "But surely your wife would object."

"She might not. Grigori can be very persuasive when he sets himself to charm, but in truth, she likely wouldn't know the difference. All his sons favor him strongly. He stamps us with his likeness. But in case that wasn't enough, he can assume any shape he wishes. Should I ever marry, it wouldn't be hard for him to alter himself to pose as me."

"That's horrible."

"It is. I won't have it," Samuel growled. "I'll be damned before I share a woman with him."

"But he would only try to take your wife?"

He nodded. "Grigori needs a legitimate heir to inherit and perpetuate the cycle. The child must seem to be mine, born within the bond of wedlock and fit to be the next puppet Lord Badewyn." Samuel ground a fist into his other palm. "That's why you are in danger. He wants me to marry you."

Her chest constricted over the pain on his features.

He'd only be in that much anguish if…if he actually did *want to marry me.*

The realization crackled over Meg's skin like heat lightning. The zinging heat went straight to her core. She and Samuel were very different, common and wellborn, human and Naphil. Maybe that was why something inside them clicked like magnets. She couldn't deny the force that pulled her toward him. Samuel must feel it, too.

Almost without her conscious volition, one stocking on, one off, Meg's feet took her around the screen. She stopped between his spread knees. Since he was still seated in the rocker, they were nearly the same height. She placed her hands on his shoulders and leaned toward him. Parading before him while she was so scantily clad wasn't a very ladylike thing to do, but she decided it was a womanly thing to do. She was meant for him. She felt it, blood, bones, and womb. If she could take upon her body even the tenth part of his cares, she'd be content.

"What do *you* want, Samuel?"

There be three things which are too wonderful for me, yea, four which I know not:

The way of an eagle in the air; the way of a serpent upon a rock; the way of a ship in the midst of the sea; and the way of a man with a maid.

~ Proverbs 30:18-19, King James Bible

Chapter Twelve

His lips formed the word, but he wouldn't let himself voice it. Still, his unspoken *You* seemed to reverberate in the air around them. The fire had banished the chill from the room, but her nipples stood out in hard points beneath the fabric of her chemise. The linen was so sheer; he could see the dark shadow of her areolas. Samuel ground his teeth together.

He wanted her, God help him. He'd never wanted anything so much in his whole life.

"If you want me, take me," Meg whispered. She leaned forward to rest her forehead against his.

Samuel would bet any amount of money she had no idea he could see down the front of her chemise, through the sweet hollow between her breasts clear to the soft indentation of her navel.

It wouldn't be fair, his light side argued. *You can't marry her.*

She wants you to do it, his dark side reminded him.

He reached up and drew a slow circle around one of her nipples. It tightened even more at his touch and she drew in a shuddering breath.

"I've never had a woman," he admitted.

Grigori had taken him to a brothel when he was fourteen, to try and "make a man" of him. To spite his father, Samuel had resisted. He'd spent the hour talking to a girl not much older than he. She only wanted to find a way to go home to her family, but was afraid they'd reject her if they learned the desperate path she'd taken to keep body and soul together.

I just knows they'd see it on me, the girl had explained. *A body can't live like I've been living without it leavin' a mark.*

During the Season he'd spent in London, Samuel wouldn't allow himself to meddle with any of the debutantes who'd flung themselves at him. It would only lead to a forced marriage and that would be as good as signing the young lady's death warrant.

His father's plans kept him from women.

Call it having a soul. Call it yearning to have one, for Samuel wasn't sure he did. But there was something within him that longed for a shining moment of honesty. His whole existence was one lie after another. He ached for one true thing.

He met Meg's clear-eyed gaze. Maybe *she* was his one true thing.

"I guess if you've never been with a woman that would make us even," she said softly, "because I've never been with a man."

Even if they came together, she still wouldn't be. Samuel

wasn't a man. He was a deviation, a misbegotten creature. He'd tried to convince her of this. But when she looked at him with her heart reflecting steadfastly in those changeable eyes of hers, he didn't feel like such a monster.

Though he ached to stop all the words and let their bodies do the talking, his light side demanded he speak one more truth.

"I won't marry you. I can't." He didn't have to elaborate. She knew why.

"Can you give yourself to me without reservation, for however long our time together shall last? Because if you can, it will be enough."

Samuel could do that. He stood and gathered her into his arms, trying to control the urge to charge ahead and ravish her in a heated rush. She deserved as much tenderness as he could muster. So he palmed her cheeks and covered her mouth with his, pouring himself into the kiss. She accepted him without question, parting her lips softly.

He'd give her all of him she could bear.

In her more wicked moments, Meg had imagined what it would be like to give herself to a man. None of those imaginings included a desperate flight and a humble inn in the hinterlands. Though Meg had always considered a match that led to the altar unlikely for a girl of her background, Lady Easton had fed her the fantasy of a storybook wedding. It was every well-bred lady's dream.

That dream could never happen with Samuel. Not with Grigori plotting to continue his "Grand Cycle." But regardless of their rustic surroundings or their need for flight from the wicked plans of a fallen angel, Samuel was here with her now.

And now was all that mattered.

His mouth was firm and gently demanding. His hands set her skin tingling as he untied the ribbon that held her chemise closed. She arched her back reflexively, straining toward him, aching for his touch. He thrummed her nipples and she softly chanted his name. After half a minute of his teasing, she practically sang it.

No matter how stolen these moments, she wouldn't change this time together.

It might not come again.

"Meg...love..." he murmured, stroking her hair as she unbuttoned his shirt. His fingertips grazed her collarbone, setting little pleasure faeries tripping over her skin. "I don't deserve you."

"No, you don't deserve me." He deserved so much more. Meg smiled up at him, determined not to cry. If only Grigori weren't...what he was, their life together might have been so fine. Then that bubble burst. Even without the threat of Samuel's father, she could hardly expect him to wed a commoner like her. She was as low-born as they came. "And I don't deserve you." But for the moment, she had him. She'd never have dreamed in a million years that she'd be with someone as wondrous as Samuel. "But that's what grace is, you know. A bit of heaven we don't deserve."

Meg had been schooled by her uncle never to pass up "the main chance." She was determined to grab this unexpected joy with both hands. She wondered for a blink what the duke of Camden, the other man who'd influenced her life, would make of her choice. Likely, he'd banish her from the Order of the M.U.S.E for good this time.

No matter.

Samuel was worth losing everything for. She blinked hard. That was what Grigori must have felt about his Atara. She'd never expected to find any common ground with that Fallen One. After all, Grigori was the reason Meg's relationship with Samuel was doomed, as doomed as Grigori's had been with his wife. She could have wept for the happy days that would never come.

But when Samuel kissed his way down her neck, she stopped thinking of what *might have been* so she could savor what *was*. Her world spun down to his lips on her skin. The rough burr of a day's growth of beard on his cheeks and jaw set her shivering in a tingly, Lord-it's-good-to-be-alive sort of way.

He'd touched her breasts earlier. She thought she knew what to expect. But when he bared one of them, bent his head, and took a tight peak between his lips, she was totally surprised by the powerful longing he unleashed. The arcing zing of desire, the urgency of his mouth threatened to buckle her knees.

"How did you know to do that?" she gasped once he released her.

"I may be a virgin, but I'm a well-read virgin," he said with a grin that was pure wickedness. "You'd be surprised at what Mr. Ingfeldt has stashed away in the secret corners of my library."

He'd been careful undressing her up till now, taking his time with the ribbons and tiny buttons. Now he tugged her chemise down past her shoulders till it dropped to pool on the floor at her feet. He made short work of her pantalets as she worked on divesting him of his rough shirt and trousers. Articles of clothing were scattered across the room until finally, they stood before each other in nothing but their skin.

Meg drank in the sight of him. His muscles rippled under flawless skin, the perfect balance of strength and masculine grace. Her gaze flicked to his maleness, checking for the star-shaped birthmark he was supposed to bear. That would certainly qualify as an unmentionable spot. She didn't spy the mark, but she did find a thick rod and bulging scrotum in a nest of dark hair. The sight made her forget all about searching for birthmarks.

"Meg, you're so beautiful."

The man must be bewitched. She almost contradicted him, but his face was so full of wonder as he gazed at her, she couldn't bear to break the spell. Or maybe it wasn't a spell. Maybe it was a miracle. There he was, with his angelic heritage shouting in every perfect line of him, and somehow he found plain little Meg Anthony beautiful. If that didn't qualify as miraculous, she didn't know what did.

Samuel closed the short distance between them and gathered her into his arms.

His skin was warm on hers, almost feverish, but she wouldn't have pulled away for worlds. They fit together, her softness and his hardness. Then he kissed her again.

Their first stolen kiss on the rooftop had stood Meg's world on its head. It had been furtive, sweet, and light by comparison to this one. This kiss took a decidedly darker turn as heat flared between Meg's thighs. An unrelenting ache began low in her belly, a drumbeat that made her want to move against him in slow undulations.

"You're so sweet," he murmured as he kissed along her cheekbone to her temple and back down to her lips again.

I love you, Samuel Templeton. My own beautiful, wicked, almost angel man.

Still kissing him, her heart sang as he scooped her up and carried her to the waiting bed. She couldn't speak her feelings, but she *thought* her love for him so hard, surely he must hear it.

He laid her out on the string bed and then climbed in beside her. Meg was deliciously warm next to him. Her whole body was on high alert as he caressed every bit of her with tenderness. When his hand delved between her legs, she bit the inside of her cheek. She'd never imagined him touching her *there,* of all places. He made her body weep for him. No doubt it was desperately wicked.

But it felt so very right.

And it made her want him something terrible.

"Please," she whispered. The ache was fast becoming unbearable.

He raised himself and settled between her legs, still kissing her as he moved closer to his goal. Meg squirmed under him and, wonder of wonders, their bodies found each other when she spread her knees to welcome him. She lifted her arms, a mute call to heaven, and then wrapped them around Samuel, encouraging him to enter.

Come to me, love. Stay with me. Never leave me ever.

She wouldn't say the words even if she thought her voice would work. They were only a beautiful dream. No matter what, she and Samuel couldn't be together forever. It wouldn't be safe. She could only have him now.

What will happen on the morrow? her heart demanded.

Samuel took her innocence in one strong thrust. In the rightness of their joining, she decided tomorrow didn't matter.

Meg lost herself in the heat and friction and the wonder of holding him inside her. She could scarcely think beyond her next breath.

As they moved together, her soul set off on a journey. It wasn't like when she went *Finding*. She was still thoroughly connected to her body and its myriad pleasures. Perhaps she'd lost the power of free will, the ability to think independently because she was feeling so much. But she was achingly aware that she sought *something* with desperation. Something for which she had no words.

Samuel seemed to know. He drove her to a pinnacle and then tumbled off it with her. Everything was suddenly lightning flashes of sensation and shuddering limbs and the hot steady throb of Samuel's life spilling into her.

It went on and on as time wove around them, loose-jointed and tottering like a drunkard. Maybe it would never end and she'd be joined to this man for eternity—one soul, one beating heart between them.

But then the glorious madness faded.

Meg was suddenly aware of the lumpiness of the mattress under her. She shifted under Samuel's weight.

He raised himself up on his elbows, his silver-gray eyes shining down at her. "I wish I could make you mine, Meg. Before God and man, I do."

She forced herself to smile. "Seems to me you've already made me yours in the way that counts. And I've made you mine."

Her heart still hammered in her chest, but not from

excitement now. Everything was ending far too quickly.

A shadow passed over his handsome face. "Grigori can assume any shape he pleases. Mine included. I think from now on if we become separated, even for a little while, we need a code between us."

"A code?"

"So you'll know it's me." He smiled. "How about if I call you 'Sunshine'?"

"Coming from a student of the stars I'd expect 'Starlight.'"

"No, let it be Sunshine. It's cheerful enough to be out of character for me, and you are just as life-giving as the sun to me." His smile faded. "Never let Grigori know we've been together like this. He'd use the knowledge for his own ends. And if a day dawns when you discover something has happened to me—"

She put her fingers to his mouth lest he speak the unspeakable and tempt the devil. "That day will not dawn."

It couldn't. There would be no dawn in a world where he was not. Or if it came, she'd make sure she wasn't there to see it.

For better or worse, the die is cast. I am hopelessly enamored of Meg Anthony. Poets who claim to wallow in impossible love have no conception of the word's true meaning.

Oh, how I wish I did not.

~ from the journal of Samuel Templeton, Lord Badewyn

Chapter Thirteen

The innkeeper rapped lightly on their door. Judging from the meaty, yeasty smell wafting through the cracks and the keyhole, he'd arrived with their supper. Samuel rose from bed, wrapped a sheet around his waist, and collected their meal at the door, giving the man another generous handful of coins. Meg dove under the covers, setting the comforter shaking while she tried unsuccessfully to stifle a giggle. Samuel figured it was nervous laughter. She was embarrassed at being almost caught in the act.

It was one thing to be swived royally. It was quite another for someone else to know she had been.

"Come out, Meg. He's gone," Samuel said as he set the supper tray down next to the pitcher and ewer on the washstand. The innkeeper had done well by them. There was a crock filled with stew, a loaf of barley bread, still warm, and two mugs of ale. "Everything will get cold if you don't come now."

She flipped the coverlet down so that her face was only visible from the nose up. "Is the door locked?"

"As much any can be in this place. The latch is pretty loose." Samuel sniffed appreciatively at the steaming crock. He tore the crusty loaf in half, pinched off a piece of bread, and dipped it in the stew. With a satisfied sigh, he popped the bread in his mouth and chewed. After their long night and day of travel, it was heaven in a bowl. "The stew will be as gone as our innkeeper if you don't come get your share soon."

"You can't expect me to lark about the room without a stitch."

He shrugged and helped himself to a bowlful of the meaty stew. "A man can dream, can't he?"

"A man could also hand me my chemise, at least."

He waggled his brows at her and grinned. "Now why would a man do that?"

"A man might not," she allowed, lowering the covers a bit, but still clutching them close under her chin, "but a gentleman certainly would. Please, Samuel."

He leaned against the washstand, continuing to wolf down his stew. Bed play was hungry work. "Don't you realize I love a chance to see every bit of you, Meg?"

"If you say so," she said doubtfully. "But now that we've...I mean, since you know all about me—"

"Oh, I highly doubt that. They say it takes a lifetime to unravel the mystery of a woman."

A lifetime we don't have.

He shoved away the unwelcome thought. It punctured the buoyant feeling he'd enjoyed since claiming Meg as his own. Making love with her was all he'd imagined the act would be and more. He hoped he hadn't rushed her, but judging from her responses, it had been just as pleasurable for her as for him. He'd never experienced such a strong sense of accomplishment over a new skill.

Of course, practice makes perfect.

With any luck at all, he and Meg would have time for more practice in the string bed. After all, the memories he made with her here would have to last a lifetime of empty nights without her.

And I've circled back to the crux of our problem again, blast it.

Samuel set down his empty bowl and retrieved her discarded chemise. Bringing it to her bedside, he delivered it with an exaggerated bow, determined to keep the mood light. "A pox upon me! Your effects, my lady."

"I'm not a lady, not really." She sat up, covers tucked under her armpits and reached for the garment. He held it just beyond her grasp to tease her.

"You are to me. Now, how does the lady propose to reward her willing slave?"

She crossed her arms over her chest in consternation. "What do you want?"

"As you suspected, I want to see you lark about without a stitch, but clearly that's not going to happen. So I'll settle for a kiss instead." He bent down and took one before she could argue him out of it. To his delight, she draped her arms around his neck and drew out their kiss. The coverlet fell, baring her breasts, so he reached for them. They were perfect, just the right size to fit his palms and topped with pink nipples that hardened in his hands. He gently kneaded her breasts and she groaned into his mouth.

Then she broke off their kiss, pulled the coverlet back up and grinned at him. "You were concerned about my stew getting cold, I believe."

"Hang the stew." He dropped the sheeting at his waist and started to climb back into bed with her, but she straight-armed him.

"No, I think you're right. I ought to eat while it's hot. Besides"—she cast him a perfectly wicked smile filled with promise—"you'll want some more, too. You'll need your strength for later."

She disappeared under the covers with her chemise and after a few moments of thrashing, reemerged wearing the garment, every button neatly fastened and every ribbon tied. Meg slipped out of bed and padded over to the fireplace. Poking the wood into a better configuration, she coaxed the waning fire back to life.

Samuel watched her with absorption.

"There," she said, dusting her hands on each other. "Aren't you thankful we have our own fire in the room?"

"I asked for the best accommodations available." Samuel had never been gladder to have more money than he could spend in several lifetimes. "But I'm more thankful that your chemise is nearly transparent when you stand before that fire."

"For shame, my lord. Has anyone ever told you you're very single-minded?" she scolded, but he couldn't take her words to heart. The corners of her mouth kept turning up.

"I never expected to become a satyr, but I seem to be. I guess it's because I've been saving up for so long." He was ready for her again and aching to see her as bare as Eve. He decided to lead by example. Samuel dropped the sheet and strode across the room toward her. In Eden, Grigori had told him, the man and his wife were naked and were not ashamed. Samuel felt no shame before Meg. He hoped she'd soon be comfortable enough around him to feel none as well. "I can't get enough of you, Meg."

When he tried to pull her into his embrace, she side-stepped to pull free of him. "Stew first, me later." She softened the rejection with a smile. "I promise."

"I'll hold you to it." He turned his back on her, strode to the washstand, and started to pour water from the pitcher into the basin.

"Oh!" The word popped out like a mouse squeak. "There it is."

He looked over his shoulder at her. "There what is?"

"Your birthmark. The one that proves you're Lord Badewyn." Meg covered her mouth to mask a giggle. "It's on your bum."

He rubbed his right nether cheek where he knew the dratted thing was. "Never seen it myself."

"I should hope not. You'd have to be frightfully limber to twist around that far." She drew closer still eyeing his bum. "It's a perfectly proportioned five pointed star the color of port wine."

"I know what it is," he said testily. It had been mortifying to have to prove himself to Malachai by displaying the blasted thing for the steward's inspection. "How do you know of its existence?"

"I heard about the mark from Cadwallader. The only thing she didn't know was where exactly it was located on your body. She just said it was in an 'unmentionable' place."

Thank God for small favors. "How could your maid

know about my birth mark? Only Malachai has seen it."

"But the help were all told that you'd been verified as the rightful heir and it seems all your older brothers had a similar mark. The story was handed down from one generation to the next," Meg said. "It's become the stuff of legend below stairs in Faencaern Castle."

"A star-shaped mark on my bum?" He chuckled. "Some legend."

"Clearly, your people are hungry for entertainment of any kind. But according to Cadwallader, they all knew about the mark and counted it as indisputable evidence that you are the right-wise born Lord Badewyn. That little sign relieved them out of all knowing," she said. "But the hiding place of the mark on your august person, well, as you can imagine, it's caused no end of speculation among those who serve you."

"It seems I shall have to find some other way to entertain them. Anything to take their collective minds off my bum." He turned back and continued to pour water into the basin so he and Meg could wash.

But before he could plunge his hands into the liquid, he began to see flickering images in the surface. He stared fixedly at them.

Meg started to shoulder around him. "If you're not going to wash, I will."

"Wait." He stopped her with an arm flung before her chest. "I see something in the basin and when a vision comes unsought, I must *Watch* it."

Meg stepped back to allow him room to peer into the increasingly still water.

The vision was a dark one. Not sinister. Merely dark. But

there was enough light for him to see a pair of fellows prying open the ground floor window of an elegant town house. Once they got it open wide enough, the older one gave the younger a shove inside. Then the younger reached back to haul his companion in after him. It was no easy trick. Neither of them were small men and the window hadn't opened very far. The last fellow in seemed to be stuck for a while until the first one put a booted foot against the wall and heaved with all his might.

Samuel never heard anything when he *Watched*, but since the intruders seemed to have encountered some difficultly, he didn't think they'd made their entry in complete silence. If there was anyone in residence at the town house, they'd have heard the pair of draw-latches bumbling about.

His vision expanded to follow them. The room they entered was well-appointed, with a long, centrally located table and twelve matching chairs.

A dining room.

The furnishings were mahogany, ornate with thick carving on each of the table legs and on the backs and arms of the chairs. There was a large sideboard whose drawers were probably filled with fine linens. The intruders didn't stop in the dining room, but instead made their way to the adjoining butler's pantry. Ornate "C's" were carved into every drawer and door panel. Samuel had seen that crest before.

Then the image faded. He rubbed his burning eyes. They always felt like glowing coals after a *Watching*.

"What did you *See*?" Meg asked in a small voice.

"It was Camden House in London." Samuel had met the Duke of Camden when he'd participated in a Season all those years ago. Unlike most of the events Samuel had attended, his evening dining with the duke had been most enjoyable. The food had been excellent, the wine and liquor top-notch and the dinner conversation stimulating. He and the duke had become fast friends, even though Samuel refused to become a permanent member of the Order of the M.U.S.E. His Grace's home, like Camden himself, was understated, elegant, and immediately recognizable.

"What about Camden House?" Meg asked.

"Two men are breaking into it."

Meg's face blanched. "Who are they?"

"I don't recognize them, but the intrusion seems to be happening right now."

"How can you tell that?"

"I can't explain it, but when I *See* something unbidden, it's usually an ongoing event." He pinched the bridge of his nose. A pinprick headache always seemed to form there after a scrying episode. "To look either backward or forward requires me to call forth a vision. This one volunteered itself."

"What were the men in your vision like?" she asked as she washed her hands. He followed her example, leaving his temporary scrying vessel scummy with soap.

"They were both large fellows. Roughly dressed." He dished up a bowl of stew for Meg and thrust it into her hands. Then he helped himself to what was left in the crock. "One is considerably older than the other. Father and son maybe."

"Or uncle and nephew," Meg said under her breath. "What are they doing now?"

Samuel shook his head. "The vision is gone."

"Can you conjure it again?"

He set his stew bowl down and peered into the soapy water. "I can try, but since I don't know the men I saw, I have no specific person upon which to focus." He wished he could call up more of the event. Even if success was unlikely, he'd attempt anything for her.

"Never mind. I think I know them. At least I know how to find out for sure." She hurried over to the rocking chair. "Bring the candle close, please."

He did as he was bidden. "What are you doing?"

"You gave me a demonstration of your gift. Now it's time for you to see mine. The duke has forbidden me to do it, but this is how I *Find*." She took his hand and put it on her shoulder. "Keep touching me until I return."

"What? Where are you going?"

"You'll see." She sat, closed her eyes, and murmured something that sounded like two names. Then to Samuel's dismay, her whole body stiffened. Her eyes rolled back in her head and then she slumped down in the chair. Her complexion took on the waxy pallor of death. When he touched her cheek, he felt it cooling. Between one heartbeat and the next, she'd left him.

He picked her up and held her limp body close. Her head lolled back. She was boneless as a cat. "Oh, Meg, what have you done?"

She hovered under the thatched ceiling, peering down at Samuel and her discarded house of flesh. He looked so distraught, she almost whipped back into her body to comfort him. She should have explained what was about to happen, but if the burglary was happening now there was no time to lose.

And besides, the sooner she went, the sooner she'd return. With both the candle to light her way and Samuel's touch to anchor her essence to her body, she was certain she'd have no trouble finding it again. She bent her will toward locating her uncle and cousin.

Free as a hawk on the wind, Meg soared through the passes of the Welsh mountains until she reached the rolling English countryside. It seemed to blur beneath her as she "thought" her way to the city on the Thames. London spread out below her, a spider's web of streets and courts. She recognized the broader ways of Mayfair and found the duke's chimney, having balanced more than once against his distinctive iron weathercock when she went *Finding* without permission. She dived down through the roof, passing through the attic rafters and the servants' quarters on the topmost floor as easily as if they were water. The butler's pantry was another two stories down.

As she feared she would, she discovered Rowney and Oswald trying to wedge open the locked drawer that held the duke's silver. The pry bar slipped and made a loud scraping noise against the fine English oak. The men froze, listening for sounds of someone rousing in the house. When they heard nothing, Rowney punched Oswald's shoulder.

"Careful, idjit!" Rowney hissed. "Just 'cause most of the household is gone, it don't mean the old geezer what serves as the duke's steward and a few other lackeys might not be about."

Oswald waggled the bar with menace. "If anyone makes to interfere with us, I'll persuade 'em to let us alone with a good clout to the head."

Meg would have gasped had she been in her body. If dear Mr. Bernard tried to stop their thievery, her cousin would damage him for sure. And maybe for good.

"If you think you can do better with the pry bar, old man, you're welcome to try." Oswald held out it to Rowney.

"Give it here then. There's a trick to is, see. It's not all muscle. Sometimes, you have to use a bit of what them Frenchies call 'finesse.'"

Rowney slipped the narrow end of the pry bar into the crack in the drawer near the lock and bore down gradually, increasing the pressure until the oak gapped.

"I see what you're about now. Hold it steady." Oswald slipped his finger in and depressed the locking mechanism. The drawer opened with ease, allowing the pair to gaze down at the sterling silverware nestled in its velvet-lined compartments.

"Gorblimey," Rowney said in the awe-filled tone most folk reserve for a supremely religious experience. "We've found ourselves a treasure trove and no mistake."

"Them titled blokes think they own the world and can't none of the rest of us get our fair share. But for all his blunt, the bloody Duke of Camden can't keep us from helping ourselves to his silver." Oswald narrowed his piggy eyes. "And he can't keep Meggie from us neither. Once we gets her back, we'll be swimmin' in lard, see if we ain't."

"Even before then. After we sells this stuff, we'll kit ourselves out like gentlemen," Meg's uncle said as he began stuffing the gleaming spoons, three-tined forks and ornate knives into a burlap bag. In his excitement, he failed to keep the clinking to a minimum. "No shank's mare for us. Mark my words, it'll be respectable coaching inns and a stage all the way. We'll be making the trip to that castle in Wales in style, my boy."

The trip to Wales? Somehow they'd discovered that the duke had sent her to Lord Badewyn, but she'd have to deal with that problem later. Now she wished she could do something to thwart their thievery, but in her disembodied state, she couldn't speak to the people she saw or move objects in the places she visited. She'd give anything to be able to fling the silver at them and send them shrieking away, crying out that they'd seen a ghost.

She was about to give up and flit back to Samuel and their cozy chamber in the Welsh inn. It was beyond infuriating to watch her family make off with the Camden House silver without being able to do anything to stop it. Although her sense of the passage of time was weak while she was in this state, she was certain she'd stretched the limits of her body's endurance. But before she could make her exit, Gaston LeGrand walked into the butler's pantry. He bore a look of utter surprise...and a glass of water.

To study the stars is pure pleasure. They are restful, orderly and, from a distance, serene. Thanks to the Italian astronomer, Giordano Bruno, we know that up close they are boiling balls of fire like our sun. A woman likewise can seem restful, orderly, and serene…but only from a distance.

Oh, how I miss studying the stars.

~ from the journal of Samuel Templeton, Lord Badewyn

Chapter Fourteen

"Meg, what are you doing? Stop it." Samuel sat in the rocker, clutching her limp body on his lap. He gave her a little shake, but she didn't respond. There was no sign that she was breathing and when he pressed his palm on her breastbone, there were wrenchingly long pauses between the beats of her heart. It was as if she were in deep hibernation, like a dormouse waiting for spring. He brought one of her hands to his lips. Her nails had a definite bluish tinge. "You need more air."

Samuel tipped back her head and covered her mouth with his. He filled her lungs with his breath, but she still didn't revive. Rocking as he held her tighter, he whispered. "Come back to me, love."

When she came back—if she came back—he promised himself he'd never let her hie off on this *Finding* business again.

Meg felt a fresh infusion of strength, as if she'd taken a deep cleansing breath. There was still a strong pull to return to her body, but she resisted it. LeGrand had stumbled upon Rowney and Oswald in the middle of their burglary. He was alone and in grave danger. She didn't know what she could do to help him, but at least she would serve as a witness when it came time to report to His Grace what had happened at his London home.

And like it or not, she'd have to confess to using her gift without the duke's permission.

"You there! What is the meaning of this chicanery?" LeGrand demanded, his French accent thicker than usual because he was clearly upset.

"I got no notion what 'shit-canery' means, but we mean to take the silver," Rowney said almost pleasantly. "If you'd be a wise Frenchman, you'll turn around and toddle back to your room. Leave us be about our business so's you won't get hurt. It's not like the duke will miss it if we help ourselves. He can always buy more."

"Whereas you only got one head and last I checked ain't nobody selling more of those." Oswald slapped the flat of his palm with the pry bar in a slow rhythm. "O'course, if you want to make trouble, ain't no skin off my nose. Been a while since I whipped a Frenchie. Expect I'll enjoy it."

Meg's uncle and cousin moved steadily toward LeGrand. Each of them outweighed him by several stone. Amazingly, the wiry Frenchman did not seem the least intimidated. Instead he tossed the contents of his water glass at them.

Oh, no. Rowney and Oswald are even meaner when they're mad.

"Now you're for it," her cousin said, swearing and

swiping his eyes.

Then a strange thing happened. The water seemed to multiply. Instead of wiping away droplets, Oswald pawed at rivulets running down his face, far more liquid than he could get rid of with a quick knuckle across his eyes. He and Rowney both looked as if they were weeping torrents.

LeGrand raised his hand and called water from the very air. It condensed in a hazy cloud over her uncle and cousin's heads. What began as a light drizzle soon turned into a drenching. Not so much as a drop reached the gleaming hardwood under their feet. As soon as the liquid reached the ragged hems of their trousers, it rose in fat droplets to start the cycle over again.

Meg watched in horrified fascination as her relatives were caught in a veritable butter churn of water, swirling in a long vertical oval to pour down on them again and again. The pry bar clattered to the floor. As the water volume increased, Rowney and Oswald lost their footing and were buoyed along by what had become a river of enchanted floating liquid. Their sputtering was punctuated by garbled yells for the Frenchman to help them.

Meg had watched Vesta use her skills as a fire mage, but she'd never seen LeGrand exercise his water magic before. Obviously, he'd been hiding his light under a bushel.

The undulating stream bore the kicking and screaming pair of burglars out of the butler's pantry, through the adjoining chamber and back to the half open window. Rowney's feet slid out of the window first, but his protruding belly became stuck and for a moment, Meg feared her uncle would drown in His Grace's dining room. But Oswald gave Rowney a boot to the face and pushed him through before

being borne out the same opening, his arms and torso
scraping along the window ledge. Meg whisked through
the upper sash to hover over the duke's front garden. Her
relatives were borne past the duke's iron gate and down the
cobbled street, still writhing and swearing as the charmed
river carried them far from the scene of their intended crime.

Meg laughed or would have if she'd had any air to do it
with in her spirit state.

It was enough to remind her that her body must be
in desperate need of a breath by now. Quick as thought,
she raced back to Wales and the little chamber above the
taproom she shared with Samuel.

When she burst through the thatched roof, she found
him seated in the rocker, holding her body on his lap. Pain
was etched on his face. Her chest constricted at having
caused it. She quickly re-entered her body and drew a deep
breath.

Or tried to. He was squeezing her so tightly, she could
barely expand her ribs enough to get a quick gulp of air.

"Come back, Meg," he chanted.

I'm trying.

She wiggled in his arms. He jerked her to arm's length
away from himself so he could look down at her face. Relief
flooded his features. It was followed hard by fury.

"What the hell was that?" he demanded. "What did you
do?"

"I went *Finding*," she said, her voice coming out a
breathy fraction of itself. Now that he'd lessened his hold on
her, she could draw a deep lungful. Her heart pounded. She
didn't try to rise. Even seated on his lap, she was so light-
headed she feared she might topple over. She'd need more

than a moment to recover after staying away so long.

"And you have to die to do it?"

"I didn't die." Meg still felt incapable of more than a three word sentence.

"You could have fooled me." He stopped squeezing her close to him, but the way his fingers dug into her arms was likely to leave bruises.

"You're hurting me," she said, her voice a little stronger now.

He released her and settled his forearms on the rocker's arm rests. "I didn't hurt you as much as you hurt yourself. You're still blue, Meg."

"It'll pass." She drew another deep breath, willing her cheeks to pinken, but there didn't seem to be any way to hurry her body along. All she could do was breathe.

"When you *Find*, what happens to you?" His voice was the soft rumble of a predator's low growl before it erupts in a roar. "Exactly."

"I…well, the easiest way to explain it is that I am able to leave my body behind for a time so my spirit can look for people and things," she said, pausing every fifth word or so for another deep breath. "I can travel great distances in a short time and pass through locked doors to uncover secrets."

He glared down at her. Why didn't he think her gift was as impressive as the duke seemed to?

"And what did you *Find* while your body lay dying in my arms?"

"I wasn't dying," she said defensively. Well, technically she was dying, but she'd only be really dead if her spirit came back too late. Of course, the trouble with that argument was that she didn't know exactly how late was too late. This time had felt chancier than most. She decided to change the subject. "If you must know, I picked up where your *Watching* left off. My spirit traveled to London and looked in on Camden House. You'll be pleased to know the robbery was thwarted with no injury to my friends in residence there."

"So no one was hurt. No property made off with. What you're saying is that you endangered yourself for nothing. No wonder the duke has forbidden you to exercise this ridiculous gift." He lifted her off his lap and prowled the perimeter of the chamber in an unconscious imitation of Camden at his most upset best.

"Ridiculous?" She latched onto the mantel to hide how wobbly her legs still were. Her vision tunneled uncertainly, but her breath hissed in over her teeth. Meg refused to give him the satisfaction of seeing her faint. "How can you say my gift is ridiculous? Was it ridiculous when I *Found* a lost child?"

"You're twisting my words."

"No, I'm understanding you for the first time. You think *I'm* ridiculous. And maybe I am." What was more ridiculous than a low born nobody pretending to be a lady?

"That's not what I said."

"Samuel, stop." She placed a hand against his chest to bring his pacing to a halt. "I need you to hear me. I am not what you think I am."

"Here's what I think you are—stubborn, willful, and a danger to yourself. You're all that and more."

And less. He still didn't know she wasn't wellborn. She needed her gift. It was all that made her special.

He grasped her hands and held them to his lips. "Meg,

you scared the life out of me."

Her insides softened at the stricken expression on his face. She shouldn't have stayed away so long, especially not the first time he saw her *Find*. "I'm sorry I made you worry."

Samuel loosed a long sigh. "Well, it's done now. It'll be all right."

He pressed a kiss on her knuckles. Relief washed over her. Everything was going to be well between them. Then he spoke.

"I trust it won't happen again," he said sternly. "I'm in total accord with His Grace. I forbid you to do that again."

"You what?" Did he think her a child?

"You heard me. I don't want you—"

"What you want doesn't signify." She pulled her hands free. "Only a father or a husband could give an order like that and expect it to be obeyed."

"What about the Duke of Camden?" Samuel said, with narrowed eyes.

"What about him?"

"He ordered you not to *Find*, too."

She laughed mirthlessly. "In case you didn't notice, I haven't exactly obeyed His Grace, either."

"But you will obey me."

"I will not." He wasn't her husband. He had no standing to order her about. And even if he was her husband, she couldn't obey him in this. It would be like hacking off a limb. *Finding* was too much of who she was.

"Why won't you do this small thing for me?" Samuel asked, his cheeks darkening with barely suppressed anger. "I defied my father for you. And since he's a follower of the Dark One, that is no light matter. I deserted my estate for you. All I ask of you is one simple thing. Something that will keep you safe."

"I might be safer if I stopped *Finding*, but I wouldn't be me." Meg straightened to her full height. "If you can't accept me as I am and that means all of me, including my ability to *Find*, you may as well leave me right now."

Samuel didn't say a word as he set a new record for a gentleman dressing without the aid of a valet. Once he tugged on his last boot, he was out the door and stomping down the narrow stairs to the taproom below.

Stricken, Meg stared after him for a few moments. Then she retrieved her bowl of stew and sat down to eat. Grease had begun to congeal on the cooling surface. She took a half-hearted bite and then set it aside.

Drawing her knees to her chin, she rested her forehead on her kneecaps and wept bitterly. She'd given him a choice, which was more than he'd offered her. But he didn't make the choice she'd counted on. He didn't choose her.

She'd lost Samuel. And no amount of *Finding* would bring him back.

"Whisky," Samuel ordered as he bellied the bar. He'd get roaring drunk. That was the thing. It always seemed to work for Grigori.

The innkeeper appeared with a half full bottle, poured a generous jigger and set it before him.

Samuel knocked back his drink in one gulp. His eyes watered, and his tongue went numb, but his chest still ached. Until that stopped, he hadn't had enough. "Leave the bottle."

"That bad, is it?" The innkeeper refilled Samuel's jigger.

Samuel promptly emptied it and held it out for more. "What do you mean?"

"Whatever it is that's happened with you and your bride."

"She's not my bride."

"Oh, so you've been married long then," the innkeeper said, misunderstanding him. "Women are the brightest and best of God's creatures, but they're devilishly difficult to understand sometimes."

"Make that all the time."

The innkeeper cast him a sly smile. "Not all the time. The walls and floors are thin hereabouts and that bed of yours creaks something fierce."

Samuel hadn't noticed. He'd been too caught up in the wonder of Meg. He took the bottle from the innkeeper and poured himself another drink. Then he offered some to the innkeeper, too.

"Don't mind if I do," the fellow said, setting a clean jigger before him and letting Samuel pour. He sipped his whisky, savoring the drink instead of bolting it. Samuel subconsciously imitated him.

"That's smooth, that is," Samuel admitted, feeling a bit calmer now. He didn't know if it was the whisky or the company, but the ache in his chest had subsided a bit. "How long have you been married?"

"Me and the missus have been together a little over thirty years."

"That's a long time."

The innkeeper nodded. "Sometimes it feels longer than others. But sometimes, it feels as if we just started. D'ye mind if I offer you a bit of advice, one married man to another?"

Samuel refilled both their jiggers. "Go ahead."

The innkeeper leaned forward and whispered, "The secret to wedded bliss lies in three little words."

Samuel nodded. "I love you, you mean." He hadn't told her. He should have.

"No, not those. O'course, they're important, too, and every woman wants to hear them, the oftener the better, but the ones I mean are even more powerful for curing what ails a marriage."

"What are they?"

"I. Was. Wrong." The innkeeper took the bottle back from him. "Mark me well. Those words will save you, lad, when nothing else will." Then he moved down the bar to serve another patron.

Samuel tried the words for size. "I was wrong," he whispered.

But he wasn't wrong. He'd only insisted she not endanger herself. What was wrong with that?

Then he began to wonder how he'd feel if she demanded he stop *Watching*. His gift came to him as natural as breathing and was just as essential. On those rare occasions when he hadn't taken the time to *Watch* the images that rose before him in still surfaces, he'd felt agitated. Incomplete. He didn't feel himself again until he went back to his scrying vessel, emptied his mind of conscious thought, and let the image rise again.

He was a *Watcher*. He hadn't asked for it. Couldn't help it. Wouldn't change it. It was who he was.

Maybe it was the same with Meg and her *Finding*. Maybe he *was* wrong.

Gravity binds planets in their orbits. It sends the stars on their nightly circular dance. But love is what binds people and sends them to do things they never expected.

It is by far the more powerful force.

~ from the journal of Samuel Templeton, Lord Badewyn

Chapter Fifteen

Meg hadn't expected to sleep, but a person only had so many tears in them before they cried themselves dry. She'd finally winked out, collapsed across the bed, exhausted in body and spirit.

She bolted upright at the scrape of a booted foot on the threshold. Framed in the open doorway, Samuel stood motionless. Firelight tipped his hair and broad shoulders with gold. His face was shadowed, but when he stepped inside the room, the whites of his eyes gleamed, flashing feral in the dimness.

Her heart skipped a beat. Swinging her legs over the side of the bed, she ached to run to his side, but stopped herself short.

Steady, girl. He may only be back to tell you he's leaving for good.

"Meg. My Sunshine."

That was all he said as he moved toward her, but it was

enough. The words were both validation of what she was to him and since they were the agreed upon code, it confirmed he was himself and not Grigori in disguise. It was almost enough to send her rushing toward him but she forced herself to remain motionless. When he reached the side of the bed, he ran his palm over the crown of her head with such tenderness, her insides melted.

"Becoming attached to another person is a vexing thing," he said softly. "I'm not sure I know how to do it."

Well, that wasn't what she wanted to hear. She stiffened under his touch.

"It makes thinking difficult because my mind is wrapped around you, my all-important Other. It makes taking action difficult because I must consider how what I do will affect you. It makes the simplest things difficult. Even something as easy as breathing because…not to be near you is to cease to care if I continue to breathe."

She was back to melting again.

"How do people bear this business of attachment?" he asked. "How shall I bear it?" He didn't wait for her answer. Instead, he took one of her hands. "I was wrong to order you not to use your gift," he said softly. "I let my fear for your safety crowd out everything else."

She released the breath she'd been holding.

He dropped to kneel before her. "My only excuse is that I love you."

There. That's it. Her other hand went involuntarily to her chest. She'd been fascinated with him from the first moment she looked into his handsome face. That fixation had grown into more with each moment they spent together. For him to love her back was more than she dared hope. But along with his love, she needed something else, too. "How can you love me, if you won't trust me to *Find* when I need to?"

He looked down as if searching for the answer within himself. Then he met her gaze. "This is hard. More than anything, I want to keep you safe. I can't do that when you use your gift. You're beyond my reach. So, when you must *Find*, I'll have to trust you."

Samuel was giving on the sticking point. It was time for her to bend a little, too. "I won't do it unless it's absolutely necessary."

He nodded. "That's a start. You know better than I what risks you run when you *Find*. Will you at least tell me when you plan to exercise your gift?"

"I can do that."

"And while your spirit is flitting about, will you remember that I'm waiting for you to return, hardly daring to breathe?"

"That's how I felt when you left me this evening," she admitted. "I thought you might not come back."

"I will always come for you, Meg." He rose to his feet, brought her up with him, and claimed her mouth.

He tasted of whisky.

"You've been drinking," she said.

"Only enough to help me see things clear."

If a few drinks made him realize and admit he'd been wrong, she blessed the innkeeper for pouring them. She kissed him again.

Every time their lips met, Meg felt the same sort of lightness of heart she experienced when she went *Finding*. Their kisses were a search, trying to discover that unique self hidden inside. But this kiss was different. It was a kiss of knowing. They'd already been found. They knew each other's secrets, bad as well as good, but they hadn't turned away.

It was a minor miracle.

When she broke off their kiss, his eyes were dark with arousal. But she remembered there was a part of her he didn't yet know. And he deserved to. "There's something I need to tell you."

"Talk fast," he said as he untied the ribbon at the neckline of her chemise.

"It's about the burglary at Camden House. The men I saw trying to steal the silver, I knew them, you see. They are my relatives."

"I don't have any living family except Grigori, but I imagine everyone has a few black sheep in their flock." He nuzzled her neck and nipped her earlobe.

"No, you don't understand. They *are* my…my flock. It was my Uncle Rowney and Cousin Oswald. I'm not what you think. I'm no lady. I was born in a barn. An actual barn. I never knew my parents. Uncle Rowney raised me. And he didn't raise me for a ballroom. He taught me to pick pockets and lie and cheat." As the words tumbled out, she pulled away from him. Feeling suddenly chilled, she started toward the fire. "I'm nothing but a low born pretender trying to fit into the duke's Order by playing at being wellborn."

Samuel grasped her wrists and pulled her back to him. "What do you think you're doing?"

"Giving you the whole truth about me," she said. "And a way out, if you want it. I can't expect a lord to love me."

He wrapped his arms around her. "Just to be in the same room with you settles me. One smile from you and I'm good for the whole day. I don't want a lady, Meg. I need you."

Samuel's breath was warm on her face as he caressed her name. "I've wanted you since I laid eyes on you, and that was before I knew you. Now I can't stay away. I'm glad you told me about your childhood, but it doesn't change a thing. We have something real, you and me. Something honest. If you think we don't, I'll walk out that door right now."

Meg stroked his jaw, his beard stubble a bristly pelt beneath her palm. The raw hunger in his eyes threatened to buckle her knees. He wanted her. *Her.* Not some pretend wellborn Meg. He loved the real one.

She stood on tiptoe to brush his lips with hers. "What we have is real."

He was on her then, claiming her mouth, his hands rucking up her hem to cup her bare bum with his palms. Then suddenly he stopped and looked down at her.

"This much is real, too," he said, his voice passion-raw. "Grigori still intends to bed the woman I wed. Because of that, I can't marry you. Not ever."

"I know," she said and kissed him softly, melting into him. "But would you have me go through life without having you? Should we never know tenderness, never know anything real? Love me now, Samuel. It will be enough."

It would have to be.

Their mouths met. Samuel held her head immobile while his tongue played a lover's game with her lips, teeth, and tongue. Her tongue darted between his lips until he groaned into her mouth. Longing rippled through her. Warmth pooled between her legs.

As they kissed, their hands found each other and their fingers entwined. Then Samuel slid his palms up her bare arms, skimming his fingertips to the hollow of her throat. A sparking trail of pleasure followed his touch.

"You're so beautiful," he whispered between kisses. "And so soft." He bent down to pull her chemise over her head. A bit of night air slipped in around the shuttered window, cooling her heated skin.

Samuel stepped back a pace and let his gaze pass over her from head to toe. To her surprise, Meg wasn't the least ashamed for him to see her. He'd seen her soul naked when she demonstrated her gift for him. What was a bare body compared to that?

"It's my turn now." Meg tugged his shirt over his head, and then worked the buttons at his hips with fingers flying. She made short work of stripping him. Taking in the strong lines of him, she reveled in his broad, heavily muscled chest and tapering waist. He stood like a statue and let her look. He was all that was masculine, all she knew of it at any rate.

She wanted to know more. He spread his arms wide and she stepped into them.

It was a little like drowning, Meg decided. She was engulfed by this man, but she didn't care a whit. She gave herself up to him. His masculine smell, the way her skin tingled at his touch, her nipples hardening against his chest—he was a whole world. She let her hands roam, learning Samuel by touch. Meg discovered clenched muscle beneath taut skin. She learned he was ticklish on his left side. She found an old scar on his ribs and pressed her lips to it, making a mental note to someday ask him how he came by it.

Of course, Samuel was discovering a few things of his own. All the tender places he'd swept with his gaze, he now explored with his touch. His hands set her skin to dancing.

He whispered her name, over and over. His voice played in her head like the wind ruffling through pines. She was warm and wet by the time he claimed the cleft between her legs. Samuel dropped to his knees before her.

Meg gasped as his tongue invaded her. He stroked. He nibbled. He took a tender spot she didn't know she had between his lips and suckled. Her knees nearly gave way.

She twisted her fingers in his hair. Her belly clenched. Inside, she was wound tighter and tighter, stretched thin as a piece of parchment. Then between one hitching breath and the next, the tightness snapped and she began to unravel. After the spasms ended, she would have collapsed, but Samuel caught her.

He carried her to her bed and stretched her out. Her spirit trembled with so much joy, she didn't care what he did with her body.

Samuel stood over her, a smug grin on his handsome face. Not trusting her voice, she lifted her arms to him in invitation. He didn't need to be invited twice. She welcomed the weight of his body, reveling in the way he sank onto her. His kisses were more urgent now, and she tasted herself on his mouth, all salt and musk.

"You are delicious." He trailed baby kisses down her neck, along her jaw line and finally nipped at her ear. "Everywhere."

"Where did you learn to do what you did to me?" Her heart still banged against her ribs, but at least she was capable of speech now.

"I told you. There's a book in my library."

"It must be some book."

"You have no idea. There are even pictures. I confess

during my younger years, I quite defiled that curtained alcove in the library while I studied the thing." He slid off her and made lazy circles around her navel.

"You took me someplace I've never been," she said breathlessly.

"Want to go again?"

She pulled his head down and kissed him. Hard.

"I'll take that as a yes," he said. "Roll over."

Obediently, she turned onto her stomach. "This was in the book?"

"This and more." Samuel ran his warm hand down the length of her spine. He teased the curve of her bum and drew something with his fingertip at the top of her crevice just below the small of her back. Tingles of pleasure streaked over her.

"Are you writing on me?"

"I am. That was my name. I claim you. You are mine," he said. "Now guess what I'm writing."

There was the straight line of an "I." It was followed by an "L." Then an "O." By the time Samuel got to the "V," Meg was trembling all over.

He finished his silent declaration of love, written on her flesh with the tip of his finger. Then he rolled her over and kissed her, settling his hand on her hot mound.

"This time, you're in control," he said. "My hand will move again only when and how you kiss me."

Lightly, she brushed her lips over his and in response his finger flicked her sensitive spot, soft as a whisper. When she gasped, he crooked a brow at her.

"And that's how the game is played," Samuel said with a grin.

Meg kissed him more deeply, thrusting her tongue into his mouth. His finger invaded her. She played with his lips, nipping and suckling and he did the same to her. She writhed under his talented hand. Finally she found a way to kiss him that set his fingers in the rhythmic motion her body needed. He took her to that dark secret place, but it didn't remain dark. She crested with a burst of light behind her closed eyelids.

Her body bucked with the strength of her release. Then as she came back to herself, she discovered he was pressed against her hip, hard and relentless. She was utterly spent, satisfied to the core of her being, but if Samuel was still wanting, she couldn't be completely content. Meg gave his shoulder a gentle nudge and he rolled onto his back.

"You've given me such joy," she said. "It's time for me to give back."

"Giving to you is better than taking." Samuel teased a taut nipple. "It pleases me to please you."

Meg nipped his lower lip. "But you're not as pleased as I intend you to be. Now stay still." She shot him a wicked grin. "If you can."

"I am putty in your hands." He laced his fingers behind his head.

Her glance flicked to his groin. "Putty was never as hard as that."

Meg had seen statues of naked men in art museums with Lady Easton, though most of them had their interesting parts covered with surprisingly small fig leafs. A leaf would have been woefully inadequate in Samuel's case. He was the first real man she'd seen, so she let her gaze wander over his long body. Stretched out in the firelight, his muscles were rounded mounds, his nipples dark, his maleness at full attention.

"If you only intend to look," he said, pulling a face, "it's going to be a long night."

"Don't worry. I'll do more than look." She climbed atop him and settled on his groin at the base of his erection. His ballocks tightened beneath her. Starting at the base, she stroked the length of him with one finger. His breath hissed in over his teeth and he rose to her touch.

"Now what?" he asked between clenched teeth.

Instead of answering, she kissed him. Then she gathered her hair in her hand and tossed its length up over his face. Slowly, she moved down his body, drawing her hair over his chest and belly. She hoped it felt like a thousand tiny fingers caressing him.

He moaned in pleasure. "Did you find that book in the library too?"

"No, of course not. I'd never ask Mr. Ingfeldt for such a thing." Her cheeks heated, imagining the little librarian's shocked face if she had. However, if they ever returned to Faencaern Castle, she might search for the book on her own. "What I did to you just now, I made that up myself. Since I've no education in these matters, you'll just have to put up with my fumbling."

"With a grateful heart!"

"No more words now," she ordered. With her fingers and mouth, she explored him, conscious of every snatched breath and quivering muscle. When he groaned softly, she showed pity and took him in her hand. She stroked him with a galloping rhythm, but he couldn't bear it long.

Samuel rolled over, pinning her beneath him and

entered her in one long thrust. They moved together as one. It was joy unspeakable to have him inside her. Holding him. Engulfing him. The bed creaked under them like a chorus of crickets as their rhythm sped up.

She sensed the pressure building steadily in him. Samuel's ballocks tightened and his whole body stiffened. His seed pulsed into her, hot and steady.

Spent and gasping, his weight sagged onto her for a moment, before he raised himself to look down at her. His heart glowed in his silver-gray eyes. Meg kissed his throat, tasting the sweat-damp saltiness of his skin.

A loud cheer erupted in the taproom downstairs.

"What in the world is that about?" she asked.

Samuel squeezed his eyes closed for a moment and shook his head. "Us, I imagine," he said with a lopsided grin. "The innkeeper warned me that this bed is noisy enough to be heard in the room below."

"You're joking."

"I fear I am not. In the heat of the moment, I forgot about the noise, but our only alternative would have been to brave the floor and, creaky or not, the bed is much more comfortable. Don't you agree?"

"I agree that I'd like to have been told we might be overheard," she said stiffly. How would she ever descend those rickety stairs and face the innkeeper again?

"After a certain point, we weren't talking much. Besides, we're supposed to be married," he said. "This is what married people do, especially after they've had a disagreement. Once I came back up here, I'll be bound the inn's patrons were laying wagers on how long it would be before they heard the bed again."

"You mean you talked to everyone in the common room about our 'disagreement'?" She would have classed it as a fight serious enough to end their relationship. After all, their argument touched on the core of who she was.

"I only confided in the innkeeper."

"Who probably can't keep his teeth together if his life depends upon it. Unfortunately, it's not his life at risk. It's ours." She gave his shoulders a shove and he rolled off her. "If your uncle comes and asks about us, you've just made us much more memorable."

"I don't think Grigori will search for us in this direction. If he follows the trail to the dead end in Scotland, he won't necessarily look for us heading toward Cornwall."

"Can you call up a vision of him to see where he is?"

"I could, but there's always the danger that he'd be looking for me in a scrying vessel at the same time. Normally, he can't see me in one, but if I open myself from this end, he might be able to. We can't risk it." Samuel tucked one arm under his head. "Grigori probably expects me to try to take you back to the duke in London."

"Which is where we ought to go." Surrounded by the other members of the Order and under the duke's protection, Camden House was the only place she'd ever felt safe.

Samuel shook his head. "There must be somewhere else. Some place not connected with the duke."

She had no family to run to. Rowney and Oswald were why she'd journeyed to Faencaern in the first place. She couldn't go back to the castle. She wouldn't be safe in London. Suddenly it was too much to bear and she burst into tears.

"Meg, love." He pulled her close to him. "Don't fret.

I'll figure something out. Trust me. I'm sorry I spoke to the innkeeper about us and—"

"Hush." She stopped him with a finger to his lips. "A little embarrassment is the least of our worries. And the bigger problems are not your fault."

"They aren't yours either. Let's let them rest for the night. The rain is coming down harder which will make travel difficult, but it'll be difficult for Grigori, too. We'll stay here a few days." He hugged her tighter. "I won't let anything harm you. As long as there is breath in my body, I swear my father will not have you."

He slipped a finger under her chin and kissed her on the forehead. His expression wasn't the least tender. Determination hardened his jaw and dug a deep groove between his brows. "You may believe me," he promised.

"I do." Meg kissed his lips. She wanted peace between them. She wanted to feel there was nothing beyond the four walls of their chamber, that no one threatened and they were what they claimed to be.

Husband and wife.

It was an empty dream. An impossible wish. But as long as she lay beside Samuel, it was one she couldn't help wanting.

I've convinced Meg that I know what I'm doing, but it's all a façade. Part of me wants to pour water into the wash basin and call up our future. A darker part of me doesn't have the courage.

There are some things no one should have to face until they must.

~ from the journal of Samuel Templeton, Lord Badewyn

Chapter Sixteen

The ducal coach slogged into the muddy courtyard and stopped in front of the sorriest excuse for a coaching inn Camden had seen since they left London. He rapped the head of his walking stick on the ceiling to signal a halt. However poor the lodging might be, it was infinitely preferable to spending another night cooped up in his coach with his disgruntled traveling companion.

Fire mages did not enjoy confined spaces for long periods.

Or the damp. Or the abysmal roads and rough fare offered at village taprooms. Or practically anything they'd encountered since he and Vesta had put the lovely hotel in Bath behind them.

She was not one to suffer in silence.

"Why are we stopping? What is this place?" Vesta asked.

"We have reached our destination," he said. "This humble spot is Gryffydd, the village where the medium Lord Badewyn recommended is reported to live."

"I can well believe he or she can speak with the dead. One would have to be half in the grave one's self in order to live in such a God-forsaken place." She peered through the slit in the coach's curtains and made a *tsking* noise. "Weren't we supposed to be going to Lord Badewyn's home?"

"We were and we still could," Camden offered. "But Faencaern Castle is another couple of days away. We might press on, but we'd likely have to spend another night along the way in the coach."

"*Ugh!*"

"To spare you some unnecessary travel, shall we see if you can bear this inn for a little while?"

Vesta pursed her lips, somewhat mollified. "Very well. But your footman will have to carry me to the door. The mud would simply ruin my lovely little shoes."

Pity her lovely little temper is already ruined.

Goodbody, Camden's footman-turned-valet, hopped down from his perch behind the coach and opened the door for them. Even mud-spattered and thoroughly damp, the corners of his mouth kept quirking up in a suppressed smile. The lad had never been beyond the outskirts of London before and seemed to be having the time of his life, no matter what his circumstance.

Camden climbed out of the coach, gave orders regarding Miss LaMotte and strode with purpose to the inn door, thankful he was wearing knee boots given the poor condition of the grounds. Behind him, Vesta was scolding the footman for letting her train touch the muck. Her voice shot up an octave. Apparently, someone had driven cattle through the place a short while ago. Then Camden heard the scuffle of leather soles on wet stone, a long wail, and finally a squelching thud, followed by vociferous swearing.

He didn't look back.

Instead he hurried into the low-ceilinged common room of the inn and demanded the two best rooms available.

"Begging your pardon, Your Magnificence," the inn-keeper said, clearly unsure how to greet him appropriately. The man dipped in several quick bows. Even bedraggled by travel, Camden's meticulously tailored wardrobe announced his high station. "But we only got two rooms, you see, and the one is occupied."

"Then evict the current tenant and quickly," he demanded. "I am the Duke of Camden. Unless the Prince Regent is in residence, I yield to no man."

"Yes, Your Grace. Right away." The innkeeper started toward the foot of the stairs, but stopped when the door to the common room swung open behind Camden. The man's eyes grew wide.

Camden turned to see Vesta framed by the opening. She was covered from head to toe in a combination of mud and cow dung. Her bonnet, once the latest bit of frufurrah from Paris, was now beyond salvation. Vesta usually moved in a cloud of jasmine and spice perfume. Instead, a decidedly barnyard-ish odor wafted from her.

Camden swallowed hard. No one could make a scene like an offended fire mage. He hoped she didn't incinerate the place.

"Camden," she said with forced sweetness. "Please tell the nice man that I shall require a bath. A hot one." When the innkeeper stood frozen, apparently dumbfounded by her appearance, she added, "Immediately!" with such force, the man's feet scarcely hit the treads as he ran up the stairs to do his new guests' bidding.

Camden gave Vesta a slight bow from the neck. Perhaps he'd misjudged her. "I must confess, I am impressed, my dear. Most women would be livid if they found themselves in your state."

"Oh, shut it, Edward."

After the innkeeper hemmed and hawed through his efforts to dislodge Samuel and Meg from their room, Samuel ordered Meg to stay put, pushed past him and headed downstairs.

"Where's the pompous ass who thinks he can have us turned out of our chamber without so much as a by-your-leave?" he thundered.

He stopped short when he spotted the Duke of Camden at the foot of the stairs.

"The pompous ass you're looking for would be me, I believe," His Grace said with unruffled dignity. Samuel descended the rest of way and shook the duke's extended hand. Others might have felt sheepish over calling a peer of the realm an ass, but Samuel had dealt with a fallen angel all his life. A mere duke didn't cow him.

"Good afternoon, Your Grace."

"Badewyn, it is good to see you. If I'd known you were here, I wouldn't have demanded your room. What's it been? Ten years? You haven't aged a day. Miss LaMotte will be trying to winkle out your secret."

The duke indicated the muck-caked lady at his side. She stared off into space, obviously either bored by the conversation or off her game over her unseemly condition.

"I've no explanation for my appearance, but I certainly can't claim righteous living," Samuel joked. It was recorded in ancient texts that Nephilim were known for aging well and reportedly lived full lives into their nineties and beyond, as hale and hearty as any thirty year old. If they were allowed to do so. In Samuel's family, Grigori hastened the end of one Lord Badewyn to make room for the next so he could restart his Grand Cycle with alarming regularity. Samuel's older half-brothers never survived the death of their wives by more than a few years.

"I'm surprised you found Gryffydd on your own," he said. "It's not on the usual routes from London."

"We didn't travel directly from Town. Before heading north into Wales, Miss LaMotte and I visited Bath. The waters are quite sublime."

"At this point, any water would be sublime," the lady grumbled.

"At any rate," the duke went on as if Miss LaMotte hadn't spoken, "according to our driver, Gryffydd seemed to be a good way point between Bath and your stronghold."

Samuel gave Camden's traveling companion a bow, which she answered with an injured sniff. Apparently Wales was not welcoming her in the manner to which she was accustomed. He remembered meeting her at Camden House all those years ago. Without a coating of mud, Miss LaMotte had been a vivacious dinner companion, possessed of a sharp mind and witty observations. She was also a courtesan, if memory served.

"This village where your medium lives happened to be only a little out of the way," Camden said. "I trust

Miss Anthony's visit to Faencaern Castle hasn't been an imposition."

"No, I wouldn't call it that," Samuel said. "For reasons I'm not at liberty to explain on the moment, she's not at the castle. She's here with me."

"Miss Anthony is here?" Miss LaMotte suddenly perked up at the mention of Meg. "I shall join her immediately. Camden, be a dear, and tell the innkeeper to find me in Miss Anthony's room as soon as my bath is ready."

The lady lifted her soiled skirts and slogged up the stairs. Samuel ushered His Grace to a booth in the corner. After the innkeeper's wife brought them ale and crusty bread, Samuel explained why he had secreted the duke's ward away in this remote village. It took a while to explain his unique familial legacy, but Camden sat quietly through the entire account, interrupting only if he needed further clarification. Samuel was grateful the duke didn't seem shocked at learning he was a Naphil. Only Camden's whitened knuckles betrayed his agitation over Grigori's plans for his ward.

"Staying in the same chamber with Meg—I mean Miss Anthony—has the appearance of impropriety, but trust me. It's the only way I can protect her from Grigori's *Watching* abilities. As long as she's near me, he shouldn't be able to see her."

"What about now? She isn't near you on the moment."

"Grigori is a creature of the night. He would be most likely to hunt for Meg in his scrying bowl then."

"Very well, but if tales of this cozy arrangement reach London, it will mean ruin for her," Camden said. "Ordinarily, I would insist you marry the girl, but so long as your uncle is a threat to any lady you take to wife, we can't have that."

Samuel nodded. "And if things were different, I would have married her already."

Camden regarded him thoughtfully. "Is that so? I trust she shared the unfortunate circumstances of her upbringing with you."

"I know she's not wellborn, if that's what you mean. It doesn't matter. I love her." It felt good to say it aloud. "I would marry her in a heartbeat if I could protect her from my father afterward."

"And you don't care that Polite Society would say you had married beneath you?"

"What Society? I am Society—polite or otherwise—as far as this part of Wales is concerned. There are only one or two other titled gentlemen within several days ride from Faencaern Castle. Besides, with a fallen angel for a father, the *ton* holds no terrors for me."

"I suppose it shouldn't for me either." Pensive, Camden templed his hands before him and his gaze flicked upward as though he could see through the rough timbered ceiling to the floor above. Samuel wondered if the duke was thinking about Miss LaMotte. The arbitresses of correct behavior would have a field day with a peer who married a "bird of paradise." Then Camden shook off his wool-gathering. "Where is this medium you are so keen on?"

Samuel stood. "I can take you to her now if you like."

"No." Camden indicated he should sit with an imperious gesture. The duke might try to present himself as an even-handed, almost democratic soul, but there were times when his ducal coronet showed in his manners with all its glittering weight. "After traveling all this way, Vesta would have my head if I went to the medium without her."

Then Camden leaned forward, his face expectant. "You believe she really can speak with the dead?"

"I have *Seen* it," Samuel explained. "In my *Watchings*, there are countless disembodied beings flocking around her home. If she cannot hear them, why would they come?"

"Why indeed?" The duke leaned back and exhaled noisily. Samuel got the sense that he was deeply conflicted over seeking out the medium, even though he'd been most adamant about finding one.

"It is not my place to remind you of this, Your Grace, but you're planning to dabble in things better left untouched. Holy writ warns against it," Samuel said. "There is only one time recorded in scripture when someone consulted a medium…and the outcome was not at all what the seeker hoped."

"You speak of when King Saul sought out the Witch of Endor," the duke said. "Don't look so surprised. I, too, have studied scripture. Saul hoped for advice on how to confound his enemies, but instead he was told that he and his sons would die on the next day."

"Then you know your session with the departed might not go well," Samuel warned.

"Not knowing will go worse. I've tried everything else. There is no other way to answer my questions," Camden explained.

"And if you don't like the answers?"

"At least I'll know the truth. It's supposed to set one free."

Samuel wondered about that. The truth hadn't helped him. He could shout his father's evil intentions toward Meg from the rooftop and it wouldn't dissuade Grigori one jot. A Fallen One knew no shame. He couldn't be bullied. He wouldn't be stopped. Samuel was only forestalling the inevitable by trying to keep her hidden.

Some truths simply wouldn't let you get around them.

Having Vesta appear at her door nearly knocked Meg's stockings off. Seeing the fire mage in such bedraggled state was even more of a surprise. Vesta had never been less well turned-out, but she still carried herself with vivacious grace.

"There you are, lovie! Don't fret. I'm not about to hug you. Heaven only knows what foulness is clinging to my person." Vesta looked down at herself and shook her head. Then she met Meg's gaze and grinned. "But on the bright side, this means Camden owes me a new ensemble and I was getting tired of this one, in any case. Believe me, my mantua-maker is not cheap. Tell me, darling, how have you enjoyed Wales? More specifically, how have you enjoyed that dashing young man I saw down in the common room?"

Meg felt all the color drain from her face. "You mean Lord Badewyn?"

"Who else? Honestly, I'd forgotten how very handsome he is or I might have come to Wales with you in the first place." Vesta waved a dismissive hand. "Oh, don't pull such a face. I'm only having a bit of fun with you. Besides, he seems to be taken already."

Meg crooked an inquisitive brow.

"By you, of course. I could tell at first sight that he cares for you. Absolutely. He looked ready to tackle a bear when he came down the stairs, bellowing for all he was worth," Vesta said. "But more to the point, do you care for him?"

"With all my heart."

"Well, then. This trip to the hinterlands hasn't been in vain, has it?"

Meg wrung her hands. "There are some problems."

"Good heavens, when is there not? You know what the Bard says. 'The course of true love never did run smooth.'"

Meg didn't know who the Bard fellow might be, but he'd hit the nail bang on the head.

A soft rap on the door interrupted them. It was the innkeeper's rosy-cheeked, and at the moment, wheezing and out-of-breath, wife. Even if she'd pressed a number of her offspring into service with her, hauling enough water up the stairs for a bath was no light duty. Meg had done it many times when she'd worked as a lady's maid. Her back ached in sympathy with the woman.

"Beggin' your pardon, miss," the innkeeper's wife said with a deferential curtsy. "Your bath is ready. Will you be wanting me to wash your dress? Reckon it will take a week."

Meg didn't doubt it. The gown was of such gossamer fabric it would need special treatment. The woman would have to remove all the buttons and furbelows and then pick apart the lining so when she laid the fabric out, it would have a chance to dry evenly. The innkeeper's wife might even have to take the gored skirt portion apart at the seams because there was no guarantee it would shrink uniformly. Then she'd have to sew it all back together and reattach all the embellishments.

Vesta's complicated wardrobe made Meg appreciate her simple bombazine afresh.

"You may have the gown. Try to launder it, if you wish," the fire mage told the innkeeper's wife. Lip curled in distaste, Vesta looked down at her ruined gown. "My advice is to burn it. How you'll ever get the smell out of it is beyond me. Now lead me to that bath and you and I shall be friends forever."

The woman seemed taken aback by this declaration, but her flushed cheeks showed she was pleased beyond knowing. The little village of Gryffydd had never seen such a fashionable lady as Vesta LaMotte and likely never would again. The gown was finer than anything the woman had ever owned. She'd try to save the gown, Meg suspected. It would become a family heirloom, probably saved for the innkeeper's daughters' weddings.

Once it was properly aired, of course.

"If you'd be pleased to follow me," the woman said shyly.

"And you come, too, Meg." Vesta crooked a finger at her. "While I bathe, you can tell me everything that's happened since you arrived in Wales." She shot a meaningful glance at the string bed. "And I do mean everything."

Regard not them that have familiar spirits, neither seek after wizards, to be defiled by them.

~Leviticus 19:31, King James Bible

Chapter Seventeen

Vesta's toilette took longer than Camden anticipated, but when she appeared, floating down the humble staircase with all the grace of one being presented at Court, he decided she was worth the wait. A breath of her perfume preceded her, beguiling and sweet. The bath had sweetened her temper, too, for the deep cleft that had been etched between her brows was gone.

"It seems the sun does shine in this remote country," Vesta said as she took Camden's arm. Keeping to the grassy edge of the lane, they left the inn with Meg and Lord Badewyn. Mellow light filtered through the limbs of a spreading oak. The forest surrounding the hamlet was filled with birdsong. "I'm inclined to think Gryffydd picturesque instead of hopelessly bucolic. Come, Edward. Give us a smile. I know your face works that way. I've seen it."

He forced the corners of his lips upward.

"Not bad, but perhaps you'll do better after this business

is done."

"It's not exactly business."

Vesta chuckled. "Everything is business with you, Camden. Perhaps that's your trouble. However, I shall make it my mission to disabuse you of the notion. A daily dose of fun should do the trick."

"Sometimes, one has to take life seriously."

"Granted. But not all the time and certainly not when I'm on your arm." Vesta's smile was contagious. She seemed to intuit that he was on pins over finally meeting with the medium, and was doing her best to keep their conversation lively and light. "So smile, Edward. I mean it."

He gave her the best smile he could muster. "I shall endeavor to accommodate you. However it's hard to appear giddy on the moment. Remember that all the other mediums have proved to be frauds." But even as he said the words, Camden began to sense the presence of a psychic entity beyond the signatures of power he associated with Vesta, Miss Anthony, and Lord Badewyn. It gave him hope that the Welsh medium wasn't just another in a long list of pretenders.

When Lord Badewyn knocked on the door of a humble dwelling, Camden's heart was pounding in his chest. Finally, he'd learn why his beloved Mercedes had died, but as he neared what looked to be the end of his quest, doubts began to fray his last nerve. The answers he received might be harder to live with than his questions.

There was no response at the door, so Badewyn knocked again, harder this time.

"Come, then, why don't you?" said a harried voice from within. "Doors were meant to be opened, you know, and I trust you've a free hand. Heaven knows, I don't."

Lord Badewyn lifted the rope latch and they all filed into the one room cottage.

In the past when Camden had sent his Extraordinaires out to assess the abilities of other self-proclaimed mediums, they often reported that sessions took place in an almost theatrically staged room. The chambers proved to be riddled with secret panels. Lord Stanstead had even discovered clockwork devices hidden beneath floorboards that were designed to make furniture appear to move of its own accord.

The humble cottage they found themselves in bore no resemblance to that sort of trickery at all. There was a spinning wheel and a three-legged stool by the hearth. A large pot of something savory bubbled over the low flames. The floor of the cottage was of packed earth, but it still looked as if someone had troubled to sweep it. No occult symbols festooned the walls. Instead, there were pegs at intervals draped with drying herbs. A string bed with curtains pulled to one side stood in a corner and a stack of blankets at its foot suggested that pallets for a number of children were made out each night.

There were only two people in the cottage at present. One was an exceedingly ordinary-looking peasant woman, bony fingered and long nosed. The other was a wiggly child with a wooden bowl on his head. The woman wielded a sharp-looking pair of shears trying, without much success, to give him a haircut.

Despite her unassuming appearance, so much psychic energy emanated from her that Camden's legs nearly buckled. If the waves of power washing over him were any indication, this medium was the genuine article.

"Make yourselves at home, if you please," the woman said. "I'll be with you in a trice if this wee fiend will only settle." Then she turned her attention back to the squirming child. "Keep still, Isaac. 'Tis a well known fact that fine folk like these eat wriggly boys for supper."

The woman winked broadly over the boy's head at Camden. Apparently, the duke and his party appeared sufficiently hungry to the boy, for her threat cured him of the fidgets. He sat still as stone for the duration of the haircut. When she was finished, she removed the bowl and gave the boy a kiss on the crown of his ruddy head.

"Take that poultice of herbs we made this morning for Goodwife Argall and see that she gets it. 'Twill do her sore hip a world of good," the woman said, giving the lad a light smack on the bum as he skittered away to collect the medicine from one of the pegs. "Tell her we expect one of the piglets when her sow farrows on the morrow. Doesn't have to be the pick of the litter. The runt will be fine."

Once the boy let the door bang shut behind him, she fixed Camden and his companions with a direct gray-eyed gaze. Not at all cowed by their obvious wealth compared to her poverty, she walked toward them. Then she stopped before each one, looking intently at them in turn as if assessing their worthiness to be in her home.

"Welcome," she finally said, directing her speech to Camden, though he had given no indication that he was the leader of the group. In fact, he'd been the last one through the door when they entered. "I am Glenys, the Witch of Gryffydd."

"Surely you're not a witch," Camden said.

"No, but that's what you're thinking I am, isn't it?"

It was. The biblical Witch of Endor had come up when he was talking with Lord Badewyn and the association had stuck in his mind. He bowed apologetically to her. "You have me at a disadvantage, madam. I cannot divine the secrets of your heart, but you seem to have a window on mine."

The woman scoffed. "If that ain't the fanciest string of words I ever heard, well, I'd hope to shout!" She heaved a sigh. "Let's get to business then before Isaac comes back. I love the boy something fierce, but he's a whirlwind with feet, that one. Don't any of the dead take to him much. Too lively, I guess."

"So you do claim to communicate with the departed?"

"I make no claim about it. I simply invite them in. If they want to come, they come. If they don't, they don't. But when they trouble themselves to visit me, it wouldn't be polite not to talk to them, would it?"

"*Hmph*...I suppose not." Glenys wasn't at all what he expected. There was no show. She was all matter-of-fact business. And since he'd thought of business... "How much do you charge for your seances?"

She shook her head. "It don't work that way. 'Tis not my seance, you see. The departed decide whether anything happens at all. Then once we're finished here, only you can decide what the time has been worth to you."

"That seems fair," Camden said. "Perhaps you'd be so good as to explain how the process does work, then."

"'Tis easy as pie. I invite a soul to visit, but I don't command. Whether or not they deign to grace us with their presence is up to them entire. To our sorrow, we are creatures with free will. We make our own choices in life. It stands to reason we will in death, too, or we wouldn't still be ourselves now, would we?"

That was as original a bit of philosophy as he'd ever heard. "What must we do?"

"Do? Why, nothing, of course. If you're too busy doing, you'll never hear the soft voices of those who've gone before. But I suppose it would help if you was to make yourselves comfortable-like. You, there." She pointed to Lord Badewyn as if he were a lackey to be ordered about instead of a baron who controlled a goodly portion of the land in this part of Wales. "Fetch the chairs from around the table and bring them closer to the fire. Then you can all take a seat."

Badewyn moved quickly to obey and soon he and the women were seated in a half circle facing the flames. An empty chair was left for the duke.

"I'd prefer to stand if it will not disrupt the proceedings." Camden narrowly resisted the urge to pace. He didn't think he could sit if his life depended upon it.

"Suit yourself." Glenys sank onto the stool by the spinning wheel. "Somehow, I didn't expect you would, Your Grace."

Camden had not introduced himself. "You know me?"

"How could I not? 'Dreamer,' says the rain. 'Leader,' says the wind. 'Powerful wizard,' say the small Voices only I can hear. That's who the Duke of Camden is." She cocked her head thoughtfully. "I'll add Man of Sorrows on my own account. I see the grief etched in every line of you. It's been a number of years since your loss, but your heart still bleeds."

Camden didn't deny it. He tried to keep his mourning private, but it was plainly evident to the witch of Gryffydd.

"You'll be wanting to speak to your wife, then," she said.

"May I have her name, so I can invite her proper-like?"

"Her Grace, the Duchess of Camden."

"No, not like that, all formal and stiff. The dead care nothing for such things. They stay away in droves when we try to force the silliness of the living on them," Glenys explained. "Speak plainly. What did you call her when your two heads shared a pillow?"

Heat crept up Camden's neck. He valued his privacy above all things. Glenys's question allowed him none, but he trusted everyone in his present company. Vesta was the keeper of so many of his secrets, he knew she'd keep these proceedings confidential. Badewyn and Miss Anthony could be counted upon to hold their tongues if he asked them not to divulge what they saw and heard here. Unbending a bit before his associates—he didn't think of anyone as his friend—was evidently what it took to speak to his dead wife. *Very well.* "When it was just we two, I called her 'my little heart,' but her Christian name was Mercedes."

"*Is* Mercedes, you mean," Glenys said. "She may have left her house of flesh behind, but the part of her that is real, the part that goes on into eternity, is still known by the name she bore in life. But before we start, I must warn you that the dead don't spare the feelings of the living. You may hear things you'll wish you had not."

"I consider myself warned. Proceed."

Glenys closed her eyes and breathed in a deep, regular rhythm. Camden had expected some sort of mystic chanting or at the very least a spell to be recited, but the medium seemed content just to sit quietly. As he watched her, some of her relaxation seeped into him. He found himself matching her breath for breath. Anxiety sloughed off him with each exhalation. Camden stared into the fire, almost mesmerized by the flickering light. He was going to see Mercedes, his wife, his love, his little heart.

What was there to fear?

"Mercedes, your Edward is here, the one who called you his little heart," Glenys said softly. Camden's gaze cut sharply to the medium. He'd not given her his Christian name, yet she knew it. "He has traveled a great distance to see you, though not so far as you will travel should you choose to meet with him here. Be welcome, spirit. We wait for you to come to us. Do not tarry, pray, but come and ease Edward's heart with your presence."

Then Glenys fell silent and her chin dropped to her chest.

Lord Stanstead had told Meg once about a Cornish medium he'd assessed for His Grace. After a great deal of fiddling about, the charlatan had finally faked a trance, altered her voice, and tried to imitate the dead. When Glenys' head finally came up, Meg expected her to speak for the duke's wife, but instead, the witch gazed silently upward.

Meg did the same. A hazy apparition was forming on the underside of the thatched roof. It coalesced into the likeness of His Grace's dead wife. Meg recognized her from the portrait hanging above the mantel in the duke's study. The ghost floated down to hover, her spectral toes only an inch or so above the floor, between the duke and the fireplace. The spirit's flowing robes undulated in a breeze Meg could not feel.

"Edward." A disembodied voice came from the apparition, though her pale lips did not move. The ghost merely smiled at him for a moment, and then her expression went as flat as an unpainted canvas.

"My little—" The duke took a step toward her but then he seemed to remember that they were not alone and stopped himself. "Mercedes."

"I think of you often, my dear one," the ghostly voice came again. "You spent so much time in your study when we were together, it is there that I imagine you. Fretting and planning for your precious Order and the governance of your estate, mindful of so many things at once you can't think properly on any of them. Settle now, darling. I would that you could be at peace, my love."

Meg wondered if she'd ever be able to publicly call Samuel "my love." *Probably not even if I was dead.*

"Are you…at peace?" His Grace asked.

"There are few things from life that remain to me here. Regret is one of them. I'm as much at peace as I can be after what I've done."

"What did you do?" Camden demanded, then moderated his tone to a more conciliatory one. "Please, I must know. Does it touch upon the circumstances of your death? It has been many years, but some details are still knife-sharp in my memory. It wasn't long after your confinement with our child. You told me you meant to venture out, to visit a friend, you said, but I forbade it. Surely, you understand I only ordered you to remain within Camden House for your health's sake. You hadn't even been churched yet and still you… Why did you disobey me?"

The apparition faded a bit, but then brightened.

"Probably because you ordered me not to leave our home. I could never abide being told what to do. If your memory is as sharp as you say, you must remember that fault in my character. I wasn't a child, Edward. You shouldn't have treated me like one." Her mouth sagged in a mournful expression, then returned to stoic blandness. "For what it's worth, I wish with all my heart I had not left home that night."

"Tell me, love. I need to know what happened."

"The telling would be hurtful to you and I would not be the cause of more grief."

Apparently the medium was wrong in this case. The duke's wife did still seem to have a care for his feelings. Mercedes must have been a tenderhearted person. Meg found herself wishing she'd known Her Grace in life.

"Nothing could hurt me more than losing you," the duke said. Meg's chest constricted in sympathy with him. "Not knowing is driving me mad. Tell me what happened and why, I beg you. Even if it hurts."

The apparition drew itself up into the exact position, gesture, and expression as the Mercedes captured in the portrait. "You love this painting, don't you?"

"You know I do."

"You won't once I tell you." She dissolved into a formless blob with only two dark holes for her eyes and another where her mouth should be. "Shame is another thing which remains with me. You see, my darling, I took the artist who painted that portrait to my bed. We became lovers right under your nose."

The duke's face paled and he looked as if someone had punched him in the gut. "But how could you do such a thing?

You were increasing when that painting was commissioned. You told me so."

"It's true. I was a few weeks gone with child before the painting began. Never doubt that the boy is yours. But after you learned I was bearing your child, you began to treat me as if I were made of spun glass." The apparition glowed a soft blue, a deeply melancholy shade. "You abandoned my chamber and held yourself aloof from me. I missed you in my bed. It was so lonely."

"I restrained myself so that I would not injure you or the child. I wish you knew how much it cost me not to come to you by night." His Grace's lips went white. Meg wasn't sure if it was from anger or embarrassment. Probably both. "It was for the sake of the child."

"For the sake of your heir, you mean." The ghost's color changed from blue to smoldering orange. Meg felt the heat of resentment roiling off Mercedes. "I began to feel I was only a means to an end for you. Alberto saw me as a woman, someone to be cherished for myself alone. Not merely a thing designed to produce a baby."

"I never meant to make you— You must believe I did not think of you like that." Then he went on more softly. "But I didn't tell you what I thought, what I felt, did I?" His Grace's fingers curled into fists, but Meg suspected his anger was directed at himself. "How long did this…affair go on?"

"About three months. It ended when the painting was finished and Alberto moved on to his next commission. I put away thoughts of my lover and focused on bearing you a healthy son. You were so happy during the months of my confinement. Even though you didn't show it in our marriage bed, you seemed to love me all the more as my time approached."

"I did love you. I still do."

"But I began to wonder if you only loved me because of little Henry."

"Never. I wish I'd...oh, never mind. It can make no difference now. I cannot change my past mistakes any more than you can." The duke's head dropped to his chest. "How did you die, Mercedes? We were never able to discover."

"I don't remember."

"Come, you must know," His Grace urged. "Why did you go to Cheapside with our son?"

"I shouldn't have taken him with me." The ghost's orange tint faded and she pulsed that soft blue again. "But I couldn't bear to leave Henry behind. A note came from Alberto, summoning me to come to him. I don't remember what the missive said exactly, but I was desperate to see him. I like to believe it was to tell him I would never see him again, to show him my son as proof that I belonged with you, Edward. But I own myself a weakling in matters of the flesh. I might have tumbled into bed with him again. I simply don't remember."

The duke's eyes narrowed. "Is he the one? Did he hurt you?"

"Truly, the events of that evening are shrouded in mist. Everything seems so long ago. When you're living life it all feels so dreadfully important, but the truth is, only a few things are." The hazy form shimmered. To Meg, it almost appeared as if the ghost of the duke's wife was shivering. "It was terribly cold. I remember that."

"It was January and very bitter," Camden supplied, clearly trying to aid her memory. "You had speech with this artist, this Alberto. What did you talk about?"

"I think we spoke. It seems he wasn't pleased with me. Yes, that much is clear in my mind. There was some matter of money to be paid, I think." The apparition began to take shape again. Meg recognized her as the woman in His Grace's prized painting again. "Oh! Now I remember. He had a nude model in his studio and I suspected she was warming his bed as well. We quarreled, him and me." She loosed a tinkling laugh. "What a strange thing to fight about. Do you think that might have been it?"

"Then what happened?"

"I remember falling. I remember holding Henry close, shielding him with my body." The ghost of Mercedes reached out her hand, but stopped short of touching His Grace. "You look sad, Edward. How much sadder it must have been for you when I was found dead."

"I grieved for you both, though I'm ashamed to admit that sometimes I forget what our son even looked like."

The apparition glowed warmly, a woman's shape in alabaster. Meg could make out her delicate features. She almost seemed to take corporeal form. "How can you say that? You must know what Henry looks like. He didn't die with me. I made sure of it."

"A dead babe was found with your body."

The ghost took on a sickly grayish yellow hue. "No. It is not possible. I would know if he were dead. Here in this realm, we all see where other souls go. If he were dead, I would have rejoiced to see his little spirit soar upward. There is no chance of him going elsewhere." Shafts of light began to shoot from her undulating form. She was clearly agitated. "Henry certainly would not be stuck here with me, betwixt and between, unable to go back, unable to move on."

"Be at peace, spirit," Glenys said quietly from her perch on the spinning stool. "There may be work yet for the living, but your labors have ceased. Rest you, now."

The churning in the apparition slowed and finally stopped. She merely glowed, now bright, now pale, in a slow rhythm that reminded Meg of labored breathing.

"Edward, you must find our son." Mercedes' voice came out as a whisper. "He lives. I swear it."

"I will." His voice was a husky shell of its usual melodious timbre. "I will devote myself to the task, heart and soul."

"Then I am content," The ghost glowed white again and her features were more plain to see. "One more thing remains to me, Edward. It is love. I did not show you the love you deserved in life, but it burns in me now like a flame." As if to prove her point, she flared a fiery red hue before settling back to a melancholy blue tint. "Though love survives death, it is not complete without forgiveness."

"Are you asking me to forgive you?"

"I have nothing to offer in exchange, so I must ask. I can do nothing to earn it. I am too poor to pay for I have nothing but my faulty memories and regret. Your forgiveness must be a gift." Lifelike color flooded the apparition and Mercedes appeared as she did in the portrait—a vibrant, beautiful young woman. "I am a fool. I was weak, despicable, blind—"

"Stop." The duke held up a forbidding hand. "I will allow no one to speak ill of you, little heart. Not even you."

"Do you have it in you to pardon me, Edward?"

"Be at peace, love. You are forgiven," he whispered. "I'm to blame for being such a high-handed excuse for a husband."

"You were never that. Not really. Your rules, silly as some of them were, were motivated by love. I see that now. If there is aught to forgive, I do it gladly with a full heart." She began to drift upward.

"Don't go."

"I am compelled to leave. Something is drawing me toward…" When she continued, her voice was different. It was the sound of a soul in ecstasy. "My chains are loosed. Mercy—both the giving and the receiving of it—has freed me from earth. Oh, Edward, I see it."

"What, my dear one? What do you see?"

"*Lux perpetua.*"

"What is *lux perpetua*?" Meg whispered to Samuel, but before he could answer Mercedes went on.

"Light. Only light. Everywhere. Moving in and around everyone and everything. Light one can drink in and be warmed and filled thereby. Light that binds us together in love." She stopped her upward progress to look back down at him. "Oh, Edward, it's so beautiful. I wish you could see."

"I see it shining through your eyes," the duke said.

"But you won't understand until you see it through yours and that will be many years hence to you. It will be but the blink of an eye to me." She began floating toward the thatched ceiling again. "Farewell, husband, until we meet in that place where we shall know as we are fully known. Remember, I love—"

And then Mercedes winked out, snatched from this world to the next without being able to finish her thought. But Meg sensed the love from that unknown place, reaching out to enfold them all like a warm soft blanket.

I used to think the stars were cloaked in mystery, distant and unknowable. Now I am persuaded they are open books compared to the human heart. For good or ill, a person will surprise you every time.

~ from the journal of Samuel Templeton, Lord Badewyn

Chapter Eighteen

In stunned silence, Camden sank into the empty chair in Glenys' cottage, drained by his encounter with Mercedes' shade. Never in a thousand lifetimes would he have suspected she'd been unfaithful to him. Even after hearing her direct confession, he could scarce believe it.

And with a common painter, no less...

Surprisingly enough, though he was wounded by her affair, he didn't wallow in assigning all the blame to Mercedes. Instead, he was mindful of his own failings and humbled by them. His dead wife's admission had brought him to his knees, figuratively speaking, but only false pride would allow him moral outrage. There had been no innocent party in his marriage. Camden might have been more sinned against than sinning, but he'd failed Mercedes in many ways. He realized that now.

Yet she had forgiven him. And he'd forgiven her.

A fresh place in his soul, shivering and new, welled up with hope. Perhaps now he could move ahead with his life, unchained by the past.

In the years since she'd been gone, he'd altered matters in his mind. Gone was any recollection of their fiery arguments and his thundering ultimatums, wiped clean from his memory so he could pretend all had been sweetness and light between them. In his grief, he'd canonized Mercedes. She'd become his saint, his ideal woman, a paragon no one else could hope to surpass. Being confronted with her essence again had shattered that illusion once and for all.

She'd been no more perfect than he was. In the eyes of the world, he was a powerful peer and wealthy noble. As the Duke of Camden, he could do no wrong. However, in his own freshly opened eyes, he was just another poor soul, no better and no worse than the next man, trying to muddle through life as best he could.

It surprised him that he could view matters so dispassionately, since the idyllic world he'd carefully constructed about his marriage had just been pulled down about his ears. He felt so detached from the past, it was almost as if his life with Mercedes had happened to someone else. But then one immutable fact from his conversation with his wife rushed back into him.

"My son is alive," he whispered.

"It certainly sounded that way to me, Your Grace." Glenys stood and wiped her sweaty brow with the hem of her apron. Though to all appearances, she'd been sitting quietly on the stool next to the spinning wheel the whole time, clearly acting as a medium was harder psychic work than Glenys made it seem. "And a very much alive son at that."

"Then why was a dead child found with Mercedes' body?" Camden asked.

"Babes die in Cheapside all the time," Miss Anthony spoke up softly. "It would be no trouble to find a dead child to leave in a live one's place."

"At the time, how old was your son, Your Grace?" Lord Badewyn asked.

"A couple of weeks. No more."

"All babies look alike at that age," Vesta said.

"Except to their mothers," Glenys corrected. At that moment, her own red-haired son burst back into the cottage bearing a toad in each hand and talking a blue streak about the piglet he planned to collect from Goodwife Argall on the morrow. His excited voice was an ice pick to Camden's brain.

He could well believe the dead didn't warm to the boy. The rowdy child was just as off-putting to the living.

Camden removed his wallet from inside his waistcoat and gave Glenys every coin and banknote he was carrying. Fortunately, his station allowed him to travel on credit. Merchants and innkeepers alike took one look at his magnificent wardrobe and the elegant coach and four in which he traveled and advanced him any sum he required on the strength of his signet ring pressed into a blob of wax.

Somehow, he didn't think Glenys would be impressed with a promise of payment. Besides, if he truly did have a living son, he owed the Witch of Gryffydd far more than he could repay.

The duke's party walked in subdued silence back to the inn and marched in eerie unison up the stairs to Samuel and Meg's chamber.

"We can decide what needs doing now without fear of listening ears," Samuel told His Grace as Meg and Miss LaMotte settled themselves on the foot of the bed. He offered Camden the lone chair in the room and His Grace took it gratefully.

Samuel needn't have worried about their plans being overheard. Everyone seemed consumed by their own thoughts and sat in stillness. There was nothing for even the most determined eavesdropper to hear other than quiet breathing and the occasional rustle of silk from Miss LaMotte.

Finally, Camden spoke. "First, I thank you, my friends, for bearing me company. The séance was a far more emotional ordeal than I expected it to be. No one need know about the content of the session but we four. I trust your discretion in this matter and appreciate it beyond words."

Samuel and Meg exchanged a glance. They were forced to trust in Camden and Miss LaMotte's discretion, too, to help keep Meg safe from Grigori. Everyone had secrets, it seemed, private hurts that would break your heart if only you knew them. Even someone as elevated as His Grace.

"There's something about your wife's story I don't understand," Miss LaMotte said, swinging a dainty foot off the edge of the bed. "Why steal a child from his dead mother? What would someone do with a child like that?"

"Sell it, most like," Meg suggested. "Or perhaps they'd recently lost their own babe and took His Grace's son as a substitute. It's true he'd be an extra mouth to feed for a while, but sooner than you can imagine, the child would be put to work to help support the family. Simple ways for simple folk."

"Then you believe my heir might be living in squalor with child thieves? This is intolerable." The duke started to rise to his feet, but Samuel stopped him with a hand to his shoulder.

"Rest yourself, Camden. You've had a shock," Samuel said. To his surprise, the duke sank back down. "At the time your wife died, did anyone try to contact you to claim they had your son and ask for a ransom?"

"I wish they had. I'd have paid anything. But it's unlikely anyone who found Henry would have been aware that he was my son. Mercedes had borrowed a plain gown from one of the maids so she could travel across town unremarked. It was some time before anyone realized the body they found was that of my duchess because of it." The duke tugged down his waistcoat out of force of habit. There was nothing awry about his ensemble. "Fortunately, a week after she disappeared, I had told the Bow Street Runners to notify me if any female or infant remains had been discovered. Thieves might have stolen my son, and the silver locket at Mercedes's throat, but they didn't think to search my wife's body well enough to remove the little gold cross she always wore under her chemise. It's how she was identified."

Silence descended on the party once again.

"It's a pity she didn't recall more about her death." Samuel wondered if that meant the actual moment of dying wasn't as bad as everyone feared. Perhaps the anxiety of not knowing what waits on the other side was worse than getting there.

"It is a shame, but at least we have some fresh information to go on. Well, then. Tomorrow, we shall return to London,"

Camden said rising with purpose. "I plan to discover the whereabouts of that painter and learn for myself if he is responsible for Her Grace's death."

They'd all heard the ghost's confession, but Camden was quick to give Mercedes her honorific as if nothing had happened. The duke was an even better man than Samuel took him for. A better man than Samuel was. He didn't know if he could be so forgiving over a lover's unfaithfulness. Meg was his. He wasn't willing to share her with anyone.

Which was why he had to keep her hidden from his father.

"Beggin' your pardon, Your Grace, but that plan won't do," Meg said haltingly. She was still clearly in awe of her mentor, but at least she had the courage to speak her mind to him. Samuel admired her pluck.

"Why not?" Camden asked.

"If that fellow Alberto did have a hand in doing away with Her Grace, he's not likely to confess it to you, is he? We need to find out did anyone else see something. And whether or not he was involved in Her Grace's death, maybe Alberto knows what became of your son. If someone of your station were to burst in and start accusing him, he'd never tell you what you want to know."

"But you think you can winkle it out of him?" Vesta asked.

"I could try." She glanced at Samuel. "With help, of course."

"But Grigori will be looking for you in London," Samuel said.

"He might be looking for me at Camden House, but I'll warrant he won't expect us to be faring in Cheapside. We'll blend in and live rough. It will pose no difficulty," Meg said.

"I've done it before."

The duke shook his head. "I can't have you endangering yourself on my account. Not with Samuel's father seeking you for his nefarious reasons."

"Don't fret yourself, your Grace. Trust me. This is something I can do for you. *Finding* is my gift, remember," Meg said. "It'll be ever so much easier than trying to be a lady."

Miss LaMotte chuckled. "I expect that's true."

"Meg, ordinarily *Finding* would be the best course of action, but in this case, I don't think you should use your special ability," Samuel said, choosing his words with care. He didn't want to upset her about it again, but Grigori had been able to see her spectral form clearly in the great hall when Samuel couldn't. "*Finding* puts you in the realm of the spirit where I can't follow and protect you. During that time, you might be visible to Grigori should he be near his scrying basin."

"I concur," the duke said.

"Well, then, someone needs to keep your father from that basin, Lord Badewyn," Vesta said. "Camden, I think you and I should continue on to Faencaern Castle. If his lordship's father is in residence there, we can keep an eye on him and discover his plans."

"Grigori is old beyond reckoning and far too wise for human trickery," Samuel cautioned. "You can't think to match wits with a Fallen One."

"Who said anything about matching wits with him? Any being who gives up heaven for the sake of a woman is susceptible to being charmed by one." Vesta batted her long lashes coquettishly. "Perhaps I can keep this Grigori fellow distracted while you two travel to London and find Camden's son."

"I can't allow that, Vesta," Camden said. "It's too risky for you."

"I'll be careful," Vesta said. "Besides, you have no say in the matter. You are not my husband. And even if you were, I've never been inclined to obedience."

"I'm beginning to think no woman is," the duke grumbled.

"It's settled then," Vesta rose and glided across the small chamber. "Camden and I will push on to the castle on the morrow and Miss Anthony and Lord Badewyn will hie themselves to London by the quickest means possible, while we create a diversion for his lordship's father."

"Still, a fallen angel is not a being to be trifled with," His Grace said. "If Miss LaMotte will not allow me to protect her, at least you should accede to my wishes, Miss Anthony. I am concerned for your safety should Grigori discover your whereabouts."

"You've naught to fear on that count, Your Grace. Grigori won't follow us to Cheapside," Meg said, grinning gamely. "There are some places in London where the devil himself won't go."

Once they were back in their own chamber, Camden started to remove his jacket. Vesta skittered across the room to help him.

"What a sweet gesture, my dear."

Vesta's laugh was a tinkling music he loved to hear. "Don't be fooled. I'm not inclined to domesticity. Never think this is a permanent arrangement. I'll be happy to give your valet's job back to him once we reach civilization again. Poor boy. Considering how rustic our accommodations are, I can only shudder at what his bed in the stable must be like." She gave herself a little shake.

"The lad is fine. Probably having the greatest adventure of his life," Camden said. "The fact that our present situation frees him from his duties to me while affording you a chance to show your domestic side is icing on the cake. I hope you don't mind."

"Not at all. Besides, it just so happens that I'm well acquainted with the best way to undress a gentleman." Ever the coquette, she cast a sly look at him while her talented fingers began working his cravat free. "But you, of all men, should know there's nothing remotely domestic about me."

"We could fix that."

She cocked a brow at him. "How?"

"You could marry me." As marriage proposals went, that one was worthy of a green lad. A duke should do better. The idea had been rolling around in the back of his mind for months, but he hadn't felt free to give it voice until he'd squared things with Mercedes. He still had unanswered questions about the past, but he was ready to turn his back on them in favor of the future. "The offer is genuine," he added when she didn't respond right away.

"Forgive me if I don't believe you. You haven't even wanted to be my lover these last few years." Vesta gave him her back, hands on her hips, a silent invitation to help her out of her gown by undoing the row of seed pearls that followed the line of her spine.

"That's not true. I've been restraining myself because

one shouldn't always have what one desires." Camden finished with the buttons and slid the gown off her shoulders. Then he bent down to her and kissed the tender skin at the juncture of her neck and shoulder. "I've wanted you for years."

"Then you have a singularly odd way of showing it." Her voice husky with longing, Vesta shivered and leaned back into him. He loved the way she gave herself over to each moment, as if this one slice of time might be all they'd ever have together and she was intent on wringing every drop of joy from it.

"I wasn't able to let go of the past before," Camden said.

"And now you can?"

Mercedes had moved on to a different plane. She would always be his first love, but now he saw her with opened eyes. He'd tried to bury his heart with his dead wife, but no more. He had some living to catch up on and Vesta was just the one to help him do it.

"Yes, I can and, starting now, I will move forward with my life," Camden said. "My heart is whole and it is yours, if you'll have it."

Her eyes glowed warmly at him. "I shall hold you to that."

Then she stood on tiptoe and kissed him full on the mouth.

In my studies of the stars, I learned that they are vastly distant from earth. Their light must have left its source eons ago, traveling through the silence of the night sky before reaching us. It is entirely possible that the star I view this evening has died hundreds of years ago. Yet now is the only time in which I may view its light, so as far as I know, it still burns hotly.

It is a lesson to be carried into the rest of life as well. The eternal "now" is all anyone has.

~from the journal of Samuel Templeton, Lord Badewyn

Chapter Nineteen

The next day Samuel and Meg parted company with the duke and his consort. Miss LaMotte and His Grace pushed on toward Faencaern Castle, while Meg and Samuel set their faces toward London.

Samuel had hoped never to see the city again in his lifetime, but if Meg was set on going there, he had no choice but to take her. If he refused to help her find the duke's son, he had no doubt she was stubborn enough to make her own way to London without him.

Still riding double on their poor mount, they headed toward the nearest coaching inn where Samuel sold the nag for even less than it was worth and paid for two fares to the city on the next available coach.

"We must not take a private room when we stop," Meg insisted, even though they were still ostensibly traveling as husband and wife. "We need to conserve whatever moneys you have for when we reach London. There will be a number of palms waiting to be crossed with coin before we wangle any information out of them."

She was right, of course, but Samuel didn't have to like it. He'd hoped to spend every night of their journey with Meg snugged up beside him in bed. Unfortunately, the best he could do while on the road was to sleep sitting up on a bench in each successive inn's common room with her head on his shoulder.

In the quiet watches of the night, when the fire dwindled and the other travelers served up a symphony of snores, Samuel treasured the warmth of Meg tucked under his protective arm. Her soft inhalations, the occasional mumble in her dreams, were a gift. He wasn't sure he had a soul, since he wasn't entirely human, but if he did, he'd have been willing to exchange it for the chance to spend all the rest of his nights on earth with this woman at his side.

When their coach finally dropped them into the middle of the city, they made their way on foot to the seedy part of Cheapside. Even in her current travel-worn and bedraggled state, Meg drew plenty of sidelong glances from the men they passed. There was something about the urgency in her sweet face that called for a second look. However, the lookee-loos averted their eyes when Samuel glowered at each one. He was a powerfully built, tall man, a fact that he'd never considered relevant before. As they pushed through the market, he used his size to advantage to keep them from being accosted by footpads and fishmongers alike. He found himself wishing again that he really was Meg's husband, that she was rightfully his to protect.

If they'd been at Camden House, it would have been tea time. His stomach rumbled in protest. He and Meg hadn't eaten since early morning when they'd breakfasted on day old rolls and strong coffee. Amid the unwashed masses, a heavenly fragrance reached out and drew him into a bakery shop.

The old woman behind the counter, who went by the wholly appropriate name of Mrs. Waddle, welcomed them to her shop. She was liberally covered with flour, which in Samuel's mind boded well for her pastries. And if she was responsible for the beckoning yeasty smell, he was willing to reckon her a goddess.

"Two meat pasties and tea," he ordered and the woman moved with surprising swiftness to serve them. Meg tucked into her pasty with a look of pure bliss on her face.

"I was going to chide you for the expense, but this is worth every farthing," she said, sweeping her top lip with her pointed tongue.

Samuel ached to capture that little tongue and suckle it, but this was not the place. Or was it? "I say, Mrs. Waddle, do you know of any rooms for let nearby?"

The baker looked them over, clearly assessing their status based on the quality of their sturdy, albeit travel-rumpled clothing. She gave them a curt nod. "Happens my tenant in the rooms above the shop moved out last week. 'Tis just a bedroom and a sitting room. No kitchen, you understand." She gave Meg a gimlet-eyed once over. "I might just see my way clear to letting your missus use the kitchen down here, after the shop closes, o' course. But mind, she'd have to leave the place spotless!"

Mrs. Waddle named a sum Samuel thought was a reasonable rent per week and he jumped on it. Pulling a couple of coins from the pouch tucked into his shirt, he paid for the first two weeks. His banknotes were hidden in his boots and another stash of coin was squirreled away in the pocket of his jacket. Meg was even carrying some of it. She'd insisted on dividing up their funds before they'd left Gryffydd.

"That way, nobody sees how much you actually have," she had explained. "And if someone picks your pocket, they'll only get away with part of your money, not all of it."

Her advice had the ring of wisdom, especially since Samuel knew she'd been on the other side of lifting a wallet more than once.

"Follow me then," Mrs. Waddle said once they finished their tea. The baker disappeared into her kitchen and led them up the back stairs.

"You should have dickered a bit," Meg whispered.

"The price seemed fair."

"We won't know that until we see the place. It may be a regular boar's nest."

Samuel doubted that after seeing the tidiness of Mrs. Waddle's kitchen. The upstairs sitting room was furnished with a pair of wingback chairs that were only slightly threadbare. The small table between them wasn't a bit worm-eaten. The place smelled strongly of camphor and carbolic soap.

At least it's clean.

The bed was dressed in fresh-looking linens and hung about with thick curtains that would help keep out the cold once autumn gave way to winter. All in all, the place was a huge step up from the common rooms with which they'd had to make do of late. An honest-to-God bedchamber would be the greatest of sinful pleasures. To lie beside Meg and feel her near him the whole night through was almost more than he dared hope.

Samuel refrained from saying "I told you so" about the rooms. He might not have much experience with women, but he knew enough not to poke the bear. Meg had been as surly as one since they entered the city. He had no idea why.

"Do you know a likely lad who can be depended upon to deliver a message to someone in a certain house in Mayfair?" he asked his new landlady as he handed her the note he'd written at the last coaching inn. He went on to explain that the missive must be put into the hand of Mr. Bernard, the steward at Camden House, and the boy must wait for a reply.

"My grandson, Timmy, can do the deed. He knows Mayfair well enough since he did a stint with the night soil wagon in that part of Town last summer." Mrs. Trott tucked the note into her apron pocket. "Not much between the ears, poor boy, but my Tim's dependable as an ox."

Samuel handed her a coin for the lad and promised Mr. Bernard would reward him similarly at the other end. "Tell him there's another half-shilling in it for him if he returns with an answer before nightfall."

The baker snatched up the coin and hurried out of the room to find her grandson, promising speedy service.

"You're tossing money around far too freely," Meg cautioned once the door closed behind their new landlady. "What we have has to last till we've found His Grace's son."

"I don't intend for it to take that long." Once they located Camden's heir, he could turn his attention to ways to best protect Meg. He wondered if she'd be willing to go with him to the Americas, or even New South Wales. Grigori seemed to possess the ability to travel on the strength of thought alone. The fallen angel often disappeared in one part of the castle and reappeared almost instantly in another, but Samuel didn't think his father's knack for rapid transport would extend to a trip half way around the globe. If they covered their tracks well enough, Grigori might never find them.

"What was that note about?" Meg asked, dragging him away from thoughts of his future plans.

"His Grace couldn't remember the full name of the artist who painted his wife's portrait. I'm sure Mr. Bernard will have record of payment and will be able to tell us the man's name. It seems reasonable to start the search for the boy by finding the last person the duke's wife spoke with in life."

"But I have the child's name. His full one. Henry George D'Lessip St. James, Lord Harrington—that's one of his Grace's lesser titles you know. I should simply go *Finding* and be done with it. Locating someone whose name is such a mouthful should be easy as pie. I don't know why you and the duke are so against me using my gift."

So that's why she was touchy.

"It's not that I don't appreciate your gift. But I more fully appreciate how dangerous it is for you and I fear you'd reveal even more than you found. Remember Grigori is still looking for you, and he is uniquely able to sense you in your spirit state," Samuel said. "Besides, the boy isn't known by any of those names now. Don't you need the name he goes by, not necessarily his birth name?"

She sighed. "You're right. Are you at least planning on having me *Find* this Alberto fellow?"

"I can do a directed scrying for him if needs be. I'm hoping Mr. Bernard will know where the artist lives and neither of us will need to use our special abilities."

"But what if *I* need to use them?" Meg plopped down into one of the wing chairs.

"What do you mean?"

"Honestly, sometimes I feel like I'm about to burst out of my own skin if I don't go *Finding* now and then. Don't you ever feel compelled to get out your scrying bowl?"

Samuel shook his head. He was never driven to use his gift. To be fair, whenever the Power that directed his psychic talents decided he needed to be shown something, a vision would find its way into his mind one way or another. Any shiny or still liquid surface—a mirror, silver platter, even a bowl of clear consommé—might become his window to a distant event. "My gift comes upon me when it wills, not necessarily when I want it to. I can force a scrying, but it's never the best choice for accuracy."

"It's the only choice for me. I have to initiate a *Finding* these days." Her face was drawn with tension and tiny beads of perspiration bloomed on her brow. "I never accidently lay my body aside any more, but from time to time, I *need* to."

"You mean it used to happen without your conscious will?"

She nodded.

Samuel thought that if he had a soul it would be terrifying to suddenly discover it had slipped away from his body, but to Meg it was simply the way she was made. "Tell me about the first time you went *Finding*."

"I thought it was a dream, actually. I couldn't have been more than four or five, but I'd lost a kitten earlier that day. I laid down that night thinking about that cat and mumbling the name I'd given it under my breath. My spirit suddenly rose up. I *Found* the cat stuck in a nearby tree and once my essence returned to my body, I wandered away from the camp my uncle had pitched for Cousin Oswald and me. I could see the very tree I thought I'd dreamed across the meadow, so I homed in on it and sure enough, the kitten was mewing on one of the topmost branches. I climbed up and brought it down and waggled it back to camp." She went silent for a moment and her face fell. "My uncle drowned it in a stream the next day. He said that should teach me not to wander off."

Anger roiled in Samuel's belly. If he ever laid eyes on Meg's uncle, he'd cheerfully strangle the man.

"After that, I used the trick of slipping away from my body to escape Uncle Rowney, if for only a little while."

"Do you need to escape me?"

"No, never think it." She put a hand to his chest and then waved the thought away. "It's just…it's hard to explain unless you've experienced it. There's such freedom, such lightness of soul when I *Find*. I need that sensation from time to time to feel normal."

"You're right," he said. "I don't understand. Not having a soul, I'm not burdened with the need to take it out for exercise."

"You do, too, have a soul. Who told you otherwise?"

It was one of the first lessons his father had drummed into his head. Samuel was Nephilim and that meant he was different. He was bigger, stronger, and longer-lived than most human males. A descendant of a *Watcher*, he was gifted with Sight beyond the common. And with those advantages came a few minor disadvantages, like not being able to sire children or possessing an immortal soul.

Meg's mouth tightened into a thin line. "You know they don't call Satan the father of lies for nothing. It stands to reason Grigori tells some whoppers, too." She palmed his cheek. "I know you have a soul. I see it, Samuel, shining behind those gray eyes of yours. And it's a fine soul, never doubt it."

She said it with such conviction he was tempted to believe her.

"And you need to *Find* now?"

"Oh, yes. I'm fair to bursting with it. Please Samuel, don't try to stop me.

He knelt before her. "Can you at least make it short? And stay close. Inside this house?"

She nodded, a relieved smile lighting her features. "Hold me tight and I'll be right back."

As soon as he gathered her close, her eyes rolled back in her head, her body stiffened and then went slack as an empty sack. Between one breath and the next, she was gone.

The black reaches of space are cold, my father says. I wish I was. It would be easier to say no to Meg and mean it.

~ from the journal of Samuel Templeton, Lord Badewyn

Chapter Twenty

"And you haven't seen Miss Anthony for how long?" the Duke of Camden said with a frown.

"Not for the better part of a fortnight," Grigori admitted. As long as she stayed close to his son, whatever power shielded Samuel from his father's distant gaze seemed to cover Meg Anthony as well. It was deucedly inconvenient that the girl's guardian had turned up at Faencaern Castle looking for her just now. "I am frankly dismayed that Lord Badewyn chose this path and regret the scandal this debacle is sure to cause."

The lie came as naturally to his lips as breathing. He was upset that Samuel had done something as unexpected as running off with the girl, but had no regret about the ensuing scandal whatsoever. Even the threat of scandal was powerful leverage in the duke's world. Grigori would use whatever came to hand to advance his plans.

Like a wolf who'd selected the weakling of the flock to

be culled, Grigori had fixated on Meg Anthony. Not having any extended family, she was perfect for his purposes. Who would miss her after she died giving birth to his child? He hadn't counted on the duke actually being interested in the ward he'd shuffled off to Wales. But, no matter. The Grand Cycle was upon him. Once his current son reached a certain age, Grigori was almost pathologically driven to sire another. He'd been so sure Samuel would simply marry the girl and things would go as he planned.

Perhaps they still could.

"I shall insist Lord Badewyn do the right thing by Miss Anthony as soon as they are found," he assured the duke. With the full weight of the girl's powerful guardian behind the match, a hurried marriage would surely be in the offing.

And then Grigori could take Samuel's place in the girl's bed at will.

"Perhaps his lordship has already done the right thing," Miss LaMotte said as she poured out tea for both the men. The woman was grace in motion, her languid movements as she stirred the tea strangely sensual. If he weren't so obsessed with possessing Miss Anthony, Grigori thought the duke's consort might make for a pleasant diversion.

"Faencaern Castle is not so far from Scotland. A wedding is as close as the nearest blacksmith over the border," Miss LaMotte went on. "There's every chance that Miss Anthony has already been made Lady Badewyn and we are all fretting over nothing."

Grigori frowned into his tea. He'd tracked a trail to Scotland already. It had proven false. If Samuel had taken her north, he'd been very clever about his route. He was about to tell his unwelcome guests as much when a vision began to form in the creamy center of his teacup. Grigori peered at the image and the world around him faded away.

All he could see was Meg, floating free of her body as she'd done before in the great hall. Her long hair undulated in a non-existent breeze. Samuel was nowhere to be seen. Grigori reasoned that his son couldn't follow her when she was in her spirit form and hence offered her no protection. He searched the image for some clue to her location. Based on the rafters behind her, she was in an attic, but the attic in question could be in Cornwall or Cork for all he knew. Then she floated upward, passed through the broken tiles of the roof, and was silhouetted before a spiky forest of chimneys.

A city.

She turned and in the distance behind her, the dome of St. Paul rose above the lesser buildings surrounding it.

London.

"Not such a clever girl after all," he muttered. Still, she'd breed. He felt sure of it. And with her unusual ability to shed her body and flit about, what a unique offspring she'd produce for him. The vision faded into nothing more than swirling milk in his tea.

"I beg your pardon," the duke said.

"Oh, it's nothing. I don't wish to speak ill of Miss Anthony, but it is a pity she was so easily persuaded to abscond with my nephew. I don't blame you for her lack of judgment, of course, Your Grace. I understand she hasn't been under your protection long." Grigori took a sip of the tea, pleased with the thought that he'd soon see Meg in the flesh instead of his cup. "Please avail yourself of the comforts of Faencaern for as long as you like. I shall leave orders that your every whim is to be indulged."

"Leave?" Camden said. "You can't mean to travel at this time, Mr. Templeton?"

"I must. I can do nothing here and meanwhile there is an urgent meeting I must attend in Wiltshire. An amateur astronomy group thinks they've located an as yet unnamed star. I will be leaving straight away. If you'll excuse me." He stood and gave his unexpected guests a polite bow.

"How unfortunate." Miss LaMotte rose, the hem of her gown swirling around her neat ankles. "No doubt that star has been shining for ages. It can wait, surely. You can't mean to gallivant about the countryside while your nephew and His Grace's ward are missing." She gave him a fetching smile. "Besides, your expertise in matters regarding the heavens is legendary. I had hoped you'd show me the finer points of the night sky some evening."

The woman was a tempting armful, no doubt about it. And the way the duke glared at her as she flirted with Grigori made her even more alluring. It would be highly gratifying to take another man's woman right under his nose. Still, the pull toward London and his next conquest was stronger. If Samuel hadn't married Meg by the time he found them, he'd haul them onto the nearest sailing vessel and insist the captain tie the knot so there'd be no need to wait for banns or a special license.

Grigori took Miss LaMotte's outstretched fingertips and brought them to his lips. "Unfortunately, I must be gone. I regret disappointing us both, Miss LaMotte. Your expertise in your chosen field is also…legendary." He'd never been with a courtesan. His fleshly urges were always tied to siring an heir, but Vesta LaMotte might tempt him to vary his sexual habits. "Another time, perhaps."

Grigori strode from the parlor and once he'd cleared the doorway, he leaned against the wall so he could focus all his energies on one thought. One point in space.

The crypt of St. Paul's cathedral.

Meg hovered for a moment above the rooftop. The last rays of sunlight glinted on the dome of St. Paul, gilding the edifice such brightness she had to turn away from it. But then, hazy and indistinct, the image of a man's face began to coalesce and swim before her.

Grigori.

She flew back to the room where Samuel was cradling her body. Sliding into it with such force she nearly knocked herself out of his grasp, she expected to land on the floor but he held on.

"Thank God you're back." Samuel hugged her so tightly she could scarcely draw breath. "And thank you for being so quick about it. I die a little every second your spirit is away, you know."

"I know and I'm sorry for it." She was sorry she'd seen Grigori, too, but she decided not to tell Samuel about that. Though she'd seen him, there was no guarantee that the Fallen One had seen her. If she told Samuel about the incident, he'd only feel vindicated about not wanting her to go *Finding*. And even if Grigori had seen her as well, surely that brief glimpse wasn't enough for him to pinpoint their location.

In any case, Samuel insisted they go out for a real meal while they waited for Mrs. Waddle's grandson to return with

Mr. Bernard's reply. On the next street over, they'd passed a tavern with a promising beefy aroma mingled with its yeasty ale, so if Grigori could somehow instantly hone in on them at the bakery, he'd find them gone.

By the time they returned, Mrs. Waddle's Timothy was waiting for them with a note from Mr. Bernard. All thought of Grigori fled from her mind.

Alberto Pontarelli was evidently still in residence in the same neighborhood where he'd lived when he painted the duchess's portrait. Mr. Bernard had received a request from the artist only six months ago, offering to do a painting of the duke as a companion piece to the one of Her Grace. But His Grace had been too busy to sit for what he considered a frivolity when Bernard informed him of the request. It was no surprise to the steward that the duke didn't know the artist's identity.

His Grace leaves such paltry details to me, the steward wrote.

Samuel wanted to head out to find Pontarelli that very moment, but Meg urged him to wait till morning.

"After a certain time of night, no one venturing out in this part of town is up to any good," Meg said.

Samuel arched a brow at her. "If we stay in, I won't be up to any good either."

"Oh, I'm counting on that." She stood on tiptoe and gave him a lingering kiss. It crowded out all thoughts of Grigori and his evil plans for her. "I'm counting on it with all my heart."

It had been several centuries since Grigori had traveled to London in a manner other than the conventional, uncomfortable, human way. He was still capable of the instantaneous transport with which angels were gifted, but it wasn't without risk since he'd fallen, which was why he normally only used the ability over short distances. If there had been changes to the place where he intended to return to corporeal form, he might find himself trapped inside a newly erected wall or under a pile of fire-charred debris. The crypt of St. Paul's in London was such a sacrosanct shrine, he could be fairly certain there had been no renovations since he was last there. Plus, since it was evening, the place where the honored dead rested wasn't likely to be occupied by anyone who might witness his unexpected appearance.

Grigori shimmered into existence next to Lord Nelson's oversized sarcophagus and stretched his arms wide. It was always disorienting to dissolve in one place and reassemble himself in another. He drew a deep breath. The place smelled of damp and must and, by reason of his hyper-acute senses, the slow deterioration of flesh. Overlaying that stale fug was a fresh application of marble polish.

A terrified sexton was near the foot of the stairway leading up to the sanctuary. With a bottle of polish in one hand and a long-handled mop in the other, he stood frozen as a statue, staring at Grigori.

"Boo!" the Fallen One said with a wicked grin.

The man's eyes rolled back in his head and he collapsed in a heap. The bottle shattered on the stone floor, the yellowish liquid, along with its distinct waxy smell, spreading alongside his body. The fellow's chest still rose and fell, though his sightless eyes didn't blink.

Only fainted.

Grigori wondered what sort of tale the man would come up with to explain what he'd just seen. He stepped over the unconscious fellow and climbed the winding stone stairs up into the empty sanctuary.

He was always mildly surprised that he was still allowed on holy ground. No warning thunder claps answered the slaps of his boots on the azure floor. No flaming sword blocking his path. Not even an indignant flaring of the votive candles. There was only the sense of a Presence moving silently in the air currents above him, swirling in the cavernous space of the dome. The manifestation brushed by him and all the hairs on his body stood on end. It was a breath of the Spirit from which he was permanently cut off.

A nearly forgotten ache throbbed once or twice in his chest, the remnants of longing for something holy. He shoved the unexpected twinge aside. There was no going back for the likes of him.

Grigori had to go forward. And that meant completing the Grand Cycle once again. It was the only way he could make sense of his existence. Lucifer may have wanted to rule in heaven, but for Grigori, seeing his image stamped on yet another son without having to grieve over a lost wife was his way of expressing a little of the creative power that belonged only to God. Tweaking the Creator's nose in this fashion gave him a reason to keep breathing. A reason not to tumble into the abyss in despair. So he would continue the Cycle.

By whatever means necessary.

It was mid-morning the next day when Samuel and Meg ventured out in search of Alberto Pontarelli. As Meg had warned, the neighborhood was filled with pickpockets and cut-purses even in daylight. Samuel shouldered past men whose dead-eyed stares warned of worse threats than losing his coins. He was careful to keep Meg on his protected side, but she didn't hesitate when the directions to the painter's studio called for them to duck down one of the narrow, dank alleyways. He wondered afresh about her childhood and how she'd managed to live in such places.

No wonder she had needed to slip away from her body on occasion.

At the end of the alleyway, the artist's house listed toward its nearest neighbor so that the eaves touched, though there was a good six inches of separation at their foundations. Samuel turned the knob on an unlocked door that cried for a coat of paint. It opened onto a long staircase leading past the ground, first and second floors, going directly to the garret. At the top of the dark stairs, they heard a man swearing a blue streak on the other side of the door. The long string of profanity was punctuated by the crash of crockery.

Samuel pounded on the door. "Alberto Pontarelli! Open up."

After a few moments, during which they could hear shuffling feet and low grumbles, the door creaked open.

Pontarelli leaned against the portal. Dark-haired and sharp-featured, he'd have been accounted handsome after the manner of Mediterranean men, except for his general slovenliness and the puffiness under his bloodshot eyes. He ran an assessing gaze over the pair of them.

"Do not be standing in the doorway. Come in and state

your business, but be quick about it," he said, waving an arm toward the partially completed canvas of a still life. "I do not want to lose the light."

"Yes, we can see that," Meg said as she moved forward to inspect the painting. Light spilled in through a row of windows cut into the roof. Judging from the half-filled pots of water scattered about, the windows leaked abominably, but Pontarelli must have accounted it a fair trade for the abundant morning sun. "What is a portrait artist doing painting a bowl of fruit?"

There was an empty table set up before his canvas, but the crash of crockery they'd heard was evidently what he'd been attempting to capture in his painting. The remains of a still life composition lay bruised and battered on the floor, with the exception of the grapes which had burst on impact and trickled in a dark stain down the far wall.

"What am I doing? That is a question I ask myself every day," he said. "There is no emotional depth in a bunch of grapes. No soul in a kumquat."

"Then why are you painting it?" she asked.

Pontarelli shrugged. "A commission is a commission."

"We're here about one of your former commissions," Samuel said. "For the Duchess of Camden."

A wall rose up behind Pontarelli's eyes. "Her Grace I have not seen in many years."

"I expect not since she's been dead all this time, but then you knew that," Samuel said, "because you were the last person to see her alive."

"Who has told you such slander?" Without waiting for an answer, Pontarelli lunged toward the open door, but Samuel was too quick for him. He caught up the artist by his paint-splotched collar and slammed him against the wall.

"What's your hurry?" Samuel said. "If you've done nothing wrong, you have nothing to fear."

"I, I know of the English justice," he stammered. "I am not one of you. To me, the courts would not be friendly."

"*I* won't be friendly, if you don't answer my questions." Samuel moved closer to the cowering artist. "Did you kill Her Grace?"

"Me?" Pontarelli's eyes grew round. "No! Never. I loved the lady."

"Then why was her body found not far from here?"

"I...I do not know."

The lie was as smelly as a polecat. "Yes, you do," Meg said. "We know she came to see you the night she died. We know you sent her a note that upset her so much she bundled up her newborn and made her way to this hole you live in. We know you were painting a nude model when she arrived."

"*Mio Dio!*" He crossed himself. "How can you be knowing such things?"

"We spoke to Her Grace via a medium recently and she told us what she remembered," Samuel said. "She sends her regards from the other side."

Pontarelli's complexion paled to the color of day old suet. "I never meant...no, it is not possible."

"Samuel, you're scaring him," Meg warned.

"Good. He ought to be afraid," Samuel said. "He murdered a duchess, didn't he?"

Pontarelli's mouth sagged. When the artist didn't contradict Samuel's accusation, he drew back his arm to strike a blow. The man's knees buckled and he slid down the wall, whimpering for mercy before Samuel laid a hand on him.

Samuel swore softly. Cowards always turned his stomach. Pontarelli wasn't worth the damage his jaw would do to Samuel's knuckles.

"Not a hair on her blessed head did I harm. I swear on my mother, on the Holy Cross, on whatever you wish me to swear," he whined. "Please do not make to beat me."

Disgusted by the sight of such groveling, Samuel took a step back. "Then tell us what happened or I'll haul you before the nearest magistrate."

"*Bene.* All right, *si*. Part of what you say is true. To my dearest Mercedes I did send a note."

"And what was in this note?"

"I was…hurt. After I finish her portrait, she toss me aside like…like day old bread. I nearly lose my mind. Food, it have no flavor. I drank to forget, but her sweet face, it was ever before me." He shrugged eloquently. "I lose more than my heart. My skill it desert me."

"And you didn't attribute that to the drink?"

A frown drew Pontarelli's brows together. "No, it was the duchess. When she take my heart, she take my gift as well."

"And you told her this in the note?"

"Not exactly. I…because I could not work, I owed people. The sort of people who do not let creditors who cannot pay continue to enjoy the good health, you see. I needed money and… I am shamed to admit… I threatened to expose our love if Mercedes did not pay. I mean, unless she make to give me a loan."

"And she refused to be blackmailed? How surprising." Samuel itched to give him a swift kick, but reasoned that it would only make him stop talking.

"No, I never got the chance to explain my troubles," Pontarelli said. "What you say it is true. I was painting when Mercedes arrived."

"At night?" Meg said. "What about the light?"

"It was a nude study," he said defensively. "Some work is better done in the soft light of a candle."

"I'll just bet," Samuel said dryly. "Then what happened?"

"Rose, she was unhappy to see Her Grace."

"I take it this Rose was your model," Samuel said.

"*Si, si.* Rose Craythorne. She did not make to charge me for sitting either. Such a good heart she have. She was trying to help me regain my skill. She was my muse, my consolation, my—"

"Your lover," Samuel finished for him.

"*Si.* But a very passionate person Rose was. She make to think that Her Grace is still my lover and that she is bringing me the child of our love. Rose, she was furious." Pontarelli sighed at the memory. "Oh, you cannot imagine how grand, how magnificent the woman was when she was angry."

"Are you trying to tell us your lover killed Her Grace?" Meg asked.

"No, no. How you twist my words. It was accident. *Si*, my Rose, she was angry, but she did not intend harm to Mercedes. She gave her the teensiest of shoves, only. You have seen the stairs. It would be easy to fall even without… help." Pontarelli burst into tears. "Oh, my Mercedes! How cruel an end for one so lovely. She did not deserve so."

"No, she didn't," Samuel said angrily. "And what were you doing while Her Grace was being attacked by Rose?"

"I am not a violent man, my lord. I could not raise a

hand to anyone…least of all an angry woman." He shook his head and gave a shuddering sigh. "When it was over, Rose, she take care of everything. She go find her brothers and they come take Mercedes away before anyone knows what happened."

"And what about the child Her Grace brought with her?" Samuel asked. "We know the infant survived the fall."

"The oldest brother's wife, she lose a baby boy only the day before and would not let them bury it. Like a madwoman, they say she was. Rose's brother, he take the living child home to fill her empty arms." Pontarelli gave them an imbecilic smile. "So you see, not all is bad."

"Where can we find Rose?" Samuel said.

The artist's smile dissolved into an anguished grimace. "Alas, she came to grief over Blue Ruin."

"Too much gin?" Meg asked.

"*Si*, gin. Cheaper than tea, it is, and my Rose she could not stay away from it."

"What about the brother who took the child? What was his name?"

"That I do not know. It was all such a nightmare. Out of my mind I have tried to put it."

"Where did the brother live?" Samuel caught him by the collar again. "You'd better get something back in your mind or I'll knock you into next week."

"No, no, do not make to hurt me. I beg you. I can remember nothing of Rose's brother." He covered his face with his hands. "On the morrow I go to paint Lady Waldgren. A bruise would make for idle talk and that lady, she does not need encouragement to carry tales. I fear she would have this story out of me in a trice."

"He's right." Meg laid a restraining hand on Samuel's arm. "His Grace would not thank us if our search became grist for the gossip mill."

"*Grazie, la mia signora.*" Pontarelli pulled a handkerchief from his sleeve and mopped his damp forehead. "I am in your debt."

"Then perhaps you can do me a favor and search your memory for one more thing," Meg said encouragingly. "What was the name of Rose's nephew, the baby who died?"

He shook his head.

"Close your eyes," Meg suggested and after a furtive glance at Samuel, Pontarelli complied. "Someone must have said something about little…"

"Wilfred!" Pontarelli's eyes popped open. "Little Willie, Rose called him. He was named for her father. She made much of that."

"Thank you. Let's go." She took Samuel's arm and led him to the door.

Once the door closed behind them Samuel said, "I could have gotten more from him."

"We don't need more. We've discovered the name His Grace's son is known by—Willie Craythorpe."

Samuel set his mouth in a hard line. The name was all she required. She intended to go *Finding* again. And there wasn't a thing he could do about it.

They say a man isn't truly a man until he stands at the grave of his father. Since mine will not have the grace to die, I cannot look forward to that moment of emancipation. But if Grigori harms a hair on Meg's head, I'll make him wish he could die. By all that's holy, I so swear.

~ from the journal of Samuel Templeton, Lord Badewyn

Chapter Twenty-one

Hovering overhead, Meg peered down at the boy in the chicken coop. It wasn't far from the bakery where she and Samuel had lodged, but it was on a much dingier street with slatternly outbuildings lining the alley behind the row of terrace houses. There were no birds at roost in the coop, but she remembered well the stench of a hen house and was thankful she couldn't sense smells when she was *Finding*. She recognized Mercedes' dark coloring in the lad, but his square jaw and the defiant tilt of his chin was all the duke.

"I'm not afraid." The lad's voice quavered only slightly.

"You better be!" The door slammed shut, releasing a choking cloud of dust. The boy blinked in the dimness.

"No, wait. Don't lock me in here!"

"Listen to me, Wilfred Craythorpe," the man's voice hissed through the crack in the door. A heavy brace slide into its iron brackets with the finality of coffin nails. "You tell me where you hid that thing, or you'll rot in there. It's all the same to me. One less mouth to feed."

"But, it's mine," Will said. "Mother gave it to me before she died."

"She never shoulda give it to you and she weren't your mother. And in any case, she's gone now. We need money."

"You mean you need more to drink." Even in the dimness, Meg saw that one of the boy's eyes was swollen almost shut and blood dripped from his nose. He swiped it on his dirty shirt sleeve. On the other side of the door, the man made a sound like a kettle, near to boiling.

"Give it to me, Will!"

"Not in a hundred years."

Silence. At first, Meg thought the man had left, but then his voice sliced through the crack, oily and mean.

"Fine," he said. "If that's the way you want it, you can just spend the night in there thinking about it. But I got to warn you, there's rats a plenty. 'Spect they'll eat a fellow's nose off before morning. Sleep tight."

Will covered his mouth to swallow the sob the man was waiting to hear. When Meg heard footsteps retreating toward the shabby house, the boy pounded the door once with his closed fist. A tear scalded down his grubby cheek, but he wiped it away angrily.

"That's right. Don't cry," Meg said, even though the boy couldn't hear her. "It's just what he wants, Will."

No, not Will. His name is Henry, she reminded herself. Her chest ached for the duke's son in such a horrible circumstance. Nothing would give her greater pleasure than to rescue this poor boy. She felt the tug back to her body, waiting in the rooms above Mrs. Waddle's bakery. Samuel would be beside himself the whole time her spirit was wandering, but she had to be absolutely certain this was His Grace's son.

Will sniffed and knuckled his eyes, wincing slightly. Then he picked up the stick leaning against one wall. He poked at each of the four corners, looking for evidence of rats. Satisfied he was alone in the chicken coop, he squared his shoulders, put his back to the door, and marched off five paces. Pocket knife in hand, he dropped to his knees and began digging in the dirt floor. When he didn't find anything right away, his digging became more frantic. Finally, about six inches down, his blade ripped into oilcloth.

He wiped the blade clean on his trousers and slid it back into his pocket. Gently, he brushed away the remaining dirt and lifted the cloth from its hiding place. Will unwound the cloth carefully.

In the slivers of moonlight that filtered through the chinks in the coop, an ornate silver locket sparkled in his hand. He fumbled with the latch and opened it to study the pair of miniatures inside.

The woman's portrait had a sweetness around her slightly upturned mouth, as if she were hugging a delicious secret to herself. Meg recognized the duchess. The other miniature had probably been of His Grace, but it had been badly scratched so that the face was destroyed. The complicated knot of the cravat beneath the subject's chin was one she'd seen on the duke. It could be no one else.

No doubt the boy's abductors knew the mother was dead so there was no harm in leaving her image undamaged. The father, however, was another story.

"Before she died, she told me you're my real mother. She kept this locket for me so I could prove it someday," he said, reciting the tale to himself more than speaking to the woman in the locket. Meg sensed he needed to cement it in his mind. It wasn't everyday a boy learned he wasn't who he thought he was. "But if that's so, why did you…"

He'd been so strong not to cry when the man locked him in there. Now his shoulders shook and he sobbed as if his heart would break.

Meg guessed what he was thinking. What was wrong with him? What had he done to make his real mother give him up? She'd wondered the same thing about herself. Of course, Uncle Rowney always claimed her parents had died, but she felt the sting of abandonment all the same.

It was past time when she should have flown back to her body, but she couldn't bear to leave the boy in this state. Then Meg heard a faint scratching sound coming from the other side of the hen house wall. It was accompanied by a muffled whine.

"Dermot?" Will said. "Is that you, lad?"

The scratching became more frantic and the dog whined again. Will hastily re-wrapped the locket and stowed it in his pocket. He fished his jack-knife out again and stabbed at the hard dirt by the wall.

Meg turned away and "thought" herself back to the bakery. She had to lead Samuel back to the Craythorpe hen house on the double quick. With the boy digging on one side of the wall and the hound on the other, they'd have a hole big enough for Will squeeze through in short order. Once that happened, the boy would run away. He'd disappear into the city and change his name, just as she had when she escaped her Uncle Rowney. Without the right name, Meg would be hard pressed to *Find* the boy again.

Back in their rooms over Mrs. Waddle's shop, Meg continued to gulp huge gasps of air, but she was slow to recover this time. Samuel claimed her skin still had a grayish undertone.

"You stayed away too long," he said with a frown. "Your lips are bloodless. Your nails are blue, too."

"Stop scolding. Am I a child to be paddled for my misdeeds?"

"Don't tempt me."

"But I had to be sure."

"And you are, you say." Samuel folded his arms over his chest, still upset with her for the chance she'd taken. "Very well. Where is the boy?"

Meg gave him directions to a house on a street not far from the bakery.

"Did you see Grigori while you were *Finding*?" he asked.

"No," she said quickly, averting her gaze.

"What aren't you telling me?"

"Nothing." At least she hoped it was nothing. As she fled back to her body, she thought she caught a glimpse of Samuel's father, indistinct and fleeting, from the corner of one eye. "I didn't see anything. I was focused on the lad." She rose shakily to her feet. "We need to go quickly."

Half-way to the door, her vision began to tunnel. Samuel caught her before she hit the floor. Then he scooped her up and carried her to the bed.

"That settles it. You're not going anywhere until I see some roses in those cheeks."

"But if we don't get there before the boy escapes, we'll

never find him again."

"Never say never."

"Please, Samuel." She tried to sit up, but the room began spinning and she plopped back on the pillows. Perhaps he was right. She'd pushed the limits of her body's endurance during her last *Finding* and now she was paying the price. "You'll have to go without me."

"Meg, I don't dare leave you. What if Grigori—"

She pressed two fingers to his lips. "Do this for me."

"Don't ask that." He caught up her hand and held it against his chest. His heart was pounding on her account, but she couldn't relent.

"The boy will be lost if you don't." She kissed him. "The sooner you go, the sooner you can return. I promise to stay right here and be as meek as a lamb. Please, Samuel."

"You aren't happy unless you're putting yourself at risk, are you?" He strode to the door, anger roiling off him. "I'll leave you this time, but if you ask me to again, it'll be for good."

Samuel arrived in time to see a boy wiggling out from under the chicken coop's wall. The lad stared up at him, his jaw sagging.

"Who are you?" he managed to whisper.

"That's not important," Samuel said.

"My mam always told me there was angels about," the boy mumbled. "Are you my guardian angel?"

Samuel supposed he might seem like a supernatural being to the youngster since he appeared so unexpectedly in the small rear garden. He was broader, taller, and, according to Meg, fairer of face than most men. If his dark hair was silvered with starlight, it might seem like a halo.

"I'm not your guardian angel. Are you Wilfred Craythorpe?"

The boy nodded. "Mighta known you're not my angel. No bloke from Cheapside ever had an angel of his own."

"You're not from Cheapside. And that's not really your name," Samuel said. "You are Henry St. James, the lost son and heir of the Duke of Camden."

Samuel startled the lad by giving him a respectful bow. But he couldn't linger long. Not when Meg needed him.

The boy barely had time to snatch up his long-legged puppy before Samuel grabbed him by the hand, hurried him down the alley and over to the next block. A cabby waited there, his cap pulled down over his eyes, clearly asleep on his perch.

Samuel woke him up with a demand that he take the boy to the Duke of Camden's town house in Mayfair. The horse whickered and stamped, clearly ready to bed down in its stall.

"I can't leave me fares, guv," the cabby said grumpily. "I brung three gentlemen from Picadilly for some… entertainment hereabouts. I'm hired for the night and have to wait on their return."

"Deliver this lad safely to the home of the Duke of Camden. Wait and see that he's received there and I promise His Grace will make a place for you in his service."

When Samuel flashed a couple of sovereigns, the cabby snapped upright. "Well, even if the duke don't make good on somebody else's promise, likely those gentlemen won't come back looking for me till first light. I'll take the boy to Mayfair."

Samuel bundled young Henry into the cab.

"Wait," the boy said. "What am I to say once I get to the duke's house?"

"Tell them Badewyn sent you. Show Mr. Bernard what you've got in your pocket and you won't have to say another word."

The boy eyed him with suspicion. "Just what is it you think I've got in my pocket, mister?"

"Your past, boy," Samuel said. "And your future."

Meg was almost asleep when the door creaked open and Samuel came back in. He closed the door softly behind him.

Please don't let him still be angry with me, she prayed silently. She could stand a great deal, but not that. Someday he'd see that she was right, that they had to put the welfare of the duke's son ahead of hers, but now was not the time to try to convince him. It was enough that he'd done as she asked. She lay as still as stone, waiting for him to speak so she could gauge his mood.

"Are you asleep, Meg?" he whispered.

He sounded like himself, always putting her first. If she didn't answer, she suspected he'd try to slip between the sheets without disturbing her. But she was more than ready to be "disturbed" by the handsome man she loved. She stretched and sat up.

"Did I wake you?" he asked.

"No, I was waiting for you."

He settled his hip on her side of the bed and leaned over her. "I've been waiting for you, too."

Alarm bells jangled in her brain. He hadn't called her "his sunshine," the code words they'd agreed upon and hoped never to have to use.

"How is His Grace's son?" she asked. *Now. Say it now.*

A slice of silence cut between them. "Spoiled and self-indulgent, I warrant. How should the son of a duke be?"

He wasn't describing the poor child Meg had sent Samuel off to save. He leaned in to kiss her, but she stopped him with a hand to his chest.

"I'm tired," she said, hoping he wouldn't feel her hand tremble. Like Lucifer who could assume pleasing shapes, other fallen angels could evidently do likewise. In the shaft of moonlight, the face Meg saw was Samuel's. The voice was his. Lord help her, the smell of his skin was even the same, but the wicked smile on his lips was all Grigori.

"Not too tired," he said hopefully, still trying to pass as his considerate son.

She feigned a yawn. "The travel has caught up to me. I can scarcely keep my eyes open."

"I don't care if you close your eyes." He untied the lace at the bodice of her chemise.

"I said no." She tried to roll away from him, but he pinned her to the feather tick with his body. "You can't trick me. I know who you are."

His smile faded. "Then you should know that, unlike my son for whom a 'no' means something, I'm used to having my way with my offspring's wives."

"But Samuel and I aren't married."

"A technicality. You should thank me, actually," Grigori said, his face morphing back into its more mature manifestation. "Once I get you with child, he'll have to marry you."

Meg started to scream, but Grigori covered her mouth with his hand. "Not yet, sweeting. I haven't begun to give you reason."

"And you won't as long as I draw breath," a deep voice came from the doorway.

Meg wrested her mouth free and cried, "Samuel."

He bounded across the room and hauled his father off her.

Grigori bared his teeth at him. "You can't stop me."

"You can't stop me from trying," Samuel said. "I'd walk through fire for her."

"That can be arranged." A ring of blue flames appeared around the bed, licking at the coverlet, but not catching.

Meg's eyes widened as the men began to circle each other. She rose to her knees to see over the flames. Samuel peeled out of his jacket and waistcoat, the better to free his arm movement. Muscles bunched beneath his shirt. His dark brows lowered as he raised his fists.

Grigori laughed. "A fist fight? Do you really think you can best me with nothing but your fingers?"

Samuel jabbed his father in the face before Grigori saw the blow coming. Blood trickled from his nostril.

"Aw, hell," the fallen angel swore softly.

And indeed in the next few seconds, all hell did break loose.

There were no rules in this brawl, no finesse, no regular punch and counter-punch. Samuel and his father hammered each other with bone-jarring strokes. Rage seemed to give Samuel extra strength for, unlike the fight Meg had witnessed in the great hall, he was giving as good as he got.

He connected a ringing blow to Grigori's temple and his father staggered back a pace, shaking his head.

"This shouldn't be happening. How are you doing this?" he demanded.

"My will is stronger than yours," Samuel said, sucking in gasping breaths. "I want to protect her more than you want to defile her."

"We'll see about that," Grigori said. He lifted a hand toward Meg and the flames around the bed died. "It's time to take this outside."

Between one blink and the next, Meg found herself transported to another place entirely. Instead of a feather tick beneath her, she was on her knees on a gravel and crushed bark path. Judging from the trees and the line of lighted lamps stretching in either direction, she and Samuel were on Rotten Row, the fashionable haunt of the *ton* for riding at certain hours of the day. Now at night, it was deserted.

Where Grigori should have been, there was now a centaur. Samuel had told Meg his father could assume any shape he pleased, but she'd never have believed this if she hadn't seen it.

The horse part of him was the glossy black of a Percheron, his flanks powerful, his sex dangling long and loose between his hind legs. Thick black hair draped from his fetlocks over hooves that were the size of dinner plates. Metal glinted on each one. He was shod with the accoutrements of a warhorse, whose four feet were as deadly as any rider's blade. Centaurs were supposed to be wise and benevolent beings, but the face on this one was the face of Grigori. His expression was a study in cruelty.

He reared and lashed out a wicked swipe of his front hooves. Samuel dodged, barely avoiding them. Meg cringed and ducked in empathy with him.

"This isn't fair," she shouted. "Samuel is unarmed."

But Meg was wrong. Even as she said it, Samuel scooped up a large stone from the edge of the path and sent it hurtling through the air. The centaur shied, sidling out of the path of the rock and Samuel ran toward him, brandishing his boot knife. He sliced from Grigori's equine chest up to his withers. Grigori loosed a long horsy squeal of pain and bucked his rear around to face Samuel. He threw out his back hooves in a powerful thrust. It was a draft horse version of a graceful Lipizzaner "airs- above-the-ground."

Samuel tried to dodge again, but one of Grigori's hooves caught him in the shoulder. He was thrown back about ten paces off the path, landing on his back, fortunately in a spongy, moss-covered patch.

Meg gasped, wishing she could run to him but a distraction of any sort might be deadly, so she forced herself to remain rooted to the spot. But she prayed. She prayed the most excellent prayer she could and hoped to heaven it would be answered.

Samuel scrambled to his feet, but one arm dangled uselessly.

Numbed by that vicious kick at the least. Might be broken. Meg's chest constricted smartly and she struggled to draw breath.

"First blood to you then, Naphil. Guess your race isn't

known as mighty hunters for nothing." Grigori ran his human hand along his horsy chest. The ribbon of red dripped down his black coat like drizzled icing. "Perhaps, I'm going about this wrong. I've given you too large a target. Something smaller, I think."

The centaur began to collapse in on itself, until there was only a small creature in its place. It was a rat. A common rodent with a sleek, dark body, sharp black eyes, and even sharper-looking yellow teeth.

"Careful, Samuel," Meg called out. "It's a trick."

The rat wiggled its whiskers at her and then began to dart about as if unsure which way to go. Samuel lowered his knife and followed its movements, but didn't seem to know what to do either. The contest was strangely lopsided, a man with a blade against a small naked rodent. Somehow, Meg knew all was not as it appeared.

"Strike!" she shouted.

"He's not armed." Samuel made the mistake of glancing toward her.

In that instant, Grigori bolted around him and leaped to the back of Samuel's knee. He sank in his long incisors. Meg heard a pop as Samuel's hamstring zinged, his thigh muscle convulsing in a bunch. The leg buckled under him. With a loud groan, he went down heavily on his good knee, letting the crippled leg jut unnaturally to the side. Samuel brought his blade down, but only managed to sever the long hairless tail from Grigori's body. The rat scampered away, but the tail squirmed like a headless snake for a moment before it lay quiet.

"I say," the rat said from a safe distance. "That was rude. I don't like having my personal tail cut off. I've been insulted.

It quite offends me." His voice grew deeper and colder with each word. "And I won't tolerate it any longer."

As Grigori spoke, he *Shifted*, passing through various predators of the animal kingdom, changing from wolf to leopard to a Kodiak bear that stood ten feet tall on its hind legs, its razor claws slashing.

"No," he said with a growl in his voice. "Even this won't do."

He continued *Shifting*, spitting light in flashes until he finally arrived at his final form. With a glimmer of green scales and a click of claws, Grigori had gone dragon.

"God help us," Meg whispered.

Grigori's eyes burned red as he looked down at his crippled opponent, but he seemed in no hurry to continue the fight. Smoke drifted from his nostrils in grayish-green puffs with each long breath. He reached over and picked up the rat's tail, letting it dangle from his long-taloned claws.

"Not much to look at as tails go, is it?" he admitted. Then he reached around and affixed it to his dragonish bum, where it promptly grew into a long snaky appendage, covered with glittering scales and barbed at the end with horny spikes.

"Now that, my son, is a tail." Grigoi thrashed it about with relish. "Want a closer look?"

He whipped it around and smacked Samuel with it, clipping him with the barbed end. Samuel toppled over, blood pouring from a wound that gaped on his forehead, but he struggled back to one knee, slicing with his knife in a counterstroke. His blade clattered harmlessly along the dragon's scales.

"You are trying my patience, Naphil. No more love pats."

Grigori swung his tale back and connected with Samuel in a ringing blow that knocked him to the ground.

Meg clapped a hand to her mouth to stifle her cry. This time, he didn't get back up. He was either knocked unconscious or…

"Too easy." Grigori tipped back his dragonish head and blew a string of self-congratulatory smoke rings into the air. Then he inhaled noisily and loosed a stream of fire after the smoke rings. The blast was like a flame thrower, the acrid stench like a whiff of hell. "And now, for the *coup de grace.*"

He stood straighter and sucked in a deep breath.

"No!" Meg bolted to Samuel. She fell upon him and tried to cover his body with hers. Realizing the futility of that, she cradled his bleeding head in her lap. She found a thready pulse under his jaw.

Just unconscious, then. She sighed with relief.

The way his leg stuck out at such an unnatural angle, she suspected he couldn't walk, though. His shoulder was already darkening with a deep bruise. She dabbed at the open cut on his forehead with the hem of her wrapper. Though the wound still bled profusely, Meg could see that the cut was shallow, stopped by the hard white bone of his skull. He'd have the "mother of all headaches" when he woke.

If he woke. She leaned over him and pressed her lips to his in a soft kiss.

"Why did you defend me?" she whispered. "You stupid, stupid man."

"Naphil," Samuel corrected. He eased his eyes open, grimacing in pain. "But I won't disagree with the stupid part."

He pushed himself into a sitting position and ran a hand

down his ruined thigh, wincing in agony.

"Hush," she said, arranging herself on her knees behind him so he could lean back against her. She looked up at Grigori, who was glaring down at them. "I'll do anything you want. Just don't kill him. Please."

"No," Samuel said through clenched teeth. "Meg, don't."

"If you die, I die," she said.

"And if you give yourself to him, I'm dead already." Samuel's gray eyes warmed to the color of burnished pewter. "You're my life, Meg. My only love."

"Then we die together." She looked back up at his father. "Do your worst. Destroy us if you must, but you cannot separate us."

"Two in one blow." Grigori bobbed his horny head. "Don't mind if I do." He sucked in another breath.

Oh, God! This is it.

They were going to be incinerated. She buried her face in the juncture of Samuel's neck and strong shoulder. Regret crushed her. She wouldn't live out her days with the man she loved. They'd never make a home together. They wouldn't grow old, hand in hand, until one of them laid the other in the arms of God. Squeezing her eyes shut, Meg held her breath, waiting for the hot blast.

It didn't come.

She peeked up and saw Grigori still poised to destroy them, but he was strangely motionless. His dragonish eyes glittered dangerously. Then great drops of steaming liquid fell from them. Suddenly, he shrank back down into his human form, and collapsed to his knees. Tears streamed down his cheeks. His shoulders shook.

"I'd have died with her too, you know. Atara, I mean,"

Grigori said between sobs. "If I could have."

"Then you know what love is," Samuel said quietly.

Grigori nodded. "I haven't seen it in millennia, but it's hard to mistake. None of my other sons loved their wives so much that they'd die for them. And their wives were more excited about being Lady Badewyn than being married. But you two have the love I can never have again."

"There are different kinds of love," Meg said. "The love of family. Of friends." If he stopped being so hateful and controlling to those around him, even Grigori wasn't beyond that brand of affection.

"But not the all-consuming love that binds two together so tightly they become one." Grigori wiped his eyes on his shirt sleeve. "Atara is gone. I'll never have that again."

"She lives on in you, Grigori," Meg said. "You carry her spirit with you."

He hung his head. "If that's the case, she'd be ashamed of me over this night's work."

"I don't think so. Not completely," Samuel said. "After all, you spared us."

He smiled sadly. "She'd have wanted me to. That's the only evidence that what you say is true, that she's still with me. If I had the grace to stop, it's because something of her still lives." Grigori rose, walked over to Samuel, and bent down to touch his knee. Immediately, Samuel was able to move the damaged leg. "She'd have wanted me to do that, too."

"You have been very alone for a long time. I see that now." Samuel stood and extended a hand to his father. "I haven't been the son you wanted."

"No, but you've been the one I needed," Grigori said.

"The only one who could help me break the Grand Cycle."

Samuel pulled Meg close and she slipped her arms around his waist. "Then you will not meddle with Meg once we're married?"

Grigori shook his head. "None of my other sons loved the women they wed as you love her. Love like that is too rare, too…holy. I may be hell-bound, but I'll not interfere with that." He turned away.

"Where are you going?" Meg asked.

"Nowhere. Anywhere. Some place where I can figure out what to do with my alone-ness."

"You don't need to be alone," Samuel said. "If you are willing, there is a group of people who may welcome you. Come with us to the Duke of Camden's house. Meg is already a member of the Order of the M.U.S.E. With any luck, they'll accept a Nephilim and his father as well."

"I am a monster. No one knows that better than you, son." Grigori stopped and without turning back to face them asked, "Why? Why do you care what happens to me?"

"We are all monsters, one way or another," Samuel said. "Derelicts and misfits abroad in the world, trying to find our home. There isn't a soul on earth that doesn't have dark places in need of restoration. Love does that." He looked down at Meg. She smiled up at him, in encouragement. She'd convinced him he had a soul. It shone in his eyes. "We are your family, Grigori. We care because that's what families do."

Meg didn't have much experience with her real family, but the Order had filled that gap. They'd accepted her despite her lowborn status, despite the fact that she'd been a common thief. No one really deserved love, but everyone needed it. Even fallen ones. Or maybe especially fallen ones.

"If you let us, Grigori," Meg offered, "we'll learn to love you, too."

She didn't know how he'd react. After all, he'd been set to immolate them both. He seemed not to have heard her at first. Grigori's chin tipped up and he gazed steadfastly at the heavens. After about half a minute, he turned around. Tears fell unabated down his cheeks. "I never thought to hear it again."

Meg looked up. The stars were brittle pinpricks in the black vault of the sky, but she heard nothing but the breeze in the treetops. "Hear what?"

"The music of heaven," Grigori said. "'The morning stars sang together, and all the sons of God shouted for joy.' I may be cast out, but I am not forgotten. Love does that."

Samuel hugged Meg tighter. "That and so much more."

The mind is its own place, and in itself
Can make a heav'n of hell, a hell of heav'n.

~John Milton, from *Paradise Lost*

Chapter Twenty-two

"Hurry it up, why don't ya?" Rowney hissed. It was a moonless night, but there was no cover for them as he and Oswald stood knee-deep in the Duke of Camden's garden fountain. Should any of His Grace's servants peer out a window they might be discovered before they had even accomplished anything criminal. "If we can't make it into Camden House this way, we may have to give up and start hoofing it to Wales. Either that or wait for Meggie to come back to London on her own."

"Keep your britches on. I'm working as fast as I can." Oswald bent to unscrew the bolts that held the thick glass to the bottom of the fountain. As it turned out, not all of the duke's servants were as discreet as he might like. After exhausting all the usual points of entry for a burglary and finding them inaccessible, Oswald had wormed the information about this secret entrance to the house from a gullible scullery maid. Apparently, there was a shaft that ran from the submerged window in the fountain down to His Grace's souterrain. It was meant as a way to provide natural light to the basement, but the man-sized shaft would also make an unexpected point of entry for a pair of determined burglars.

"There, now," Oswald said. "The glass is loose. Once the water's drained, we'll have no trouble lifting it."

The duke would have a damp cellar since all the water gushed down the sloping passage. "Should make sliding down it all the easier," Rowney said. A wet ride down the slope was a small price to pay for entry into such a rich storehouse of goods.

As soon as the last bit of water was gone, Oswald worked the bolts completely free and lifted the thick glass from its cement casement.

"After you, nephew."

The younger man didn't have to be told twice. He wiggled into the shaft and disappeared from sight. Rowney could hardly wait to see what treasures someone like the Duke of Camden might have squirreled away in his souterrain. No doubt there would be more than a few bottles of wine he and Oswald could liberate. The Duke of Camden was wealthy beyond reason. Rowney figured a wall safe wasn't near enough space to house His Grace's stash of coin and jewels. Such fine stuff was easily portable and Rowney had a fence in a sketchy part of town who would ask no questions.

Rowney tapped his toe with impatience as he waited to follow his nephew down. He'd enter the shaft once Oswald had a head start so they wouldn't get jammed up, but he wouldn't emulate him completely. The younger man had slithered head first into the damp opening.

"Bollocks to that!" Rowney was still the brains of the outfit. He started down after his nephew feet first. He'd only slid about ten feet when he heard the first scream. It was horrible. And it was Oswald making the ungodly sound.

Rowney dug his fingers into the moss-furred walls of the narrow space. He tried to catch a heel on one of the mortar joints, but the soles of his boots were so worn, he could gain no purchase. There was a time, and not so long ago, that he'd have been unable to even fit into this shaft, but his stomach had been empty more often than not of late. Now he could bend his neck and see over his flat belly.

There was light below—a ghastly, yellowish light.

The screams didn't sound like Oswald any more. It was like a cat being turned inside out. Still, Rowney was sure his nephew was the one making the noise. His heart threatened to pound out of his chest. He tried bending his knees to wedge himself in place, but he kept sliding downward, inch by unavoidable inch.

It was no use. He couldn't stop his descent to whatever evil befell his nephew. And just when he couldn't imagine anything worse, the screams stopped.

"I discovered them when I brought down Mr. Pascal's breakfast tray," Mr. Bernard said. "As you can see, Your Grace, the miscreants are still here."

"But not quite unscathed, are they?" Camden peered through the iron bars that held the time thief prisoner.

Andre-Simon Pascal was seated at the harpsichord Camden had provided for him, playing a Mozart sonata as if nothing untoward had happened.

Some months earlier, Pascal had sacrificed his youth to give back time he'd stolen from Lady Stanstead, a member of Camden's Order of the M.U.S.E. Now the time thief no longer had the appearance of a man approaching middle age. The silver was gone from his hair. His frame was trimmer. Only his hands were unchanged. They were as supple and talented as ever. Pascal finished the last cadenza with a flourish and then turned on the swivel seat to face Camden.

"Ah! Your Grace," he said with evident pleasure. "It is some time since we last played a game of chess. I have missed you."

"I have been unavoidably away from London." Camden gave him a quick bow from the neck. Just because he was holding the dangerous entity captive didn't mean he couldn't be civil to him. "My apologies. I trust your needs have not gone unmet in my absence."

"Not at all." Pascal tugged on his trademark pair of scarlet gloves and flexed his fingers. "These two have given me a bit of diversion you never could."

Camden glanced at the would-be thieves, who cowered in the corner of Pascal's cell. Both men were balding and frail-looking. He'd supposed Miss Anthony's Cousin Oswald to be much nearer her age than her uncle's. "Which of you is Rowney Jackson?"

"That'd be me." The younger looking of the pair hauled himself to his feet and tottered to the cell bars. He lowered his voice to a frantic whisper. "Get us out of here, Your Grace. Throw us into Newgate. Have us transported. Do what you will. God knows, we deserve it, but nobody deserves this. For Christ's pity, don't leave us here with…that." The man shot a terrified look at Pascal and crossed himself.

Pascal laughed, but sobered quickly when Camden shot him a warning glance.

"What happened to them was their own fault," Pascal said. "They came down the skylight shaft as I slept and that one"—he pointed to Oswald—"attacked me. I merely defended myself. I cannot be held to account if my touch took a couple of years from him."

"A couple of decades, it would appear." Twenty or thirty years at the least, perhaps more, Camden estimated. Pascal was a boyishly handsome man again. He'd look completely at home sitting for any class at Oxford or Cambridge.

"I did not lay a hand on the other fellow," the time thief said. "If he appears older, it is from shock only."

"May one point out to Your Grace that Mr. Pascal did not, in fact, initiate this encounter?" Bernard said. "He did not continue to siphon the life away from these two common brigands when he might have easily done so. And he was actually defending Your Grace's home, and perhaps your very life, by intercepting the invaders and detaining them here."

Pascal rewarded the steward with a toothy grin.

"Perfectly true," Camden said. "It seems I owe you a debt of thanks, Pascal. Will you allow us to take charge of Mr. Jackson and his nephew, at this time?"

Pascal stepped away from the door and gave a sweeping bow. Rowney Jackson toddled back and helped his elderly nephew to his feet. The pair shuffled out of the cell with as much speed as they could muster. Pascal made no attempt to leave with them.

"Do not contemplate escape, Mr. Jackson," the duke warned. "At the top of the stairs, there is a pair of able-bodied footmen waiting to escort you to the magistrate."

"It'll be a mercy," Rowney muttered.

"That'll be all, Bernard." As his steward left the underground chamber, Camden turned back to Pascal. "I notice you did not escape through the same shaft the Jacksons came down. I suspect it would be a challenging climb but one of your youth could have managed it."

"In truth, I did, Your Grace. Your garden is lovely by starlight, but then I began thinking that running off at the first opportunity would be a poor way to prove I deserve your trust. And so I voluntarily returned to this cell." Pascal gripped the bars and leaned his soulful face between them. "I have lived for centuries—always alone, constantly moving about and having to reinvent myself. My life may have been long, but it has been without meaning. Full membership in your Order, doing something useful, something...good, would give me a measure of purpose I have heretofore lacked."

"I thought we'd agreed that you could not become a full-fledged Extraordinaire until I found a companion, a guardian of sorts, for you. Someone who was not only immune to your time theft, but who would also ensure you did not begin stealing time from others again."

"We did, Your Grace, but I doubt you can find such a one." Pascal looked sadder than a dog that had just piddled on the carpet. "Haven't I proven to you that I can be trusted, even without such an overseer?"

"Perhaps." An inkling of an idea bloomed in Camden's

brain. "But changing your situation will require the consent of the entire Order. I will summon them tonight."

It gave Camden great pleasure to survey the bevy of unique individuals gathered in his parlor. Most were psychically gifted. All were precious to him.

Lounging on the fainting couch, there was his beloved Vesta, his fire mage, all-consuming lover and since they had taken secret vows over a Scottish anvil after leaving Faencaern Castle, his unacknowledged duchess. He'd have been pleased to shout their union from the rooftops, but Vesta insisted on concealing the marriage for his sake. Ever the vivacious charmer, she chatted animatedly with Lady Westfall.

Lord Westfall's viscountess possessed no special gift but she was privy to the Order's business on account of her marriage. Lord Westfall no longer heard the thoughts of others all the time. He was now in full possession of his gift, being able to selectively listen in on the minds around him. Camden was glad for him. Relaxed and finally at ease in his own skin, Westfall was almost unrecognizable as the high-strung fellow Camden had arranged to have released from Bedlam into his charge last spring.

Cozy on the settee, Lord and Lady Stanstead were deep in conversation with Gaston LeGrand, the water mage who leaned against the fireplace mantle. Camden still remembered how tentative Cassandra, now Lady Stanstead, had been about joining the Order after her future husband had all but abducted her from Almack's. Since then, the pair had worked together to protect the Crown's interests and had been instrumental in capturing Pascal before he could harm the Prince Regent. Thus far, LeGrand hadn't used his facility with water in service to the English royal family, but his help to Camden and other members of the Order had been invaluable.

Lastly, there was Meg Anthony.

No, Camden corrected himself. *Lady Badewyn.*

He was still concerned over the risks she ran when she used her gift of *Finding*, but he'd be forever indebted to her and her new husband for bringing his lost son back to him. He and young Henry had many lost years to make up, but Camden had hope that they could. The lad had his mother's sweetness along with her eyes.

As for the way Meg courted death each time she slipped away from her body, Camden finally agreed it was *her* life to hazard. She should be allowed to run the risk of *Finding* if she deemed it necessary. And she'd brought her devoted Lord Badewyn and his valuable distant vision into the Order as well.

Along with the problem of what, if anything, Camden and his friends could do for Samuel's father, Grigori, now that he'd foresworn the continuation of his "Grand Cycle." The fallen angel stood in the far corner of the room. He reminded Camden of a pike hanging motionless in the shadows, watching the smaller fish dart in sunlit waters.

Still dangerous.

But he gave his word, Camden reminded himself. Millennia had passed since anyone had trusted Grigori. He was still a ruined creature, beyond redemption, yet there was a craving for something good and decent in him, the desire to find himself on the side of right once more. The chance to be proven dependable was not one the fallen angel would give up lightly.

Camden was betting a great deal on his belief, but then so was Grigori's son and new daughter-in-law.

The door to the parlor swung open and Pascal entered, flanked by the footman James and Mr. Bernard. He was wearing his gloves, as usual. When he was a concert pianist, Pascal's admirers once believed the red gloves a dandified accessory. The fact that even then, he wore them to protect others gave Camden hope that the fellow would live up to his promises now.

"Well, I must say, life above ground certainly has its charms. Good evening, ladies." Pascal smiled at each of the feminine members of the Order. His gaze lingered on Lady Stanstead. "Cassandra. Forgive the familiar address, but I was so in hopes we would meet again. You were always kind to me. I like to think I may count on your support at this time."

"That very much depends on whether your incarceration has changed you," Lord Stanstead said, taking his wife's hand possessively.

Pascal's smile no longer reached his eyes. "How could it not? Am I right, Lord Westfall? Didn't your time in Bedlam, which was no doubt worse than my cell in His Grace's souterrain, change you?"

"It did," Westfall admitted. "But not for the better."

"Well, one of the things my imprisonment has taught me is that anything is preferable to being shut away. Because of that, I am willing to submit to His Grace's conditions for my release. I promise faithfully that I will no longer siphon so much as a minute from anyone…" The time thief arched a sly brow. "Unless, of course, the Order deems it necessary."

"Which, rest assured, it will not. Civilized society has other ways of dealing with those who would harm the royals besides sucking the life out of them," Camden said.

"There are those who might argue that Newgate prison or transportation to New South Wales amount to the same thing," LeGrand muttered. The comment made Camden wonder about the water mage's past, but decided that warranted a discussion at another time.

"The other requirement was that we find a guardian suitable for you," the duke went on, "Someone to make certain you are living up to your part of the bargain."

"And this is my cue." A bare hand extended, the fallen angel strode toward the time thief. "I am Grigori Templeton. Take off your glove."

Camden nodded when Pascal looked askance at him. "Do as he says."

When Grigori took Pascal's hand, the time thief's jaw sagged. Camden sensed a transfer of raw power between the two. It was like watching a pair of Titans meet, measuring each other's strength in their grip. Pascal was first to try to pull back.

"My God," the time thief said as his knees buckled slightly.

"Not quite," the Fallen One said with a chuckle, "though I was once on rather familiar terms with Him." Then all traces of levity drained from his features. "The will to endure is all that binds a fallen angel to earth. What you feel in my handshake is the weight of my years in exile. Should you break your word to His Grace, I will deposit all of them into your soul. At that point, I'll have exhausted myself so thoroughly, I'll have no will left. I will no longer be able to fight the downward pull that is ever upon me and will tumble into the abyss." He tightened his grip on Pascal's fingers. "If that happens, rest assured, I will take you with me."

When Grigori released the time thief's hand, Pascal massaged his knuckles as Grigori continued, "You will accept me as your companion and I will take you as my charge. You are an old soul, I'm told. I suspect we'll find much in common. When we are not being of service to the duke's Order, we will travel the world. Contrary to Solomon's opinion, there are still a few new things under the sun for such as we."

"I accept your offer and will bear you company, Mr. Templeton," Pascal said.

"Good," Camden said. "Before you joined us this evening, the Order voted to allow you both full membership if this agreement between you was reached. Now, on to other busi—"

A burst of raw psychic energy cracked over Camden. A hazy impression descended upon him. It was too indistinct for him to describe. More a sensation of loathing and malice than anything. Something malevolent had wakened from a long sleep and had bent its eye toward the English court. The object which contained the evil intent flashed a warning toward him and he sank into blackness.

When he came to himself, he found that someone had carried him to the fainting couch and his lovely Vesta was pressing a perfumed handkerchief to his forehead.

"Oh, my dear Edward," she said, "what is it?"

He sat up. "It appears the psychic lull we have been enjoying is at an end. Someone has been searching for the

Honours of Scotland."

"Ah, yes, the royal jewels," Samuel said. "After the Acts of Union in 1707, the crown, scepter, and sword no longer had a ceremonial role to play. Someone hid them away so well, their location remains a mystery. Never say the Honours have a psychic bent."

"I don't know. As far as I can tell, they are still missing," Camden said. "But the people who are looking for them have stumbled upon something else, a set of bagpipes from the time of Robert the Bruce with a decidedly dark inclination toward our king."

"What are we to do about it, Your Grace?" Grigori asked.

"Do? Why, we go to Scotland, of course. If my read on the situation is correct, this is a task of such herculean proportions it calls for the entire Order. Mr. Bernard, see to the travel arrangements at once."

The Order planned its strategy into the wee hours of the morning. Once the meeting broke up for the night, Samuel and Meg retreated to their chamber in Camden House. He closed the door behind him and threw the bolt. "I wish I could lock out the world as easily."

He took her into his arms. She melted into them with the rightness of a homecoming. "Now that Grigori is no longer a threat to us, I'd hoped we'd have a bit of peace together."

"We will. But as long as we serve the Order, we'll just have to have it in small bits," Meg said. "You know, I never thought myself worthy of love. Either because my gift made me a freak, or because without it, I wasn't special enough for someone to love."

"You're more than special enough for me, with or without your gift. I'll love you till the last star falls." He nuzzled her neck. As he breathed in her fresh scent, it was as if he took her in, too. "Before you came to Faencaern, I had convinced myself I was a hollow husk. A hybrid freak. A Naphil. I had no love to give. No soul."

"You know that's not true." She palmed his cheeks.

He nodded. "You taught me different. You gave me a new version of myself. Now I'm returning the gift. I'm not as much as you deserve, but all that I am, or ever will be, is yours."

"You're all I'll ever want." Her smile turned wicked. "And I want you right now."

"Good. I plan to love you from here to Scotland and back."

"All through my childhood, I was on the move. I hated traveling and slogging to and from Wales did nothing to change my opinion," she said.

"That sounds like a challenge." He hefted her up with his arms under her bum. She bent down to kiss him.

"Nothing you can't handle. As long as you love me, I'll go wherever you take me."

"Right now," he said as he strode across the room, "I'm taking you to bed."

"My favorite place."

He laid her down to sink into the luxurious feather tick. "Mine too. As long as we're in it together.

OTHER BOOKS BY MIA MARLOWE

The Curse of Lord Stanstead
The Madness of Lord Westfall

Author's Note

I've always been fascinated by the cryptic scripture verses that deal with beings called Nephilim. There are only a few passages and all of them are sunk deep in antiquity. Before the Flood, the biblical writer tells us that the "sons of God" went in to the "daughters of men" and sired children on them. I have no idea what that really means. For the purposes of this book, I have decided that "sons of God" refers to some of the angels who rebelled against God by following Lucifer.

I'm usually a stickler for historical accuracy, but I'm the first to admit, I really don't know in this case. You are welcome to endorse a different interpretation. My dad, for example, would say the Nephilim might have been ancient aliens. (Clearly, he needs more channels on his satellite TV package!) Anyway, I hope you enjoy a love/hate relationship with my fallen angel Grigori and his doomed love for his human wife.

A few of you may be skeptical that the Duke of

Camden would actually marry Vesta LaMotte, his off-again-on-again mistress. Such a misalliance is not without precedence. Consider Charles James Fox, second son of a baron and speaker of the House of Commons, who secretly wed Elizabeth Armistead, former mistress of the Prince of Wales. They made the marriage public after seven years, but she was never fully accepted by polite society. Fox could not have cared less what anyone thought about his private life. And neither does the Duke of Camden.

If you enjoyed Vesta and Camden's romance, which arcs through the entire Order of the MUSE series, be sure to visit http://www.miamarlowe.com. I've posted a love scene between them that didn't make the final manuscript.

Samuel and Meg are two of my favorites, probably because they both feel unworthy of love. What they don't realize, at first, is that no one is worthy. No one can be. Love is a gift we can't deserve. It's a grace. When it comes to us, we should grasp it with both hands. And a thankful heart.

Wishing you love in all its unexpected glory,

Mia

Acknowledgments

Writing is a solitary activity, but that doesn't mean I didn't have lots of help with *The Lost Soul of Lord Badewyn*. I need to thank a few of the special people who also have their hand in this story:

Erin Molta, my editor. She never gives up and never stops nudging and prodding until the story is as good as it can be. She has an amazing sense of story and hones in on the details that make a book better.

Louisa Maggio, my cover designer. She did a terrific job of capturing the essence of not only this book, but the entire Order of the M.U.S.E. series. And thank you to Amanda Faris, my copy editor. Any errors that slipped through her grammar gauntlet are my fault.

Natasha Kern, my wonderful agent. She handles all the nuts and bolts of business so I can spend my days playing with imaginary people. I don't know what I'd do without her!

Ashlyn Chase and Marcy Weinbeck, my critique partner

and my beta reader. Not only do I count on their feedback, I'd be lost without their friendship. You two are the best!

My husband, my friend, the love of my life. Anyone who can romance the same woman for almost 40 years is definitely hero material!

And last, but not least, I want to thank YOU, dear reader. You invested some of your hard earned money in my story and more importantly, a few hours of your life. I'm thrilled we've shared this story together. Thanks for bringing your imagination along for the ride. It means the world to me. Truly.

About the Author

Mia Marlowe didn't intend on making things up for a living, but she says it's the best job she ever had. Her work was featured in the Best of 2010 issue of PEOPLE magazine. One of her books is on display at the Museum of London Docklands next to Johnny Depp memorabilia. The RITA nominated author has over 20 books in print with more on the way! Mia loves art, music, history, and travel. Good thing about the travel because she's lived in 9 different states, 4 different time zones. For more, visit www.miamarlowe.com.

www.ingramcontent.com/pod-product-compliance
Lightning Source LLC
Chambersburg PA
CBHW020645030726
47498CB00002B/371